17 &
GONE

Also by Nova Ren Suma

IMAGINARY GIRLS

17 & GONE

NOVA REN SUMA

DUTTON BOOKS
AN IMPRINT OF PENGUIN GROUP (USA) INC.

DUTTON BOOKS
A member of Penguin Group (USA) Inc.

Published by the Penguin Group
Penguin Group (USA) Inc., 375 Hudson Street, New York, New York 10014, USA
Penguin Group (Canada), 90 Eglinton Avenue East, Suite 700, Toronto, Ontario M4P 2Y3, Canada
(a division of Pearson Penguin Canada Inc.)
Penguin Books Ltd, 80 Strand, London WC2R 0RL, England
Penguin Ireland, 25 St Stephen's Green, Dublin 2, Ireland (a division of Penguin Books Ltd)
Penguin Group (Australia), 707 Collins Street, Melbourne, Victoria 3008, Australia
(a division of Pearson Australia Group Pty Ltd)
Penguin Books India Pvt Ltd, 11 Community Centre, Panchsheel Park, New Delhi–110 017, India
Penguin Group (NZ), 67 Apollo Drive, Rosedale, Auckland 0632, New Zealand
(a division of Pearson New Zealand Ltd)
Penguin Books (South Africa), Rosebank Office Park, 181 Jan Smuts Avenue,
Parktown North 2193, South Africa
Penguin China, B7 Jiaming Center, 27 East Third Ring Road North,
Chaoyang District, Beijing 100020, China

Penguin Books Ltd, Registered Offices: 80 Strand, London WC2R 0RL, England

Published simultaneously in Canada

CIP Data is available.

Published in the United States by Dutton Books,
a member of Penguin Group (USA) Inc.
345 Hudson Street, New York, New York 10014
www.penguin.com/teen
Designed by Danielle Delaney
Printed in USA First Edition
ISBN: 978-0-525-42340-9

10 9 8 7 6 5 4 3 2 1

For my mom,

who's helped so many

— — —

And for Erik,

who found me when I was eighteen

17 & GONE

GIRLS go missing every day. They slip out bedroom windows and into strange cars. They leave good-bye notes or they don't get a chance to tell anyone. They cross borders. They hitch rides, squeezing themselves into overcrowded backseats, sitting on willing laps. They curl up and crouch down, or they shove their bodies out of sunroofs and give off victory shouts. Girls make plans to go, but they also vanish without meaning to, and sometimes people confuse one for the other. Some girls go kicking and screaming and clawing out the eyes of whoever won't let them stay. And then there are the girls who never reach where they're going. Who disappear. Their ends are endless, their stories unknown. These girls are lost, and I'm the only one who's seen them.

I know their names. I know where they end up—a place seeming as formless and boundless as the old well on the abandoned property off Hollow Mill Road that swallows the town's dogs.

I want to tell everyone about these girls, about what's happening, I want to give warning, I want to give chase. I'd do it, too, if I thought someone would believe me.

There are girls like Abby, who rode off into the night. And girls like Shyann, who ran, literally, from her tormentors and kept running. Girls like Madison, who took the bus down to the city with a phone number snug in her pocket and stars in her eyes. Girls like Isabeth, who got into the car even when everything in her was warning her to walk away. And there are girls like Trina, who no one bothered looking for; girls the police will never hear about because no one cared enough to report them missing.

Another girl could go today. She could be pulling her scarf tight around her face to protect it from the cold, searching through her coat pockets for her car keys so they're out and ready when she reaches her car in the dark lot. She could glance in through the bright, blazing windows of the nearest restaurant as she hurries past. And then when she's out of sight the shadowy hands could grab her, the sidewalk could gulp her up. The only trace of the girl would be the striped wool scarf she dropped on the patch of black ice, and when a car comes and runs it over, dragging it away on its snow tires, there isn't even that.

I could be wrong.

Say I'm wrong.

Say there aren't any hands.

Because what I sometimes believe is that I could be staring right at one of the girls—like that girl in my section of study hall, the one muddling through her trigonometry and drawing doodles of agony in the margins because she hates math. I look away for a second, and when I turn back, the girl's chair is empty, her trig problem abandoned. And that's it: I will never see that girl again. She's gone.

I think it's as simple as that. Without struggle, without any way to stop it, there one moment, not there the next. That's how it happened with Abby—and with Shyann and Madison and Isabeth and Trina, and the others. And I'm pretty sure that's how it will happen to me.

MISSING

ABIGAIL SINCLAIR

CASE TYPE: Endangered Runaway

DOB: June 20, 1995

MISSING: September 2, 2012

AGE NOW: 17

SEX: Female

RACE: Caucasian

HAIR: Brown

EYES: Brown

HEIGHT: 5' 7" (174 cm)

WEIGHT: 120 lbs (54 kg)

MISSING FROM: Orange Terrace, NJ, United States

CIRCUMSTANCES: Abigail, who more often goes by the nickname Abby, was reported missing September 2 but may have been seen last on July 29 or July 30 on the grounds of Lady-of-the-Pines Summer Camp for Girls in the Pinecliff area of New York State. She was said to be riding a blue Schwinn bicycle off the campground after the 9 p.m. lights-out. She may have been wearing red shorts and a camp counselor T-shirt. Her nose is pierced. Her family does not believe she returned to New Jersey.

ANYONE HAVING INFORMATION SHOULD CONTACT

Pinecliff Police Department (New York) 1-845-555-1100

Orange Terrace Police Department (New Jersey) 1-609-555-6638

–1–

SHE'S Abigail Sinclair, brown hair, brown eyes, age 17, from New Jersey—but I call her Abby. I found her on the side of the road in the dead of winter, months after she went missing.

Abby's story started in the pinewoods surrounding my hometown. The seasons changed and the summer heat faded, and no one knew yet. The dreamland hung low in the clouds, smoke-gray lungs shriveled with disease, and no one looked up to see. The snow came down and the bristly trees shuddered in the wind, sharing secrets, and no one stopped to listen. Until I did.

I was forced to stop. My old van made it so, as if someone had tinkered with the engine, knowing it would hold out down my driveway and onto this main stretch of road, until here, where the pines whispered, it would choke and give out and leave me stranded.

I drove this road practically every day—to school and to the Shop & Save, the supermarket on the outskirts of Pinecliff where I stocked shelves and worked the registers on Saturdays and a couple afternoons during the week. I must have passed this spot where the old highway meets Route 11 hundreds of times without realizing. Without seeing her there.

She came visible seconds after my engine gave out, as if a fog had been lifted from off the steep slope of our railroad town that mid-December morning.

Abby Sinclair. There at the intersection. I'm not saying she was there in the flesh with her thumb out and her hair wild in the wind and her bare knees purpled from cold—it didn't start out that way. The first time I saw Abby, it was only a picture: the class photograph reproduced on her Missing poster.

When the light turned green and traffic started moving, I wasn't moving with it. I was arrested by the flyer across the road, that weathered, black-and-white image of Abby, with the single bold word above her forehead that pronounced her MISSING.

I remember being dimly aware of the cars behind my van honking and swerving around me, some drivers flipping me off as they blasted past. I remember that I couldn't move. The van, because the engine wouldn't start, and my body, because my joints had locked. The green light dangling overhead had cycled through again to yellow—blinking, blinking—then red. I knew this only from the colors dancing on the steering wheel, which I held in two fisted hands, so my knuckles that had been green, then yellow, were now red again.

Ahead of me, where the old highway halted in a fork, a stretch of pine trees braced themselves against the biting wind. The pines were weighted down by weeks' worth of snow, but they still moved beneath it, unable to keep still. The slope of ground between them and the road was white and pristine, not a footprint to mar it. Centered within all of this was the telephone pole and, hung there as if displayed on the bare walls of a gallery, the missing girl's face.

I left my van door swinging open, keys in the ignition, backpack on the front seat, and abandoned it to run across the intersection toward the stretch of pines. A pickup truck skidded; a horn shrieked. A car almost met me with its tires, but I moved out of the way before I could feel the bumper's touch. I was vaguely aware of a big, yellow vehicle stopping short behind me—the school bus, the one I rode before I got my license and saved up to buy the old van—but by then I'd made it to the pole.

I trampled through the snow to get close. The flyer was old, the date she was last seen long passed. Her photocopied picture had been duplicated too many times for much detail to show through the ink on ink, so with all those layers smudging away her face, and with the snow spatter and the fade, she could have been anybody really, any girl.

By that I mean she could have been someone who had nothing to do with me. Someone I'd leave attached to the pole on that cold day, someone I'd never think of again in this lifetime.

But I knew she wasn't just any girl. I had a glimmering pull of recognition, burning me through and through, so I couldn't even sense the cold. I'd never felt anything like it before. All I knew is I was meant to find her.

The flyer had only facts. She was 17—like I was; I'd just turned 17 the week before. She'd gone missing from some summer camp I'd never heard of—though it was around here, in the Pinecliff area, near this place that overlooked the frigid, gray Hudson River from the steep hill on which our town was built. The commuter train that ran alongside the river stopped here nearly every hour during the day, and crept past at night. The summer camp had to be close.

I tore the page from the pole, ripping it loose from where it was stuck fast with packing tape that had been wound and wound around the pole to keep her from falling face-first into the snow, or from getting carried away on a gust of exhaust and escaping into the traffic leading to the New York State Thruway. It was the clear tape covering the details on the flyer that had kept it from disintegrating for all these months. It was also the tape, so much of it, that made it almost impossible to tear her free.

When I crossed the intersection again—more horns honking—and reached my van, I saw that some Good Samaritan (or a creeper disguising himself as a Good Samaritan) had stopped his own car on the shoulder to offer help. There was some tinkering with the engine, mention of a possibly busted fan belt, and a plume of gray smoke that spat itself into the man's face and then lifted up into the bone-white air overhead, a blot of hate on the sky that already threatened more snow. There was a tow I couldn't afford, and an hour waiting on a greasy folding chair in the back of the garage because it was too cold to wait outside. It wasn't until they fixed my van and I was headed in late to school that I had a moment alone to take a closer look at the flyer.

I didn't tell Jamie or Deena, or anyone. There wasn't anyone I wanted to tell. This discovery was mine, and I wanted to hold it close.

My heart had an irregular beat that I can almost hear again now, like an extra thump was thrown in to make me think there were two hearts in the van, thumping.

There were—but I wasn't aware at first. This was before I knew she followed me.

–2–

I'D parked in the senior parking lot even though I wasn't a senior, cut the engine, and was sitting there holding it. The flyer. The paper was the same temperature as my fingers—cold—so I couldn't feel either.

I tried to flatten the paper against the steering wheel, smoothing the tears and wrinkles from her face as best I could to study what they said about her.

"Endangered Runaway" they called her. A sliver of fear entered me when I saw they said she was in danger, but now I know that everyone under eighteen who goes missing is called endangered. On Missing posters, if you're not an "Endangered Runaway," you're "Endangered Missing," but you're always in danger—it's never a "She's Probably Doing Okay, But We Have to Check Since It's the Law" missing girl.

Besides, Abby *was* in danger. I felt it.

I pored over her flyer again, learning her hometown, her

hair color, her eye color, her weight and height. I learned that she was gone before she was reported missing, and I didn't understand why. I learned of her pierced nose. I didn't learn about her habit of writing the name of the boy she liked on the inside of her elbow, then spitting on it and rubbing at it till it was clean. That information wasn't on the flyer, and this was before she told me.

I would have pocketed the piece of paper and gone into the school building, and maybe all of what happened next would have been different, but that's when I saw the light.

My Dodge van had one of those cigarette lighters built into the dashboard, a knob beside the stereo that you press in to heat. It glows orange, and then when it's ready to use, it pops back out. I'd had the van a couple months, but I'd never used the lighter.

Now the knob was pressed in. An orb of fire-orange was blazing from the dashboard as if someone had reached out an arm to light a cigarette. A phantom cigarette and a phantom arm, because I was alone in the van. I was alone.

I told myself I must've knocked the lighter when I parked. Or the mechanic who'd fixed the engine got it stuck. It's been lit up, I assured myself; it's been on the whole time.

I looked out at the quiet parking lot, a white expanse beneath the rising ridge above the school. Nothing stirred.

This was when something streaked past outside: a fast-moving blur, as if someone were sprinting the length of the school property. Someone wearing red.

My temples hammered, and I screwed my eyes shut. I lost my grip on the flyer and felt it fall to the floor. There were stars clouding my vision, stars that became one star, until then, *there*: the sparkling cubic zirconia in her left nostril.

She was visible in the van's rearview mirror when I opened my eyes. Bright and searing like a sunspot, until my eyes adjusted, or her heat dimmed enough so I could see her clearly.

She'd taken the middle bench seat, the collapsible one I hadn't bothered to collapse all week, as if I'd known to expect her company. This seat was just behind mine, but I didn't turn around. I could say that I didn't want to make any sudden movements, that I was trying not to scare her away, but truth is I couldn't. My body wouldn't move for me at all.

Her reflection in the rearview showed her face at eye level. Her shoulders hunched. Her two bare knees folded to her chin, purplish blooms of bruises on her shins like she'd crawled across the icy asphalt lot, slithering between parked cars, to reach my black van.

This was Abigail Sinclair from the Missing flyer. I could smell her, harsh and hot like a tuft of hair burning.

She uncrossed her arms and lowered her knees, and I noticed that her T-shirt had the name of the summer camp and a picture to go with it: a veiled lady lifted up above a trio of pine trees, as if in the midst of being taken herself. The shirt was covered in grime and streaked with mud, so the words COUNSELOR-IN-TRAINING could barely be made out above her heart. Below the shirt, I saw she had on a pair of shorts. Red ones, with thin white racer stripes. She had been on the home team in Color War that day—I found that out later.

She was letting me see what she was wearing on the night

she disappeared, but I knew, even then, that this wasn't about what a girl was wearing when she found herself gone. Nothing she could have worn on that night would have made a difference. Not these shorts or another pair that were longer or less red. Not a bathing suit. Not a bear costume. Not a short skirt. Not a burqa.

There was so much more to her story I didn't know.

"Abigail?" I said. It came out in a whisper.

Without a word or warning, my vision shifted. I was soon seeing through some layers of smoke and coughed-up haze into what she herself saw the night she went missing. This seeing was more like knowing. I didn't have to question it—in the way that I can be sure, without needing to check first, that there are five fingers on my hand.

What I came to know was this:

She didn't like it when people called her Abigail. So I wouldn't, not anymore.

And she did ride away on that bike, though it was green, not blue as had been reported. What I saw of her—what she willed me to see—was a moving image spooling out in the frame of my rearview mirror, a home movie projected in an empty theater for me and only me.

There she was, riding a bright green bicycle into a sea of darkness. That was her, coasting on a gust of wind and letting her long hair untangle and fly. It was a rusty old bike, one she borrowed from the counselor's shed; it was an empty road, one on which no cars passed; it was a slick, sweet-smelling summer's night.

That was it, that was the last of her. She lingered on it, and so did I, holding the memory between us like something sweet slowly licked off a shared spoon.

I watched the reflective light mounted on the back of the bicycle catch and glow and grow small as she traveled into the dark distance. Watched her pedal, quick at first, then slowing to coast down the hill. Watched as she lifted both arms from the handlebars for a heartbeat of a second, then put them back down and held on. I watched her go.

Then I lost sight of her. The bike dipped under, but the image of the road stayed still. I was leaning forward, trying to see farther, when the mirror went dark and I realized someone was pounding on the window of my van.

My neck turned until I was face-to-face with the intruder.

It was Mr. Floris, ninth- and tenth-grade biology teacher by trade and prison guard in his dark dreams and deepest fantasies. Everyone knew Mr. Floris loved trolling the school grounds during his free periods, itching to hand out detentions. And even though it was no surprise to find him in the parking lot seeking to foil late sleepers and slackers, it was still a shock to be caught. I'd forgotten where I was.

He rapped his knuckles on the glass, then lowered the red scarf that he'd wound around his face to keep out the cold. When his mouth was free, I saw the chapped lips beneath his mustache shape out the words: *You. Roll down this window this instant, young lady.*

There was only a single layer of window glass between us, but I couldn't hear him. I heard nothing but the distant whirring of two bicycle wheels. Then he pounded again, and I heard that and flinched and was rolling down the window and saying, "Sorry, Mr. Floris. I didn't see you there."

At the same time I was taking another glance in the rear-view mirror, needing to know—was she still in the van with me? Was she huddled behind my seat, in the dark cavern in back? But something was blocking my view: the reflection of the pale girl in the mirror who must have been rubbing at her eyes again, a bad habit. She had smoke-gray tracks of mascara streaking down her cheeks as if she'd been holed up in the van crying. She wasn't. I hadn't cried in years.

On top of my head was the puffy wool hat my friend Deena Douglas stole from the mall and didn't like on herself and so gave to me. The hat was pulled low over my eyebrows, hiding my ears and hiding the view of the backseat where Abby still could be.

"Miss Woodman," Mr. Floris said, "you do realize it's third period and you should be in class? Get out of this van and come with me or I'll have to write you up."

I'd never been written up before. This was before I started skipping all that school, before the "marks" on my "permanent record" that I'd "regret" for the "rest of my life." This was before I shattered into the particles and pieces I'm in now.

Even so, I didn't get out of the van.

"But . . ." I said, pausing there, waiting.

Because didn't he see?

I was expecting him to notice her behind me. He was close enough to my window that he must have been able to see the bench seat and who was in it. There . . . the apparition of a girl hiding behind her hair, wasn't she there with her grimy face and her scratched-up knees?

I could still smell her. I could sense her breathing, too, her mouth sharing air with my mouth even though logically I knew it wasn't possible.

But Mr. Floris's eyes landed on something else: The lighter in my dashboard had thrust itself out with a hard *pop*.

"That's it, Lauren, get out. Now. I'm writing you up."

He didn't see—he was blind to it. To her. Soon enough he was opening the door for me and waving me out onto the icy pavement. I glanced directly at her only once, when I was reaching down to rescue her flyer from the floor.

Her long hair was tangled with leaves, I noticed then, stuck through with loose green leaves and pine needles and matted with twigs and sap. One bruised knee was bleeding, and the trail of blood had wound down her leg to between her toes. She was wearing one flip-flop. The other had been lost somewhere I couldn't imagine.

I knew she fell off the bicycle; I could see it happening, a loose rock under her tire catching her off-balance in the dark depths of the night. But did she get up again, or did something stop her? What and who did she meet at the bottom of that hill?

She didn't say. I wouldn't have expected her to tell me in front of him, anyway.

I stepped out of the van, closed and locked the door, and followed Mr. Floris to the front office, where I was about to be awarded a block of after-school detention. But I did look back. I kept looking back. Nothing would keep me from looking for her now.

— — —

That was the first time I was visited by Abby, who met her fate outside the Lady-of-the-Pines Summer Camp for Girls. Now, there are so many more things I know about her.

She's Abigail Sinclair of Orange Terrace, New Jersey. Yes, there's that. But she's really only Abigail to her grandparents and her homeroom teacher. To everyone else, she's Abby.

Abby with the smallest speck of a stud in her nose, so it looks like a sparkling star has been plucked from the sky and hung low beside her face, a star that follows her wherever she goes, night or day. Abby who chews her nails, just the ones on her thumbs. Abby who never wears skirts. Abby who's afraid of clowns and isn't kidding when she says so. Abby who doesn't mind when it rains. Abby who played flute, for three months, then quit. Abby, solid C student. Abby, still a virgin, on a technicality, which *does* count. Abby who can tap-dance. Abby who can't whistle, no matter how hard she tries. Abby who likes, maybe even could have loved, Luke.

Abby with brown hair, brown eyes, 120 pounds, 5'7", small scar on her right knee from tripping over the back step when she was five.

Abby: age 17, reported missing September 2, but gone before that, gone in summer and no one went looking.

Gone.

–3–

I don't know how I made it through the day I first found Abby.

My memory holds on only to vague pieces, because other, sharper things have since come to take their place. I remember the detention slip for cutting class and smoking in the parking lot, torn ragged on one side so it looked like someone had taken a bite out of my sentence, but I don't remember the detention itself. I don't remember what happened in my classes or what I learned, if anything. I don't remember lunch period with Deena, and what particular kind of slop-on-a-tray I carried to our table and then put in my mouth. Or what plans she made for her eighteenth birthday party, which was all she could talk about even though it was weeks and weeks away. Or anything else she said.

At one point there was my boyfriend, Jamie Rossi, at my locker, asking what happened and why I was late, and I remember this because it was the first time I had ever kept something from him.

"Just engine trouble," I heard myself telling him, "that's all." I didn't say anything about a girl taped to a telephone pole, a girl hidden in the back of my van. It was still possible I'd imagined it. Imagined her.

I have this freeze-frame of Jamie in my memory, this picture. In it, the hood of his sweatshirt is popped up over his head, and the dark curls over his forehead are spilling out because he needed a haircut again like he seemed to practically every other week. He's leaning in, eyes closed so I see how long his lashes are. And there are his lips out to meet mine. His stubble showing, but only on his chin, because he couldn't grow a full beard, not if he tried. I can't tell what he's thinking—if he believes me—because his eyes are closed. Not that I could ever guess, with Jamie. He's a guy, so he's used to keeping things close.

Then the picture of Jamie's face falls away, and I must have kissed him back, or a teacher came by and stopped us, but I don't remember that part.

I was outside myself, as if I were standing at the dip in the highway that led to Pinecliff Central High School, the last place you could turn before heading to school, all while some shadow-me was inside the building going to my classes, kissing my boyfriend, answering to my name when it was called.

I couldn't get Abby out of my mind.

During my free period, I did a search online, on one of the library computers, and found a listing in the missing persons database for an Abigail Sinclair from New Jersey. That flyer on the telephone pole may have been a few months old, but she was still out there somewhere. She was still 17 years old. Still missing.

There was also a public page online that her family or friends must have made for her—a memorial of sorts where anyone could post a message:

> ABBY! IF YOU ARE READING THIS! Come home! We miss you.
>
> ---
>
> Abigail, it's your cousin Trinity. You have Grandma and Grandpa so worried you have no idea. Where are you????? Call me if you're reading this. We just want to know you're ok!
>
> ---
>
> Dear Abby, I have never met u but I am praying for u every night
>
> ---
>
> Abbz U R missed @ school <3
>
> ---
>
> luv you girl come home!!!!

It was when I was scrolling through this page of notes left for Abby, notes I felt sure she'd never seen, from some people she didn't even know, that I realized a person was standing behind me, waiting for the right moment to speak.

When I turned in my chair, I watched this girl's gaze peel

away from my computer screen and go to me. I didn't recognize her at first, and then her face took on shape and I realized she was a freshman, a girl I'd seen around school. I was more aware of the fact that she was breathing, undeniably alive, than of anything else. This girl wasn't missing; she was right here. And all I wanted was for her to go away.

"Hey, Lauren," she said, "we saw you this morning. Are you, um . . . okay?"

"You saw me? Where?" The thought of being watched while I was in the van alarmed me.

"Before school? You were in the middle of the road? The bus almost hit you? We all saw you and we called out the window to you." She waited. "Didn't you hear us?"

I shook my head. A feeling of cold came over me as she brought me back to that moment—so immediate I could have been out on the windy highway beneath the snowy pines right then. I shivered involuntarily.

"We were all like, 'Hey what's going on, why'd we stop?' And the bus driver was like, 'Whoa, there's a girl in the road.' And then I was like, 'I know her, that's Lauren Woodman! From school!' You know we used to be on the same bus and—"

"My van broke down," I said, so she'd stop talking. I'd already clicked away from Abby's page and filled the computer screen with the library's search catalog. But the flyer—Abby's dirty, crumpled flyer—was on my lap under the desk, and I twisted it up and rolled it into a tight tube.

"Yeah, but you ran across the road. We saw you—"

She was a tiny girl, with warm brown skin and warm

brown hair, and she seemed harmless enough, she seemed genuinely concerned, but I couldn't listen to her anymore. What caught my attention was the movement out the window: not the flurries of snow but the flash of red. A gloveless hand on the glass that left streaks of mud in its wake.

She'd left my van and come close to the school, even though she couldn't get inside. There she was, a girl dressed for summer, though all around her was a white stretch of December snow. Her face was clouded with dirt, her long hair woven with brambles, with sticks and leaves and other indecipherable things gummed up and glimmering through the glass. The expression on her face—that haunted look in her eyes—made it seem like she'd seen things I hadn't, things not many of us had. Bad things.

The hand to the glass, the gesture, palm out, five fingers spread, insinuated so much to me: I should say nothing about her if asked, not to this random freshman and not to anyone. And it said she wanted something from me, needed it, and that I was the only one who could give it to her.

Help. Abby Sinclair needed my help.

"What're you looking at?" the freshman asked. She followed my gaze to the window and when she said, "Oh . . ." my heart seized, and I wanted to block her view with my body. But then she added, "Gross. Someone's got to clean that window—so dirty." She looked back at me and shrugged.

She wasn't able to see Abby, but she could see what Abby had left behind: the handprints, if not the hand that made them.

– 4 –

THAT night I had the dream.

In it was a house. I could try to explain it like it's an actual place that could be found on some street somewhere. Narrow and made of brick. Abandoned. Four floors rising up to disappear into shadow-smogged sky. The broken iron gate. The cracked and collapsing set of stairs leading up to the dark front door.

Even though the dream starts with me standing out on the street, I know it's not a street I could find anywhere in the waking world. There's no town or city beyond this place. The sidewalk begins and ends in a prickling patch of darkness. I can only go inside the house. And I always go in.

That first night, I was at the door in no time. Though the windows were covered in boards, and though a shroud of silence enveloped the building, curling out from the cracks and gaps in the brick, gagging me with it, I lifted my hand to try the bell. It was grown through with rot, so when I pressed the doorbell my finger sunk into something soft and wet, as if plunging into an open, oozing wound.

I pulled my hand away, then tried the door itself. It gave. One push, a few steps in, and there I was standing in darkness. I didn't realize I was in the foyer, beneath the dangling skeleton of a once-grand chandelier. I didn't know what was above me, or beside me, or shuffling down near my feet.

But I could smell something: the distinct scent of smoke. It tickled my throat, made my eyes water. Coming from close or far away, I couldn't tell. The hush of it was simply in the air, like a hot breath exhaled.

I should have been afraid, want to race out of there, even if I met my end where the sidewalk did. But I stayed put. It may have been dark, too dark to see my own hand before my face; and it may have been quiet, so quiet someone could have been hidden in the shadows observing my every move; but I felt the need to stay.

Soon I'd come to know the space of this dream like I know the house I live in with my mom, the carriage house we rent from the Burkes who live on the other side of the hedge, that little house with its unnecessary closets and stacked cupboards, its creaky steps and crooked doors. But on this night, my first night visiting, I didn't know what I'd find in this place. Or who.

When the smoke thickened, the oppressively hot air filling my lungs, I began to think I was in danger. That I could die. But no, actually. The dream wasn't that.

Soon I'd know this dream wasn't about anyone dying—it was about living on, forever. The house was a place where you could be remembered, even visited. A home for you when you lost your own. If you ran away. If you got taken. If you steered your bike down the wrong dark road.

All the girls ended up here.

When I'd visit on other nights, I'd come to notice the patterns decorating the wallpaper in all the rooms, the prickly vines of climbing, choking ivy. I'd see the gaps in the patterns, the blackened gashes where the rot had licked the walls away.

I'd know the layout of the rooms, even the upstairs, once I got the courage to climb the staircase without fearing it would turn to dust under my weight. There were many bedrooms, all down the hallways; enough rooms to make me wonder how many people had once lived here, how many people could fit here now.

I'd see the other girls there, each of them bound to this place. But that was later.

This was the first night. And the first night I ever had this dream—after I found the flyer with Abby's face on it—it was Abby I was looking for.

I could sense her, a shrinking, quiet presence breathing from some pocket of darkness. The scent was the same from the van. But stronger, closer. She moved and the floorboards creaked; that's how I knew she carried weight here. She was substantial here. Here, she was real.

I took a step toward the noise. "Abby? Is that you?" My voice scratched, but sound still came out.

I could make out a figure near a window in the next room. When I'd been standing out on the sidewalk I hadn't been able to see that there were curtains, but from inside I could see the long, dark sails of the closed drapes. The light was brighter in this room, somehow. The curtains had a sheen that seemed to fight the darkness, folds that could hide bodies, grimy tassels that trailed the floor.

She had her back to me.

Her hair wasn't matted with leaves and sticks, as it had been in my van—at least, as far as I could tell. The curtains hid her enough so I couldn't be sure. She felt familiar somehow, in a way I couldn't pinpoint.

I was trying to reach her through the smoke, because I had questions. Questions like: What is this place and what's burning? Is she really Abby Sinclair from the Missing poster? Does seeing her here mean she's dead, or is she still alive? Am I supposed to find her?

But it was a dream. And legs don't work in dreams the way they're meant to, and my tongue wouldn't shape the words collecting in my mouth. All I could get out was "Abby?"

The figure didn't turn around or make any kind of reply. This told me the answers weren't there in that scorched house. They were outside, somewhere near Pinecliff, my hometown, waiting for me to go out and find them. And for that, no girl in the smoke could help me.

I'd have to wake up.

– 5 –

THERE it was, down a road I'd driven before. To find it, I only had to hang right at the fork instead of left. From there, the winding road led deep into the pines and the entrance I was seeking was just past a blind bend, marked by a cluster of white firs and a blue sign. Most of the sign was obscured by a fresh covering of snow, hiding the words, so only the cutout of the lady herself rose into the darkening sky, two palms raised as if to catch the drifting flurries. She wore a pale blue head scarf, like the Virgin Mary, and had no face, like a ghost. Behind her was a locked gate as tall as the trees.

This was Lady-of-the-Pines Summer Camp for Girls: a place where people from suburbs and cities sent their daughters. The campground was buried in a valley of mosquitoes, pine trees, and poison oak, skirting the edge of a tepid lake. The mountain ridge cut off a view of what was on the other side, beyond this camp, so the girls—and their parents—

would have no idea what stood within miles of them. All that nature they'd spend the summer embracing was closer than they might guess to one of the state's maximum-security men's prisons, which housed, last I checked, more than a thousand violent offenders, including murderers, rapists, and child molesters.

According to the Missing flyer, this summer camp was the last place Abby Sinclair had been seen. Here, past the gate and beyond those trees.

I pulled in and cut the engine, but Jamie's car behind my van almost kept on going. He braked in the road and had to back up, scudding over a snowbank. The snowplows hadn't made it up here since the latest storm, so all the snow made it difficult to find a place to park. When he was closer, he rolled down his window and called out to me in the cold.

"What's wrong? Why'd you stop?"

"Nothing's wrong," I called back. "Just get out of the car. Come here."

I was already climbing out of the van and testing my flashlight. Night came sooner in winter, especially up here with the ridge blocking the sun. I knew it could be mere minutes before the dark dropped down all around us, and I wasn't sure if the electricity would be working on the closed campground during the off-season. Without a flashlight, we'd be out there unable to see.

The flashlight flickered, and I smacked it against my thigh. Light. I waved it at him, signaling to get him out of the car.

"Your engine didn't die again, did it?" he called.

I shook my head. He didn't know why we were here. I hadn't bothered to tell him that the spot I'd wanted him to follow me to wasn't a restaurant, as I'd insinuated, but *this* place. Through the gate was a snowed-out road leading in to what I assumed were the main grounds of the camp, where Abby had spent those summer weeks before she vanished. Only that locked chain-link fence was keeping us from it.

Jamie gave me a look I couldn't read, but he shut off his engine, pulled up his hood, then stepped out into the cold with me.

I pointed the flashlight at the fence opening, indicating the padlock secured by rings of thick chains. "Can you do something about that?" I asked. "So we don't have to climb over?" I let the light reveal the top of the tall fence, the razor wire glittering in the falling darkness.

"You're saying I dressed up for nothing, then?" Jamie tugged at the shirt collar under his coat, his one good gray button-down that he might have even ironed for the night out. But he didn't seem mad about it, I could tell.

Jamie and I had gotten together over the summer (the same summer Abby, mere miles from us, had been swatting away gnats and rowing canoes and singing campfire songs in repetitive round-robins). It happened fast, between Jamie and me.

Before I discovered Abby, and soon the others—before a fundamental piece of who I am shifted to reveal itself inside me, like an iceberg rising up to show its true and monstrous size from the frigid depths of the sea—I'd been the girl Jamie fell for. Whoever that was. It wasn't so long ago, but she and I were different people now.

He and I were different, too, but I don't want to forget all the good things about him. Like how he's fearless when it comes to braving heights, or breaking and entering; he once scaled the side of my house to reach an open window when I'd locked myself out, balancing on a flimsy gutter high up over the backyard, holding on by his fingertips. There was the way he'd go ahead and do something with me, simply because I asked him to. He didn't need to know why.

Like right then, in the snow. He was lifting the lock to take a look. A puff of his cold breath hung between us, as if reaching out to touch me, but I was just out of range. Just.

There I was, watching flurries fall and catch in his hair, those unruly curls of his poking out from under his hoodie, wishing I could tell him about Abby. But Jamie didn't believe in things like ghosts. And how do you tell a sane, rational person that you've had an encounter with one? That you've connected somehow with a girl whose face you found on a poster? A girl who went missing *right here*? How she's reaching out to you, you're sure of it? How she's trying to communicate something, though you can't quite make out the message?

I think bringing him with me was my way of telling him—but no matter what screamed out in the dark of my head while we stood there together at the gate, I guess he couldn't hear if I didn't open my mouth and let it out.

NO TRESPASSING signs hung on the chain link above us, glowing, practically nuclear, in the night. Snow dusted the shoulders of his green army peacoat, the one from the thrift store that was made for someone much bigger than him (but he wore it anyway, because I got it for him). He was silent for too long; I thought he'd given up and would say we should just go to the restaurant. Then his face lit up.

"So I can't pick this lock," he said, with a small smile. "But the chain? It's busted." With one hard tug, he got the chain open. The padlock fell into the snow.

Jamie was trying to meet my eyes, and I was trying not to let him. "So what is this place, anyway?" he asked.

"A summer camp, for girls," I said as I shoved the gate open into a snowdrift. "They close it up for winter, but I wanted to see."

I didn't give him the chance to ask why. I pulled him through to the grounds of Lady-of-the-Pines, abandoned for winter, though from the way it looked that night, expanding into the dark distance, it could have been abandoned years ago, before my mom and I moved to the area, before I was even born.

Jamie and I walked along what I guessed was the main path inside. He took my hand. I don't know what he thought we were doing there—what my intentions were, seeing how cold it was. It was starting then, my need for distance. I could feel this crawling sense in my skin whenever he touched me, the need to put some molecules of air between us. I could feel the cold sweat on his palm and something greasy, like he'd gotten goop on his hands when he was playing with the lock on the gate. There was an ultra-awareness of him, prickling and uncomfortable. Something so much more important was crowding out all thoughts of him.

We passed a shed and a white structure with the words MAIN OFFICE carved in over the wooden door frame. We went slowly, my flashlight exploring anything of interest, no words between us. Paths split off into the trees, the levels of snow lower to give hints of where they started, but not where they led. The quiet, except for our boots swishing through the freshly fallen snow, grew more and more intense.

Jamie startled me when he spoke. “I thought you said this place was closed.”

He’d found a set of prints, or really a series of indents over which the day’s snow had fallen. A small, squat building made of cinder blocks was to our left, and to our right a fenced-in square with a sign noting it as the compost, though whatever had been in there, rotting into the soil months before, was now frozen solid and shrouded in white.

“Probably only an animal,” I said, and as soon as the words left my mouth, a rustling could be heard, fast and loose like someone breaking into a panicked run. Then we saw it wasn’t someone at all—it was some*thing*. A fat little creature trundled out from the darkened patch of woods, over a fallen branch, to the edge of the compost, watching us with two yellow eyes as if waiting for the right moment to pounce.

“Is that a—” I started. “Oh, please no. That’s a skunk.”

“It’s a fox,” he said. “I think.” We backed away slowly, putting distance between us and it.

This might have been our only encounter of the night on that vacant campground if the wind hadn't shifted and let me know she was close.

"Do you smell that?" I asked. "Like something's burning?" It drifted—the scent of fire—from an unknown source. Faint and far-off, but familiar enough to remind me of the dream. Of her. Of how I felt sure they were tangled up together.

"No, I—" he started, but I didn't give him the chance to say more, because I was moving faster now, searching now, the smoke-thick veil between my world and her world loosening enough to let me slip in.

At some point during this, I let go of Jamie's hand.

–6–

SHE'D been here.

Abby Sinclair walked this very path, I could sense it. She'd spent whole weeks of her summer in this place before she was gone. She'd raised the flag on this pole and counted out change for candy at that canteen.

The farther in we went, the more it came clear to me. What she saw here, what she felt and experienced and breathed. I sensed, in an abstract sort of way, Jamie following behind me, but I didn't look back after him, I didn't explain.

I could feel the sweaty air that hung thick inside the mosquito netting of the camp's cabins. There was a dampness on my skin, the humidity that clings to this valley in summer clinging now to my clothes. I kept hearing flashes of activity through the trees, remembered noises echoing at me from the darkness. A series of splashes in the lake, the clatter of forks on plates in the mess hall, the satisfying *thwack* of an archery arrow into a target's heart.

We kept walking. It felt like we did so without a word to each other, but Jamie could have been saying things and I could have not been responding to what he said.

We found the mess hall and the arts-and-crafts cabin and the sports field. On a raised hill, we could see the ring where fires had been built. There was a large circle of stones, and I imagined the campers gathering here on the hottest nights, here where the thick cluster of pines broke open and the air thinned and where, overhead, there was a clear view of the blanket of stars.

Nothing appeared to be burning, and the scent I thought I'd caught in the woods had drifted, but still I brushed off a stone and rested my weight on it, gazing up. Night had fallen enough by now that the stars had come out. The jagged ridge in the distance was only a fuzzy and faintly shimmering outline, as if not a part of the mountain at all. I tried to see this place the way Abby might have. She was a visitor to this area. Not from here. Not used to this. Maybe our sky looked different to her, outside the suburb she was from. Everything was so much darker up here, away from stores and streetlights. And in the dark, out of view of traffic and neighbors, practically anything could happen.

Jamie cleared his throat. He was right next to me and I'd forgotten. Again.

"What are we . . . are we looking for something?" he asked.

He was occupying himself by throwing stones into the

woods beside the fire pit. Sometimes a stone would hit a tree—I could hear the thump of impact, or a whistling rustle into a thicket of branches—but sometimes the stone found only air.

I stood up. She wanted me to keep looking.

"We're exploring," I said to Jamie. "We're just seeing what's here."

"Hey, c'mere, hey, Lauren." He was grabbing for my arm, or my hip, or some part of my body, to pull me closer. But he missed me in the dark, and I made it past him and away from the fire pit and headed down the hill. The decline forced speed on me, and I started running.

I followed the pathways between the sleeping cabins and peeked in through holes in the sagging skins over the windows: the screens and mosquito nets that couldn't be that much help in keeping back the mosquitoes. The steps leading up to the cabin doors were buried in snow. I noted more animal prints—tracks from deer and raccoons, claw marks that had to be from birds, and a larger set that could belong to a giant owl hiding in the trees. Nothing human, not until me.

There were only five cabins for campers to sleep in. It took three visits with the flashlight to find it.

Cabin 3. Abby's cabin.

But I didn't know that at first.

All the furniture had been left inside the cabins for the off-season, the rows of beds with their plastic-cased mattresses stripped of sheets and their yellowed, lumpy pillows left behind in zipped pouches for next summer's girls.

Jamie was the one who helped me discover Abby's bed.

He'd followed me in, as he'd been following me around all the cabins, and he said, "Hey, check out the walls."

This was how I discovered that the girls at Lady-of-the-Pines liked to carve their names or initials and the dates of their stay onto the rough-hewn walls beside their beds. Over the years, enough girls had done this that there was a yearbook of sorts, an inmates' record on the walls of a prison cell.

I circled the cabin hoping, taking my time to check the latest set of names marking each metal-framed bed, which were arranged in two long rows against the walls.

I had a feeling I'd find her, somewhere, and then I did. Abby hadn't just carved her name into the wooden wall behind the bed she slept in. She didn't bother to note the year she spent here the way the other girls had. What she'd carved was a clue:

abby sinclair
♥
luke castro
forever

Jamie said it before I did. "Weird. Remember that Luke Castro kid from school? What a douche."

I knew who he meant—some guy who'd graduated a year or two ago. He played on some sports team, or hung around with the guys who did. I didn't really remember.

"Maybe it's the same Luke Castro," I said, and even as the words came out of my mouth I knew it had to be the same

Luke—this carving of his name together forever with Abby's told me so.

I don't think Jamie noticed how I lingered at this particular bed over all the others, how my finger reached out to trace the shape of the lopsided heart Abby had carved into the soft, splintery wood near where she rested her head each night. He had no idea I was trying to picture how she'd carved it, and with what. I was looking back into memories I didn't own, wanting in.

I heard him down at the other end of the cabin, talking to himself—or, no, someone must have called his cell, because he was talking to someone on the phone. His back was to me and his voice was low, like he didn't want me to know who it was.

It was then, with no one looking, that it began.

I stood up. I walked on legs that didn't feel like mine toward the back of the cabin, where there was a line of empty cubbies and a dark bathroom. I kept going, toward the bathroom. I couldn't hear Jamie on the phone anymore. My ears picked up on something else: a rhythmic *slap-slap-slap* coming from floor level. Startled, I stopped. The slapping sound stopped. I started walking again, and the sound picked up as before.

It was coming from my own feet, the noise of my own footsteps traveling the floor into the tiled room that held the showers. I could almost imagine that I didn't have on my combat boots and was wearing summer flip-flops instead. Flip-flops like the one Abby had on in my van.

As I stood in the shower room I realized I wasn't cold anymore. It was so far from cold, it was stifling, and I needed to undo the buttons on my wool coat to let my neck breathe. I opened my coat all the way. I shrugged off my thick scarf and let it drop.

There was a single window in the shower room, so small only an arm could fit through, but I went to it and shoved it open for some air. It revealed a view of the woods behind the cabin, but not the snow-covered tree branches I expected, not the heavy-loaded pines and the blanket of white gleaming in the winter darkness. What I saw was green.

The impossible green of summer.

I turned away fast and slid down the tiled wall—warm with humidity against my back—until I was sitting on the shower floor, beside the drain.

"I'm in here," I said aloud, letting the words echo and find their way to whoever was also there, listening.

I became aware of her breathing, as if she'd sidled up the tiled wall beside me, her bare, bug-bitten shoulder millimeters from mine.

Her story rose up in me, fully formed and practically kicking.

The summer she stayed here, Abby did sleep in that bed in Cabin 3, where I'd found her name and Luke's name. She did have the bunk pushed closest to the farthest wall and below the last of the windows. She slept curled into a ball. The pillow in the plastic pouch still on the bed was the pillow she'd hug between her knees.

I would soon know more and more. Like how when Abby left camp late that July, no new girl came to claim her bed.

Though Cabin 3 was minus one counselor-in-training with Abby gone, they had to make do; it was too late to fill her spot. The girls at camp were simply told she'd quit. The counselor in charge of Cabin 3 removed Abby's clothes in their neatly rolled stacks from her cubby and packed them into the paisley suitcase stowed under her bed to return to her family, who didn't seem surprised she'd run away. None of the counselors wanted to tell the kids that she'd run off into the night with only the clothes from Color War on her back. That she'd left no note to say why. No explanation.

Even so, the girls in Cabin 3 suspected more. They avoided uttering her name and stayed away from the things she'd touched. No one took advantage of the extra cubby or used the tropical shampoo she'd left behind in the communal bathroom. Abby's bed was in a prime location, more private than the beds in the middle, yet no one wanted to sleep there after she had, as if it had been cursed.

The only way I knew I'd gotten up and started walking was the *slap-slap-slap* that followed me as I went.

The bed was just as I'd left it, but on the mildewed pillow trapped inside the plastic case was something I hadn't noticed before. My hand reached out and unzipped the pouch. My fingers plucked it from the stained surface of the pillow and drew it out. It dangled before me.

A single strand of hair.

From Abby's head.

I knew this fact like I knew all the other things I knew. Besides, the piece of hair couldn't be mine—due to its light brown color and the spring to its spiraling curl. My own hair was dyed black and coarsely straight.

Something made me sniff it, some disgusting level of curiosity. I knew what it would smell like even before I lifted it to my nose, the faint but acrid hint of smoke as if this piece of hair had been held over a lighter and set ablaze. Everything connected to Abby seemed to smell like that.

I left Cabin 3, and with the *slap-slap-slap* of the flip-flops on my bare feet I wandered out again to the campground, feeling the hot summer sun on my shoulders. I lifted my hair and tied it in a knot. The sky was bright blue and dotted with fluffy, drifting clouds. The sounds of girls shrieking, splashing carried over from the lake in the near distance.

There were traces of her everywhere. Abby peed in these woods. She trampled these flowers. Here she scratched at a mosquito bite. Here she scratched at the same mosquito bite until she bled.

The spot on the campground where she first saw him was hidden from view by pine trees, but I found it from the way the branches grew sparser there and how the ground gave way, as if I'd seen it in pictures. Or, more, as if she were handing over this memory so it didn't have to be hers any longer. So now it could be mine.

He was on his motorbike, which you could hear way out in the trees, a sawing sound that made it seem like the whole forest was under siege. None of the girls in Abby's group out picking wildflowers knew what the noise was, or where it was coming from, until there he appeared atop that speeding, screaming machine. He sailed over a hump of tree roots and skidded to a solid stop in the clearing, front tire braking inches from a girl's toes.

"This is private property," one girl said. "You're not supposed to be here."

"I live here," Luke Castro said. As he said it, I remembered. Luke Castro from school *did* live somewhere around here—I was pretty sure.

The glare from the sun, or from her memory, made it so I had a hard time looking directly at his face, but it was him, the same guy from school.

He was checking out Abby in her camp-issue tank top. Out of all the girls there, he eyed her and only her—because she was older than the others, because she'd gathered up the most flowers, or simply because she had on the tightest shirt.

"I live down the hill, that way," he said.

He gestured out into the trees, though none of the girls knew where that could be, or what direction. Was it toward Pinecliff or away from Pinecliff? Near the train tracks or far from them? The counselors hadn't taught the girls how to judge direction by the sun or to use a compass yet, and Abby should have figured out how to make this a teaching moment. But she couldn't care less.

Abby had come here to train to be a camp counselor. On her application, she'd written that she loved kids. She didn't actually love kids; she'd wanted an excuse to get away from Jersey for the summer. She had no idea how much she'd *hate* kids after just the first week, after all the yelling through megaphones; eating slop, or trying to; burning through her arm muscles rowing those canoes. Right then she wished the girls would just wander off into the woods and entertain themselves with twigs and pinecones or something so she could have a moment alone with this stranger here.

But the girls were telling Luke to get off camp property, and he did, with one last glance at Abby.

These girls couldn't know what was communicated in that glance and in Abby's. The *Hey*, the *Hey yourself.* The *What's up with all the weeds?* The *Oh my God, don't even ask*. The *What're you doing with these losers anyway?* The *No freaking clue, I'm sooooo bored*. The *Yeah?*, the *Yeah*. The *Then maybe you should come out later and hang with me*.

Luke Castro rode off, his motor buzzing in the trees all around them like he could come crashing back and run them over at any moment, crushing toes this time, leaving carnage. But he didn't come back, not that day.

All Abby remembers is how she said, under her breath, "Who was *that*?" And how she had no idea she'd find out soon enough. She'd find out.

— 7 —

SHE wanted to show me another memory of hers before I left the campground that night, something more about Luke.

That was Abby's giggle scattering in the air like pine needles. We were rolling. It was too dark to see, and I'd lost track of my flashlight, but I could feel the warm grass through my shirt, the mud and leaves leaking through my clothes. The ground had given way to some kind of hill, and the decline went on until it stopped at a soft bottom, where another body dropped next to us, as if this other person had gone rolling down the hill, too. Even though I felt connected to her—she and I, me and Abby—I was also aware that there were just two bodies at the bottom of that hill: the boy, who was Luke, and the girl, who was Abby. I was only watching.

She took his hand then—it felt like I, too, took his hand—and she held it tight. She spit out pine needles and smoothed the leaves from her hair, even though it was too dark for him to see her hair, and she said—she said it and my mouth echoed the shape of it: "Oh my God, I totally love you, Luke."

It had just come out. She didn't mean to say the words out loud, but something from the fall down the hill made her tongue loosen. Because there it was now, a creature hovering over them in the night, and she couldn't unsay it.

I didn't hear what he said back, and at first I assumed that my hearing was going in and out of this memory, but it wasn't that I was losing sound and connection. It was that he didn't say anything. She'd told him she loved him and he didn't bother to respond. He silenced her with his mouth instead.

The last time I was kissed, it was Jamie, who tasted like cinnamon, which was the way I was used to a boy tasting.

But being kissed by Luke wasn't what I was used to. He didn't use his tongue at first, and that made Abby want him to. He teased with his lips, pressing his mouth to her neck. One side of her neck, below her ear, then the other. Then down her neck, down and down to her collarbone, and lower, to between her breasts, which is when I realized her shirt was wide open. Then he brought his lips up again, climbing, climbing, and his tongue entered her mouth, finally, and she tasted him, I tasted him, and he tasted us. It was sweet, a faint and faraway sweetness, and it was much wetter than I expected, so much so, I had to wipe my mouth off after. So did she.

He wanted more than the kiss, but the night wasn't over yet. Up above, at the top of the hill, was Abby's borrowed bicycle. I know this like I knew the grass was tickling the backs of her thighs because she had on shorts, but it was too dark to see if they were the red ones with the white racing stripes or another pair of shorts. If this was *the* night or another night.

And then his mouth left hers and she had a moment to catch her breath. She pulled back, dropping her weight to the soft ground, the grass wet with dew from the night, and gazed up to the darkened sky over her head. All those stars: the very same ones I was seeing almost five months later.

This was what Abby remembered. She liked returning to it to keep herself from thinking of what came after.

–8–

JAMIE was shaking me. He had me by the shoulders and was calling my name, his voice cracking, like this had been going on for a long time. He'd taken my coat—which had somehow detached itself from my body—and was holding it over me, like a blanket. My skin was slick with chilled sweat underneath the wool coat, my chest sticky with it, and my buttons were all undone, my shirt flapping open. I put the buttons back together as quickly as I could and wrangled myself out from under Jamie's grip, so I could stand up by myself.

I was at the bottom of a hill that was covered in snow. There was no bicycle at the top, and no Luke Castro.

"Did we just—" I said, motioning at my mouth, then his mouth. My lips felt swollen from kissing, wet.

"What? No!" Jamie said, standing up beside me and trying to help me get my two arms into my coat. "You were freaking out. You ran. You started stripping in the snow, then you fell down the hill. Don't you remember?"

I didn't know what would be worse . . . if I told him I did, or if I told him I didn't.

I was saved by a harsh light in my face. Not Abby's memory of a blazing summer's day come to distract me, but an actual light, vivid and aimed straight.

A police officer was waving a flashlight at Jamie and me. "Those your two vehicles out by the front gate?" his voice shot out.

Jamie hesitated. Then he said, "Yeah. The car's mine. The van's hers."

My hands were cold; that's what I was thinking. And my ears. So cold. I must have lost my hat when rolling down the hill, and my scarf somewhere, too. My legs were soaked and streaked in ice and snow. I had ice in my hair; I had ice up my nose.

"This is private property," the officer said, averting his eyes while I adjusted my coat and cleaned myself up. "There are signs up all over the fence."

Now that he was closer, his light bright enough to illuminate the whole area, I tried to make out the name on his uniform, but I couldn't. He was a dark blur, the brim of his hat keeping his eyes in shadow.

"We were just going," Jamie said, taking me by the elbow.

But I was realizing something: the opportunity here before me. Abby wouldn't want me to pass it up. I found my voice. "Officer . . ." I waited for him to give his name.

"Heaney," he said, after a long moment.

"Officer Heaney, we're actually here for a reason"—I felt Jamie tense up beside me, alert and on guard—"we, I mean, *I* just wanted to see what was out here. Since the summer."

"Uh-huh," the officer said, putting out a hand. "ID."

He made us open our wallets and show our driver's licenses. Jamie wore a deathly stare in his photo, like he'd been planning to set a pipe bomb in the DMV. I looked inexplicably sad in mine, which was strange, as I remember being pretty happy that day, the day I got my driver's license.

Seeing our IDs—that we were both 17, and both local—the officer seemed satisfied enough, though he still wanted us off the property. He said he'd remember us. He'd remember and arrest us for trespassing next time.

He motioned for us to start walking, ushering us toward the gated entrance, where we'd parked.

I found myself lagging so I could keep pace with the officer, leaving Jamie alone up ahead, the officer's flashlight a white-hot force against his narrow back.

"Officer Heaney," I said, "were you around here over the summer? When the girl went missing?"

With the light on Jamie and not on me, I could see more of the officer's face now, making him less of a uniform and more of a person. Only, Officer Heaney was nondescript in the way middle-aged men often are, with their bloated, stubbled faces and their shedding heads. I wouldn't recognize him out of uniform. He could be anyone.

I noticed Jamie slow down a little ahead of us, listening. But I had to ask, even if Jamie heard me.

"Which girl?" the officer said in a low voice.

He said it like there could be a great many girls, a whole jumble of thin, coltish legs and heads of long, blown-out hair, and I could select the one I most wanted from a model casting. He was only testing me. He knew which girl.

"The girl who stayed here over the summer," I said, and then let the name stumble off my lips for the first time. "Abby Sinclair. *Abigail* Sinclair, I mean. The girl who disappeared."

The officer was moving us quickly off the property. As we passed the naked flagpole, its rope hanging slack and then flowing upward with the wind, I caught Jamie glancing back at me. His face had gone bone-white in the beam of the flashlight, a piece of understanding settling there. He now knew why I'd stopped the van, that I'd planned this and kept it from him.

The officer had stopped mid-step, as if trying to decide what he could say, but when he spoke, it was with recognition and with authority, like I didn't have a legal right to ask for her by name. "Yes," he said. "Abigail Sinclair. Why are you asking about her?"

I didn't like the way he said her name.

"She's an"—I was avoiding Jamie's gaze—"old friend of mine. I heard she was up here this summer, and then I heard what happened, and I thought I'd come here and look around . . ."

The officer nudged me to walk faster. We'd passed the compost now and were coming up close to the front gate. "From what I understand," he said, "you're looking in the wrong place."

I shivered from the slap of a cold breeze. My feet had gone numb, and I was almost surprised to look down and see I did still have my boots on, and not Abby's flip-flops, because I could have sworn my bare toes were buried in snow.

"What do you mean, the wrong place?"

"The girl ran off. Her family knows that. Everyone knows that."

"You're wrong. She didn't run away."

"You sure about that?"

I was, all at once.

We'd reached the chain-link fence out front. He held it open with an arm out level with my chest, and there seemed to be a fraction of a second when he was keeping me from stepping through the broken gate.

"I *know* her," I said lamely. "I know she wouldn't."

Jamie spoke up, surprising me. "Didn't anyone see anything? Where she went? Who with? Anything?" He gave me a sidelong glance, assuring me we'd talk about this later, but for now he'd go along with it.

"And did you ever search the area?" I added. "The woods? Did you look for her bicycle, did you—"

"If you're only curious and that's all this is, I'll tell you," the officer said, looking only at Jamie's face, I noted, not mine. He revealed a couple details I didn't remember from the Missing poster, and I drank them in, holding them close for later.

It was Abby's grandparents, her legal guardians, who said she ran away—that's what they told camp officials and the police—and that's why there was no urgency to propel anyone to keep searching.

The officer pointed off the campground toward the old highway, now called Dorsett Road. A witness—he didn't share who—had seen Abby take a right on her bicycle down this road, and that was the last anyone saw of her. He shook his head like there was nothing that could be done. She'd done it to herself.

Besides, I could sense him thinking, what was she? She was only a 17-year-old girl. And 17-year-old girls vanish all the time.

Soon after this the officer closed the gate, made sure we got in our separate vehicles, and then took off. He drove an unmarked car without any lights on top, and I wondered if he'd been off-duty when he noticed our cars parked here. But as soon as his taillights were swallowed by the night, Jamie got out of his car and strode over to my van.

"*What* was that?" he said, taking a seat on the passenger side. My engine was idling to get the heat running, and he cupped his hands to the vent.

And here was another opportunity for me to tell him. Here—in the quiet night, minutes after I wore Abby's body, or she wore mine, when the two of us together rolled in a bed of pine needles, in the arms of the boy she said she loved. Now that Jamie knew she existed, I could have told him how connected I felt to her, this stranger who wasn't a stranger to me.

I could have. But all I said was, "I saw her Missing poster. I looked up this place. I was . . . curious."

(I did *not* tell him I had the Missing poster, folded as many times as a piece of paper could be folded, in my backpack, near his feet. I felt Abby in the trees, and I felt Abby in the air. I felt the exhale of her breath through the heating vents, and I felt the inhale in my head. She didn't want me to show Jamie, and what she wanted felt far more important than what I wanted.)

"So you don't know her," Jamie said. "So you lied."

"She didn't run away," I said. "She didn't. She—"

"*How* can you possibly know that, Lauren?"

I was staring down into my hands. The light from the dashboard lit them up enough for me to be able to see the lines of my palms, and yet when I gazed at them, there were no lines. My palms were smooth and unmarked as if I had no past, and no future. I had a moment of wondering whose hands were on that steering wheel, whose body walked out of the Lady-of-the-Pines Summer Camp for Girls and climbed into my van.

"I don't know for sure," I said. "It's a feeling I have, that's all."

I couldn't read his face.

But I'm going to find out, I thought but didn't say. She wouldn't leave me alone if I didn't.

He moved toward me then. I felt his hand on my chin, and his mouth on my mouth, and before I knew it I'd pulled away, putting some needed inches between us. A hand was out, shoving into his chest. That was my hand, making it impossible for him to get any closer.

I watched confusion cross his face, then something worse that looked a lot like anger. I'd never shoved him away from me before; I didn't even know why I had.

"Who was that who called you?" I blurted out randomly. I hadn't been bothered by it then, in Cabin 3 when he'd answered the phone, but in this moment something told me I should be.

"When?" he asked. He was frozen, leaning over my seat as if suspended in midair. My arm was still out, my unlined hand pressed up hard against his chest as if I were the one keeping him there, dangling. And I was.

I watched him move away from my hand, shrink back and retreat. It felt like witnessing something die between us, a stop-animation visual of a rotting and shriveling thing turning to particles of gray dust, then the wind lifting that dust up and away until there was nothing. I knew I should care. Only a few days ago, I would have fought it, leaped to close the distance, said I was sorry. Yet I did no such thing.

"Who called you? On the phone?" I repeated. "In the cabin before. Someone called."

"Oh, just my manager at work. Telling me my schedule for next week." He was in his own seat by this point, not even looking at me.

"Really," I said. "Who did you say it was?"

"My manager. At work," he said again. He waited tables at Casa Lupita, a Mexican restaurant across the river, and it was true he never knew his schedule until the week before. "Next week I'm on Tuesday night, Thursday night, Saturday day."

"Okay," I said. "Right."

Something told me not to believe him. And that something was irrational, and that something was unexplainable, and that something had never entered my mind before this night, and yet it was there, related to everyone and anyone. Even the boy I'd lost my virginity to, the one I'd talked about staying with after graduation, into college, which was as far ahead as we'd ever let ourselves think into the future. Even Jamie. Even him.

Jamie's neck snapped around, and there was a light in his eyes I didn't recognize, like I'd struck a match and lit him up.

"*What* is going on here?" he said.

"I really don't know," I answered honestly. My voice felt so cold.

"But something is," he said. "With us. First bailing on the restaurant. Then this place, this thing with that girl you never even told me about. Now—whatever the fuck this is."

He didn't wait for me to confirm or deny it. He slammed the van door, got back into his own car, and drove off. He made a left down Dorsett Road and let the trees steal his tail-lights and the wind steal any sound of his engine and the night steal my chance to fix it, not that I knew how to, or was even sure I would.

It happened so fast that I sat there waiting for him to come back, and when he didn't I was surprised, and then that surprise sunk lower and lower until it turned into a hard, black coal inside me that harbored three leaden words: *Told. You. So.*

I didn't have him when I needed him, which meant I didn't need him at all. He left me alone so I could be free to find what came next.

Though the truth is, I wasn't alone. After he was gone,

there was Abby, in the bench seat behind me as if she'd witnessed the whole scene and had been holding her tongue until she was sure she had me to herself.

Our eyes met in the rearview.

In this instant, a thought planted itself in my head in a voice I didn't recognize.

It's good you got rid of him, it said.

– 9 –

I was standing in the middle of the road where Abby Sinclair went missing. Jamie had left minutes ago, or an hour ago; all I knew was that he'd left.

I'd pulled out of the Lady-of-the-Pines parking lot and turned right, the direction the police officer said Abby had gone. I'd driven for a short distance looking for a hill, and since this was a mountain road, it wasn't long before I found one. I'd decided it could be *the* hill, it had to be, the one Abby had coasted down on the bicycle the night she disappeared. I pulled over, wanting to feel my feet on the asphalt she'd traveled that July night. I made myself walk the center of the road, following the decline, and as I did I imagined the speed of her bike picking up, how she stopped having to pedal, how she began gliding down, faster and faster, down and down . . . but to what?

As I descended to the bottom of the hill, the pines rustled, and it sounded like they were whispering again, spilling secrets I couldn't understand. They held their breath as one, keeping still, when I got close.

I remembered how, in the rearview mirror the morning Abby showed me her story, it came to a stop at the bottom of the hill. I wanted to see what went on after the end, when there was no one watching.

The narrow road was flat here, a pocket of darkness without streetlights or the glow of any nearby houses. There was nothing here. Just the shallow gully running alongside the stretch of pine trees on the left side, but nothing to separate the pines from the road on the right. Even so, the forest appeared to be brightly lit—glowing from the recent snowfall. All was quiet; all was alight.

What did I expect to find?

There wasn't the ghost of Abby herself, ready to talk and spread herself open for the reveal. Not her shimmering figure, standing in the shallow dip of snow to my left maybe, a hand lifted and its fingers slowly curling in to beckon me closer. Not her bicycle—leaned up and rusting against the bristly trunk of a towering pine tree, where the police were too blind to spot it. Not the man who grabbed her—if it was a man—or the car that hit her—if it was a car. Not an answer in a box with a bow on it, left there on the asphalt for me to find.

In fact, standing in the middle of the road told me nothing.

Still, I stepped into the gully, my eyes searching. I bent down, to inspect closer. Snow was in the way, and any evidence left there in summer would be long washed away or buried, but I kept looking. As if, somehow, I'd find a spot and a feeling would come over me and I'd know.

At some point I happened to turn and look back up the hill.

My van was parked on the side of the road where I'd left it, but what startled me were the bright beams of the headlights on high, cutting through the deep gloom.

I'd left the lights on?

I was sure I hadn't, was sure I'd turned off the lights and the engine and then gotten out and started walking, but I must have forgotten, because who else would have climbed into the van and flicked on the headlights?

I felt myself shiver. My van was black, with windows only in the very front and the very back. The main cavern was windowless, which made it seem like the kind of vehicle a serial killer would aspire to drive, to make it easier for transporting a body. I'd never noticed how ominous the van looked from the outside, how threatening.

It stared at me from up on top of the hill, eyes blazing.

And I think this was the first time it came over me—the reality. I was being followed. Haunted, by another girl the same age as me. She needed me to do something for her, and she wouldn't leave me alone until I gave her what she wanted. Would she?

She knew every little thing I did, could see me here on the dark road right now. She could hear my thoughts. She could feel my heart and how furiously it was beating. She could feel the panicked sweat dripping down my spine.

I never felt so alone, or so crowded.

I had to keep looking.

When I turned my attention back to the bottom of the hill, I saw things in a new light. It was golden and it was warm, thick with the heat of summer. Everything was tinged this color, even the night sky.

I noticed how the snow had vanished, so the road and the gully running alongside it was brown with mud, and green with protruding weeds. Then I realized I was on the ground, on the asphalt, because I'd fallen off the bicycle, and my hands were pocked with gravel and my knees were bleeding.

My hair was longer than usual, and I swept it out of my face so I could see. I noticed the front fender of the car—rusted, one headlight gashed in—and I used it to help myself to stand up. I heard a door open, and I heard a voice, and I heard a response come out of my own body, in a voice that wasn't mine, saying I'm okay. That was not me talking, that was someone else.

I was someone else.

It was over as soon as it had begun, the light around me turning colder and more blue. I was wavering on my two feet, in the middle of the icy back road, completely alone. There was no car here, no bicycle, no glimmering specter of a girl. My raw knees through my jeans burned, as if I'd really fallen to the ground as she had, and the palms of my hands were pricked with bits of snow and grimy pebbles of tire salt. But these were my knees again, and my hands, and my own breath billowing out in visible wisps from my own lungs into the cold.

That's when I saw it. There, close by, was a glow that

seemed to hum from the edge of the road. A light that, once it caught my attention, turned smaller, shrinking in on itself until the tiny thing I was meant to find focused and came clear. It looked like an oddly colored rock at first, and then I blinked. And realized what it was. Someone had dropped . . . a piece of jewelry on the side of the road.

I crept closer and lifted it from the blanket of snow. Impossibly, it had been perched there, half buried and glistening in the darkness. This stone pendant on a broken strand of silver chain.

Once I climbed the hill back up to my van, I let the pendant drop into my palm so I could study it under the dome light. I'd thought it was a rock, but it wasn't, at least not the kind of rock or stone that would be found just lying in the dirt in the Hudson Valley. Maybe it was a moonstone, but it wasn't so much a silky-smooth, gray gemstone as a round bubble of glass translucent enough to show its gray insides.

Gray like swirling smoke.

If I moved the circular pendant—which wasn't a real circle but a lopsided, handmade attempt at a circle—I could see the insides shifting, like I'd woken a dormant volcano. Other than this otherworldly aspect to the pendant, the smoke that moved as the stone moved, it was a plain piece of jewelry mounted crookedly on a backing of thick silver. The broken chain was crusted with dirt and green with rot, and wasn't even that nice of a chain to begin with. The pendant wasn't expensive. It wasn't beautiful. But it meant something.

It belonged to Abby.

– 10 –

MY mom caught me with one of Abby's flyers. It was the one I'd found in the Shop & Save where I worked after school. In the days leading up to visiting the camp, I'd discovered more of them, more and more, everywhere I checked in town.

This particular copy had been within my reach for months. It had been pinned up in the break room on the board between the two vending machines, the machine with the petrified ice-cream sandwich stuck in its craw and the machine that dispensed the same kind of soda, over and over, out of every hole. I'd seen only the top of the flyer on the bulletin board, only part of the headline that read: ISSING. But the rest quickly filled itself in for me, even though corners of other pages were blocking most of her face. I went to dig it out from beneath the layers of announcements for unwanted kittens and needed roommates, staff notices saying who can park in what section of the parking lot, and the store's holiday hours. There, beneath all that and pierced with hundreds of old pushpin holes so the page seemed to flicker with starlight, was a Missing notice for Abby Sinclair.

She'd been here waiting for me to find her all along.

My mom got home from class late that night, after I'd visited Lady-of-the-Pines. I was in our living room, curled up in front of the TV, waiting for her to come in so I could heat up a frozen pizza. Jamie hadn't called or e-mailed or left me a message, and my mom found me in an immobile ball.

"Hey," she said, pausing in the doorway. She dropped her schoolbooks on the side table and shrugged off her coat, then asked how my night out with Jamie went.

I shrugged. It went fine, I told her, and by the expression on her face I could tell she knew it didn't and she also knew I had no desire to talk about it. She digested all of this and restrained herself from asking more.

"How was class?" I asked.

"Good," she said.

In the moving light from the television screen, I watched the dance of her tattoos—for all my life, she's been covered with them. There are the vines that wrap around her arms and grasp her shoulders; there's the pinup girl on her back, the tendrils of the painted girl's yellow hair peeking out from beneath my mom's real hair, which she kept a brilliant bottle burgundy; and the flock of birds soaring up her neck and into the sky beyond her ear. All of these tattoos were as much a part of my mom as her two blue eyes.

But as I was looking at her, she was also looking at me, noticing the furious motion of my hands. "What's that you're holding?" she asked.

I realized I was still fingering the flyer, running over every rip and prick of a pin and gouge in the paper, acting like I was trying to memorize Abby's story in Braille.

"Oh this?" I said. When I heard myself, it sounded so artificial. "It's nothing."

I knew it wasn't nothing, but I also didn't yet know how, in a way, it was everything. Abby might have been the first, but she wouldn't be the last. All the girls are 17, the same age I'd turned that month. Soon I'd have flyers like this for so many of them. I'd be able to recite their names, their identifying details (birthmarks and hairstyles, fluctuations in weight and height), their hometowns and possible destinations, and sometimes the outfits they were last seen wearing (sneaker brands and jacket colors, specifics like the silver heart necklace, the turquoise hat with the pom-pom, the zebra-print belt). I'd know and understand their vanishings, but I wouldn't have the end to their stories, I wouldn't have the why.

"Can't I see?" my mom said, reaching out as if I'd actually let go. And that's when I crushed it—Abby's Missing flyer—crushed it fast into a hot, damp knot in the palm of my hand.

She pulled back her hand as if I'd bitten her. "Never mind," she said. "You don't have to show me. So I was thinking of heating up a frozen pizza. You want?"

I nodded, and watched her drift off to the kitchen. I want to say I offered to help, but I stayed put where I was. I kept the balled-up flyer safe, wedged in under my body, and I didn't fight it when my eyes began to close.

It was almost like I wanted to have the dream, like I was calling it closer. Before I knew it, I was on the sidewalk outside the brick building, and I was climbing the cracked and crumbling stairs, and I was at the door trying to decide if I should ring the bell or just let myself in.

Oh wait, I was in already. I was coughing and coughing and batting at the smoke to get it away from my face. When the air settled—when my eyes and lungs got used to it, or when I realized I was lucid enough to communicate to myself that I was dreaming and this wasn't actual smoke—a sense of calm came over me. I let myself see where I was.

The house had shifted its arrangement of rooms, with some doorways I didn't remember, and some rooms in places there hadn't previously been rooms. Up above, the ceiling creaked with the weight of movement. A rotting chandelier, covered in moss and spiderwebs, misted with smoke, shook as if a person were stomping heavily right over it.

"Is someone up there?" I called. "Abby?"

That's when I caught the drapes moving at the far end of the giant room. Someone was hiding near the windows, like last time. The same figure, the same girl.

I could see her more clearly now.

The long curtains were in tatters, so it wasn't entirely possible for her to fully conceal herself behind them. Holes in the mealy fabric showed pieces of her body—she was still wearing the too-tight jeans she'd been wearing on the night I last saw her; the jeans that said *FU* on the thigh (upside down, because she'd scrawled it without thinking of how other people would read it, or because she meant it for herself more than anyone else)—and the gutted hem of the drapes showed me the bottoms of her legs in those jeans and two bare, dirt-blackened feet.

All this time I'd been looking for Abby, and here I'd found someone else.

In the dream, I found myself doing things I'm not sure I could have done in real life. My dream-self picked her way through the room to get closer to those drapes. My dream-self had no fear. She ignored the growing sense that there were others behind her, others she hadn't been introduced to yet. She found the edge of the drapes and moved slowly along the length, searching for a cord. When she found it, hidden in the tatters and held together by a few tangled threads, she took it in both hands and she pulled. The drapes slid open, and the girl, Fiona Burke, was revealed.

There she was—not an animated and gruesome corpse, dead the way she surely should have been if the stories were to be believed. And not years older, either, the way she would be now if she'd survived.

Fiona Burke hadn't aged a day.

Her hair was red with the black roots, gone pinkish in some spots. Her eyes were liquid-lined. Her bare stomach was visible, but it wasn't that she'd grown out of her shirt in the years since I'd known her; that's how she liked to wear her shirts, one size too small and no shame for what was showing.

With the drapes open, Fiona Burke stepped out into the room because there was nowhere to hide. There was glass all over the floor from a window that must have been shattered—and as she walked closer to me she stepped right on the shards. Pain didn't reach her face, if she felt any at all. I realized, now that I'd grown up and she'd stopped growing, we were about the same height.

She spoke then. She recognized me.

Happy now? You little brat.

I could have asked her how she knew it was me, after all these years, because I dyed my hair black now, blue-black from a bottle, and didn't I look any different from when I was a kid?

Before I could utter a word, she grabbed my hand and shoved something into it that was hotter even than her skin, sizzling like a coal burning from a fire, and hard, like a knob of bone. My sole reaction was to get it away from me as quickly as possible. My hand opened and let go.

What dropped to the ground was a pendant made from a smoke-gray stone.

That's when I remembered I'd seen something very much like it before. Fiona Burke used to wear a choker with a similar stone around her long, thin neck.

My dream-self didn't have the wherewithal to make the connection, but my waking self, the self bursting out of sleep on the couch before the flickering TV at the sound of Mom saying the pizza was ready—my waking self needed only an instant to connect the dots and connect the girl.

There was me. There was Abby Sinclair. And now there was a girl I last saw when I was eight years old. Fiona Burke used to be my next-door neighbor, but she ran away from home when she was 17 years old.

MISSING

FIONA BURKE

CASE TYPE: Endangered Runaway

DOB: June 17, 1987

MISSING: November 13, 2004

AGE NOW: 25

SEX: Female

RACE: Asian

HAIR: Black

EYES: Brown

HEIGHT: 5'3" (160 cm)

WEIGHT: 125 lbs (57 kg)

MISSING FROM: Pinecliff, NY, United States

CIRCUMSTANCES: The photo on the right is a composite image to show how Fiona may look at twenty-five years old. She was last seen on November 13, 2004. When she was last seen her hair was dyed red. Her hair is naturally black.

ANYONE HAVING INFORMATION SHOULD CONTACT

Pinecliff Police Department (New York) 1-845-555-1100

– 11 –

WHEN I look back, I can see the hints. The hints that were there all along—like the time I was eight years old and my mom left me in the care of the girl who lived next door. The girl who told me to stand very still with my face squashed up against the yellow wallpaper and to not turn around and to not dare look. To stand against the wall in my My Little Pony pajamas while she made plans to ditch town for good.

That was the first time I came in contact with someone who went missing.

Fiona Burke was the daughter of the couple in the big house next door. They'd adopted her when she was a baby, from an orphanage in China. I don't know what her name had been before the Burkes rechristened her and brought her back to the Hudson River Valley, to where they lived in the small town of Pinecliff, New York. Even today, the Asian population in Pinecliff is only 1.34 percent. Fiona Burke was likely one of only a handful of Asian kids in school, and she was the only person I knew who'd been adopted.

I don't know what the Burkes were like all those years before Fiona, when they were childless and tucked away behind their lace curtains, shopping for someone else's offspring to bring home. They were an older couple, older than anyone would expect to be raising a teenage daughter, and the only reason we knew them is because we rented our house from them. It was small and separated from their much grander house by a pruned hedge. They called it the "carriage house" and wouldn't let my mom and me paint it a color because they wanted it white, to match theirs. Apparently, a long time ago, it used to be the garage.

This meant the Burkes were our landlords; my mom used to send me over to their palatial front porch on the third or fourth of the month—never the first, never on time—to ring their bell and hand-deliver an envelope containing the rent check.

Only, the Burkes never came to the door. I'd ring the bell and Fiona would answer before the chime even stopped sounding, like she kept herself pressed up behind it, waiting for any excuse to let in some air.

She'd open the door, see it was only me, and her face would fall. She'd hold out her hand so I could give her the envelope, and she'd say, "This from Tamara?"

And I'd say, "Yeah, that's from my mom."

Fiona Burke wasn't particularly friendly—she never invited me in; she never said thank you. But, in the beginning at least, she wasn't mean. She'd simply put the envelope containing our rent check on the sideboard, and the whole time she'd be looking up over my head, past me at the road, a visual ache showing in her face. Then she'd close the door.

She was nine years older than me, so it seemed she'd always lived there in that house with the Burkes. She belonged in Pinecliff, our small town set upon the steep hill, with the railroad station down at the bottom and the mountain ridge hovering above. To my mind, she belonged there more than I did.

When we spent any amount of time alone, like when she'd do my mom a favor and babysit me for a few hours, she was quiet, perched on the edge of the couch near the television, making surreptitious calls on the phone. But something changed the last year I knew her, around the time she turned 17. I know because my mom said, "Don't take it personally, honey, she's 17—that's just how girls are at that age."

But were they?

The shift in Fiona Burke's personality came fast, it felt to me. It altered the look in her eyes, and it chilled the tone in her voice. It changed everything. She liked to tease me about something that year, telling me she could evict me and my mom anytime. All she had to do was make up a good, steaming lie about us to tell her parents, and my mom and I would be out on the street. We'd have to live in a cardboard box and beg for handouts at the train station, she said. And maybe my mom would decide I was too much for her to take care of, and she'd sell me off to some passing businessman on an

Amtrak train bound for Penn Station, and who knew what would become of me then.

I cried the first time she said this, which made her enjoy repeating it. Of course I know now she didn't have the power to evict us, not by her word alone, but I used to believe she did.

But my sometimes-babysitter and longtime next-door neighbor Fiona Burke appeared as innocent as she ever would in the photograph her parents selected for her Missing poster. In it, she had straight teeth and straighter hair, not yet dyed. Her shirt buttons were done all the way up to her neck and there were two pearl earrings fastened in her ears. She wore a blameless smile and sat there on a stool with her hands folded. Her favorite necklace was tight around her throat, and the flash of the studio camera happened to catch it at the exact right angle to make it look lovely and not like a ghastly, dirty thing hanging over her shirt.

She was who they wanted her to be, in that picture. That was before she turned 17. After, a whole other side to her emerged, one that was out in full the night I saw her last.

Fiona Burke's parents saw one thing, and the world saw another.

When she disappeared, I remember seeing her picture in the news, being aware that people were looking for her. But, as the years went on and she didn't come back, as her Missing posters came down from bulletin boards and other announcements for yard sales and ride-shares and rooms for rent went up in their place, people forgot about her and stopped asking.

She'd lost herself to that place where the missing kids go, the kids no one finds, even when lakes are dredged and woods combed. The ones computer-aged into adulthood who never make it home.

She didn't call. She didn't write.

She was just gone.

And I guess I'd forgotten about her like everyone else in town had, until she showed up in the dream and tried to give me that stone, the one that looked a lot like the broken piece of jewelry I'd recovered from the gully on the side of Dorsett Road. I was sure it meant something, and it wasn't until I was alone again later that night, after the frozen pizza with my mom and trying to deflect her questions about Jamie, that I closed myself in my room and dug it out from where, the second I got home, I'd stowed it inside a sock that was wrapped in a sweater and buried in the bottom drawer of my dresser. It wasn't until then that I really let myself remember.

– 12 –

IT was a chilly night in November, the night Fiona Burke disappeared. Her parents were down in Maryland for the weekend, so she had the house to herself, and it was clear she'd wanted—planned—to keep it that way. Until my mom asked her parents if she could watch me, and they said yes without confirming it with Fiona first. I'm guessing that my usual babysitter must have flaked like she did sometimes, and my sudden appearance at my landlords' house was a last-minute surprise—to both Fiona and me. Because with her parents out of state, this was the night Fiona Burke had planned to run away from home, and all of a sudden I was there, in the way.

My mom wasn't in school then. She didn't have the job at the state university or even the certificate to get that job, so this must have been when she worked nights, when she was still dancing at the club across the river.

I want to say I could pinpoint exactly what Fiona Burke looked like on that night she gave my mom the finger behind her back and then said she'd take great care of me. I should have an image of her cleaning out her mother's jewelry box and her father's suit jackets, dredging for pawnable brooches and misplaced gold cards.

But she was a fiery blur. Her hair was livid, dyed the red of a sugar drink. Her mouth was a deep, dark streak slathered in gloss that was manufactured to look wet long after it dried.

I remembered this:

Fiona Burke on the landing of her parents' circular staircase, leaning over and looking down to the floor far below. Her scraggly flame-red hair with the pitch-black roots hung upside down in the air like living thorns, and through the thorns she was yelling at me to come help her.

I realized she was really doing it and not just saying she would. Leaving. She was actually running away. She'd packed up her things; the few bulging bags up above were the possessions she'd decided to take with her. Before I was ready, she began to fling the bags one by one over the banister.

Dropping her bags down from that height made each one land with the sickening smack of a suicide on the tiled foyer floor. I dragged them off to the side as soon as it was safe to grab them.

When she leaned over to drop the last bag, the odd, murky pendant she always wore got caught on the banister. She pulled herself free and flung the bag, and I guess at that point the black cord that kept the necklace choker-tight against her throat snapped, and the pendant itself slipped off and fell, too.

It sailed through the air over me, and though it must have dropped fast, because it was an actual stone and not made of something lighter, my memory holds a picture of it still falling. I'm standing below, in the middle of the foyer beneath the glittering chandelier, gathering her bags in a pile as instructed, and I look up. I should have moved, but there I am with my face turned upward and the dark object hurtling straight for me.

I must have covered my head and ducked at some point, because the broken pendant did reach bottom, where it hit me in the shoulder, leaving a searing pink whop of impact. From there, it dropped to the floor, glossy face up.

I seem to remember, if I peer back through the years of carefully buried distance, that the stone was as gray as a trail of exhaust smoke, and it had a surface that shone and bounced the light to trick you into thinking it was beautiful. I also seem to remember that I didn't get such a good look at it before Fiona Burke descended the stairs and snatched it out of my hands, shoving it in the slim pocket of her jeans to take with her.

That's how I know she had the pendant with her when she went. And yet somehow, impossibly, there I was, more than eight years after she'd gone, holding her signature piece in the palm of my now much larger hand.

– 13 –

AFTER seeing Fiona Burke so distinctly in my dream, I cornered my mom. I wanted to ask about Fiona in a way that didn't seem rehearsed, to know if my mom had ever heard anything about the girl, after all these years. For all I knew, Fiona Burke had safely made it into her twenties and was living in a perfectly nice house somewhere far from here, like North Dakota, studying to be something admirable, like a veterinarian.

My mom looked up from her psych textbook. "Did you say Fiona Burke?" she asked absently, yawning and marking her place with her highlighter. "I haven't heard her name in years." She pulled her hair off her neck and stretched, and as she did the flock of birds tattooed near her ear lifted their wings for the ceiling. The green vines encircling her arms came alive with her movement, and I admired their twists and turns and flowering details until she lowered her arms and her sleeves dropped closed and hid the pictures from me.

Our cat, Billie—for Billie Holiday—leaped up on the back of the couch. Her long gray hair made her appear even larger than she actually was, and her green eyes held on me warily. We'd had her almost as long as Fiona Burke had been missing.

"Yeah," I told my mom. "I hadn't thought of her in a long time, either."

She asked a simple question next. She asked why.

This is how it's been between me and my mom since I was a kid: I'd tell her anything. I'd tell her things before she asked. I told her the first time I tried a cigarette, at thirteen, and never again. And as soon as Jamie and I were getting close to taking it to the next level, I confided in my mom and she made me an appointment at Planned Parenthood.

That's what happens when it's only you and your mom and no one else. There's a trust you share that no one can get close to. My mom had a tattoo on her left arm of two blackbirds in a knotted tree; that was the piece she got for her and me, after I was born. We were in this tree, together, she liked to say.

Something breathed in the living room with us, and I was the only one aware. Was it Abby, whispering through the hollow spaces in the walls? Was it the rising voices of the other girls, who I didn't know were coming yet, so I didn't know to listen for them? Was it Fiona Burke herself, haunting this property and reminding me she could still have us evicted from this house?

All I knew was something—someone?—didn't want me to tell my mom why right now. I felt sure of that, almost as if I could hear a voice breathing these commands into my open ear:

Don't tell her. Don't tell her about the dream.

I knew I shouldn't tell her about Abby's Missing poster rescued from the telephone pole, or about the summer camp where she'd gone missing. Not about Luke Castro, either, who I'd now tracked down and would go visit. And not about Abby's grandparents' address in Orange Terrace, New Jersey, and how I'd mapped my path there from our front door. Not about the pendant I was now wearing on a long string that hung under two layers of shirts and felt warm, oddly warm, against my bare skin.

I was not supposed to tell my mom any of these things.

I spoke carefully, as if there were someone keeping tabs on me from the shadows, making sure.

"I don't know why," I said. "I . . . I just thought of her. Like randomly. For no reason. And I wondered if Mr. and Mrs. Burke ever got any word about what happened. Did they?"

My mom had gotten to her feet by this point and stood there worrying the tattoos at her wrists, winding her fingers around and around them, as if she could rub off the vines and start over with fresh skin. This was a nervous habit she had, when she was finding words for something difficult.

She drifted to the window, the one facing the hedge that separated our house from the Burkes' next door. The night was glistening white and as silent as an unsprung trap. Billie wove herself through my mom's legs and tried to look up and out the window herself, though she was far too short to reach and a little too fat lately to go leaping.

Obviously I assumed my mom was going to tell me that

Fiona Burke was dead. But she only confirmed what I already knew: Fiona Burke had run away, and no one had ever heard from her again.

The Burkes' house was dark, as if they were away—and maybe they were, like the night their daughter took off—but my mom studied its windows as if expecting a light in one of them.

"It's so sad," she said, turning back to me. "I still don't know what to say to Mr. and Mrs. Burke, now, after all these years."

"Me either," I said.

"I could have helped her," my mom kept on. "Fiona. I could've done something. If I'd known."

I could see how she took it in, what happened to the girl who'd once lived next door, knotting it up into her own little ball of knots she carried around inside, lifting it out every once in a while to dwell. She was studying to be a psychologist at the university where she worked; it would take her years to get the degree, as she could only take a couple night classes a semester with her tuition reimbursement while she worked days in an office on campus, but I believed she'd make it. I believed she'd get to help people.

Still, I don't think she could have helped Fiona Burke.

"You two were close," my mom said.

"We weren't close. I hardly knew her."

"It wasn't your fault, you know. Not by any stretch of the imagination was that your fault."

She was thinking about the night Fiona Burke left, and

then I was thinking of it, and then there it was, that almost-nine-year-old memory, itchy and oily like wool.

"I know it's not my fault," I said.

Fiona Burke had been babysitting me the night she ran away, that's fact. Her parents didn't come home that night, so my mom was the one who found me after, and she never once blamed me for not stopping the girl from getting in that truck, mainly because she didn't know about the truck.

Besides, I couldn't have stopped Fiona Burke, I told myself. She'd been watching the road for a good long time. Once on it, I don't think there was anything that could have turned her back around.

So it was no one's fault. There was nothing I could have done.

This is when the idea came to me, featherlight and drifting through the room like tufts of Billie's shedding fur. What if that's why all this was happening—starting with my van breaking down on the side of the road so I could find that flyer—was it so I could do something for someone else? For Abby?

My mom touched her cheek, absently, as if she knew the exact spot where her beauty mark could be found, the distinct circle so black it was almost blue, on the left side of her cheek, beside her lips. She put her fingernail to it like it itched.

Her beauty mark wasn't inked on in a tattoo parlor; she was born with it. That's why it was my favorite piece on her.

It was then that Billie hissed at no one, as if someone had entered the room who only she could see. And then, when my mom turned her attention back to her studies, I saw them, the twinned shimmering outlines in my living room, though it looked like they didn't know they were in my living room, that they didn't see me or us or even our furniture, since they stood in the same space already occupied by the couch.

My mom looked up because I was staring. "What?" she said. "Still thinking of Fiona?"

"No," I said. My eyes weren't on Fiona; they were on the girl beside her.

I now knew for sure that Fiona was connected to Abby and Abby to her, somehow. They were reaching out from wherever they were now, trying to let me know.

They stood wavering like a two-headed mirage in the space where the couch was. Then, when my mom reached out to turn on the reading lamp, like shadows do when the light hits, they disappeared.

14

THERE was a witness. The officer said someone saw Abby Sinclair ride the bike off the campus of Lady-of-the-Pines and into the night. He didn't say who the witness was. Of course he didn't; why would he tell me? But Abby did.

It was another girl—a kid. She was one of Abby's campers in Cabin 3, and happened to be the only soul who knew that Abby would sneak off after lights-out, and who she'd go to meet. This girl carried around the secret about Abby and Luke for weeks, first because she got up to pee in the middle of the night and caught Abby tiptoeing into the cabin with a blazing smile on her face that illuminated her teeth even in the darkness. And then because Abby wanted someone to confide in, and she believed that this girl—with her frizzy braids and her thick glasses, her lack of friends and her innocent sense of devotion—would never betray Abby to the counselors.

And so, the girl ended up witnessing more than the last bike ride. Nights previous, she'd seen Abby slip back in beneath the mosquito netting with her eyes full of stars, her lipstick smeared, and the grass stains riding up the back of her shirt. The girl wasn't there herself when it happened, but she heard it recounted later, how Abby and Luke almost did it. *Almost.* This girl was young enough to wonder, for hours on end, in vivid-if-anatomically-impossible detail, during games with balls she was supposed to be in the outfield to catch, just what "almost" could even mean.

It wasn't so much a premonition but simple curiosity that made her follow Abby that night. The faint *slap-slap-slap* of Abby's flip-flops were what had woken her, as if Abby were being careless and begging to be caught.

When the cabin's front door swished closed and the shadow of her favorite counselor-in-training sneaked past the window, she slipped out of her bed and tiptoed outside. She felt the crunch of leaves and pebbled dirt beneath her bare feet and wished she'd thought to bring shoes. Once she saw Abby make a run for it past the mess hall, where the counselors had gathered to be loud and reckless now that the campers in their charge were asleep, she knew she'd have to run, too. And again she longed for shoes.

Somehow she made it past the counselors—in there laughing and popping bottles, not one of them glancing out the windows to catch Abby or the girl streaking past—and she caught up to Abby by the bike shed near the edge of the road. What did she expect Abby to do once she saw she had company?

Welcome her with open arms? Let her ride the handlebars of the borrowed bicycle and join her on the hill past the fence with Luke, lying between them and making a game of searching out constellations in the sky? Even better, making it so Abby changed her mind and didn't go see Luke at all?

She didn't exactly know. But she sure hadn't expected Abby to get so mad.

Abby snapped at her, called her a nosy brat, and a few worse names besides, and told her to get her butt back to Cabin 3 before she got them both kicked out. The girl happened to mention that the bicycles in the bike shed were for counselors only—she believed in following rules—and since Abby was only in training to be a counselor she wasn't allowed to ride them, and that made Abby madder still.

The girl backed away, stung, and then watched dejectedly as Abby pedaled off on the old, rusted Schwinn bicycle toward the main road.

That was how I pictured it.

I could put myself in place of either girl: the witness, willing her not to go, or Abby herself, the wind in her hair, the blur of the road, those last moments of gorgeous freedom.

—15—

WHEN I pulled up in my van, Luke Castro was in the garage, the sliding door raised open so I could see him from where I'd parked at the bottom of the driveway. He was a pair of legs under the body of a car, so still it seemed at first the car had fallen and crushed him.

I knew it was Luke, the guy Abby liked and maybe could have loved, in the way I knew that Abby had been to this house before. I could sense what patches of lawn she'd walked on, because the ground was still warm months after, snow melted through to grass in spots no larger than a size-eight shoe.

He must have heard my van pull up, because he wheeled himself out and sat up, staring down the driveway at me. He didn't wave.

From that distance, I wasn't sure at first if I recognized him from Abby's memory, but I did recognize him from school. Jamie was right: Luke Castro had graduated a year ago, and apparently he hadn't gone off to college or he was home on a break, because he was still here at his parents' house, the same address listed in last year's school phone book.

Luke glared at my van, his gaze drilling holes through the windshield. I wondered who he saw in the driver's seat, who he thought I was. I got out and started walking.

I'm not so tall, and I'm not so short. I've got long fingers, I've been told, and long legs for my height, and, I've noticed, a long nose. I was earringless and lipstickless, but the pendant was there around my neck, the round, smoky stone mounted on the long string and hidden under all the layers of my clothes where no one could tell it was hiding unless they pressed a hand up to my chest. Then they'd feel its hot, hard lump.

From where Luke was in the garage, though, I would have only been a hooded face outside an unmarked van. I lowered the hood of the sweatshirt I wore under my coat—one of Jamie's hoodies, his red one; he'd left it in my room weeks ago and I hadn't washed it or given it back—and when Luke saw my face, saw I was just a girl, his stillness broke.

He lowered a wrench and moved out of the garage, coming closer. I realized he didn't exactly look like he had in Abby's memories. For one, his body was . . . thicker. He probably had thirty pounds on Jamie. He was also less glowy than I remembered, the shimmer of Abby's gaze noticeably absent, making him just some guy standing in a driveway in broad daylight. He was good-looking in that obvious, overly symmetrical way I'd never been into, and I found myself wondering about Abby then, about what kind of girl she was if she'd gone all gaga over a guy like him.

Was this the same Luke that Abby had known? I thought back to the declaration of love carved letter by letter into the wooden wall against where she rested her head:

abby sinclair
♥
luke castro
forever

That's what I'd seen. Luke Castro. This guy. This guy, here.

My legs walked me over to him. "Luke? Do you remember me? I'm Lauren. I'm—"

"Jamie Rossi's girlfriend," he said, stopping me, like that's how I'd introduce myself to someone, my identity in relation to a boy's. "Yeah, I know who you are. What's up? What'd I do this time?" This last added with a grin, as if he were happy to be known around town for doing mischievous things.

"I don't know," I said, "what did you do?"

His smile cracked wide open, my tone lost on him. Besides, he wasn't even looking me in the face. "Hey, I like the van," he said. "No windows. Good and private. Nice." He wasn't looking at the van, either. His eyes were running up and down my legs. His eyes took their sweet time finding their way back up to my face, and when they did the arrogant look there showed me he didn't care if I had a boyfriend. Or who I was. I could have been any female in skinny jeans standing in his driveway and he'd assume he had a shot at tugging them off. I pulled the coat down and lifted the hood of the sweatshirt.

That was what my body did and what my brain thought, but then what Abby wanted took over. It was having Luke Castro so close that had brought her out again. Her breath fogged up my mind.

For a second, as if Abby's nails were digging into my skin to keep me from squealing, I didn't want to say why I was there. I wanted to do what she would've done. To be her. To take over from where she would have landed, had she made it all the way here on her bike that July night. To lean in and kiss him and let him tug off my skinny jeans and see what his body looked like under those clothes. It was cold outside, but with these thoughts in my head, it was warm. I'd never been with anyone but Jamie, and there was only the thinnest thread holding me to him. How easy it would be to break it.

But I shook my head and wrestled back control of my mind. "I'm here because of Abby. I heard you knew her."

The sound of her name turned his face an unnatural shade of blank. The kind of expression someone would have when trying to hide something.

"Abby Sinclair," I said, watching his face carefully. "I heard you guys hung out this summer."

Still blank. So blank I thought he'd deny it. And then I'd have to remind him.

Abby's memories of Luke, of the nights she snuck off the campground to see him before the night in question, are full of lips pressed in darkness, and the way his neck smelled, which was musky from his cologne, and the way the planes of his face caught the barest patches of light in the darkness. How he looked under a streetlight. How he looked in the beam of the tiniest flashlight, so small it hung from the ring of his keys. How he looked under the light of the moon.

"Abby?" I repeated. "Pretty girl? From New Jersey? Long brown hair?"

He straightened, and a shadow could be made out, slinking across his eyes and cheek, cascading down his chin. "That girl from that camp down the road?"

"Yeah. Abby. I know you know her. She told me."

"You a friend of hers or something?"

I nodded. I was way more than a friend. He had no idea.

"Well," he said, shrugging. "Took you long enough." He turned his back on me then and walked up into the garage. I had no choice but to follow.

Abby was deathly silent as I trudged up the driveway behind Luke Castro. I couldn't see her anywhere in the snow and I couldn't feel her behind me.

Was she in the house? Had Abby Sinclair been hiding here in Pinecliff all along?

Once in the garage, where it was warmer because of the space heater, and darker because the sun didn't reach, I tensed, expecting him to open the door leading into the house and then there, all cozied up in a winter sweater knitted by his grandma, would be Abby herself, alive and well and rolling her eyes at my intrusion. She would have known my thoughts all this time, have been listening in as if over a radio, playing with me, teasing me, pushing me to see how far I'd go.

I felt like a fool. I questioned her face in my rearview, her shadow skirting the edges of rooms. I questioned all of it, everything about her, for the first time since all this started. And then as quick as the doubt had come, anger replaced it. My insides flipped and seethed. Oh, it had been Abby, haunting me ever since I found her picture on the side of the road. But not so I could help her. Not so I could find out what happened. Not because we were connected, somehow, through Fiona Burke, who knew me, who somehow knew her. She wasn't communicating with me because I was meant to help her, because out of everyone in the town of Pinecliff, in all of Dutchess County, in this state, in this country, in this world, it had to be me. No. She was fucking with me.

All of this rushed over me, and I lost sight of if she was a ghost or not a ghost, a villain or a victim or a messed-up teenage girl.

"What's your problem? Don't you want this or what?" Luke was asking me.

And him. He'd been a part of it. I wanted to punch him in his chiseled nose, break it clean across the middle so he never recovered and he lost some of his luster and people called him ugly sometimes. How would he like that? But before I could make a fist, I realized what he meant. There was no door open into the house. There was no Abby in his grandma's hand-knitted sweater leaning out, laughing at me for trying to save her when she didn't need saving.

We were alone in the garage as before, and he was balancing a blue Schwinn bicycle, holding it upright by the handlebars. The frame was doused in rust, and one of the tires was punctured.

"What's that?" I said slowly, putting it together. "That's not . . ." I eyed the rest of the garage. My panic soothed when I heard her breathing. She must have trailed me so closely, I hadn't even seen her shadow.

"Abby's bicycle," he said. "Isn't that why you're here?"

"No," I said. You see, the bicycle in his hands was blue. Sure, it was a Schwinn, but I could have sworn, when I saw it in her memories, that it had been green. Bright green. Green like the trees surrounding the road she'd been riding. Green. "That's not it."

"Uh, yeah, it is," he said, rolling it as best he could with the flat back tire over to me so I had to take it. Its metal frame was very cold, and its seat was gashed open, spilling yellowed fluff and a protruding wire spring.

"If it's her bike, why didn't you give it to the police?"

"What do you mean? Why would I?"

"Because she's *missing*," I said.

"She ran away," he said, and shrugged. "That's what I heard. Some girl at that camp told me."

I couldn't speak. Why could no one who knew her see that she hadn't run away? How was it that I hadn't met her in real life and yet I, of all people, knew?

"She rode this over that night," he said. "Then she had a conniption when she heard me on the phone—she was late, I didn't think she was coming, so I called some other chick. So what?"

"She . . . She *did* see you that night?" I wasn't expecting that. "She rode all the way here, on her bike? That night? Are you sure?"

"Yeah, but like I was saying, she didn't stay long. She started bawling, the whole freak show. Then she gets on the bike to go and runs over something in the driveway and *this* happens." He kicked at the flat back tire. "And—get this—she dropped the bike and she took off. I went after her, but I couldn't find her anywhere on the road. Maybe she took the shortcut through the woods, dude, I don't know." He shrugged. "We weren't exclusive. What did she expect?"

I was still trying to understand. I'd seen her reach the bottom of the hill, but nothing beyond that, nothing outside that patch of darkness, and I'd assumed that's where it had ended.

Instinctively I touched the pendant, resting beneath my clothes. How did it get in the gully then? Was it when she was walking back? Did I misunderstand, get the whole trip reversed, shuffle the events out of order, confuse the whole night?

Luke seemed happy to get rid of the bike. I was the one holding it upright now, and he used his free hands to fix his hair.

"You're . . . giving this to me?" I said.

"I figured she'd come back and get it, but yeah. Then I heard she was gone, so. It's a piece-of-shit bike anyway, but take it. It's what you came here for, right?"

"But, Luke, that was the night she disappeared. You were the last person to see her."

"Wasn't me, Officer." He put up his hands in surrender, laughing, but when I didn't laugh back he lowered his hands. "Seriously, though. Everyone says she ran away or whatever. You don't think I—"

I wasn't sure what to think. It depended on what Abby thought. And I needed her to tell me what that was.

"Why'd I keep her bike all this time then, huh? That should prove I didn't do shit to her. I'd have thrown it off a cliff by now if I had."

I didn't say anything, so he kept talking.

"Lauren, you know me. C'mon now. Be serious."

I closed my eyes. I wished I could will the dream to life. That I could climb the steps of the house, no matter the time of day, awake or asleep or in the middle of conversation. If only I could control it, the smoky space that controlled me. I could be in the dairy aisle during my shift at the Shop & Save, stacking the 1 percent and the 2 percent milk cartons beside the whole and then the smoke would start sifting in, up from the floor like that time the little kid broke open the bag of flour, and the pale cloud would be a curtain through which I could visit the dream. Or here, now, in Luke Castro's garage. I'd step through and ask Abby my questions. I'd find out what I needed to know. I'd come back, I'd know all.

This time it worked, in a way. Because the place in the dream *was* near. I could smell its smoke. Or someone who reeked of it.

"Who are you looking for?" Luke asked. "My parents are out. It's just you and me."

It's just you and me, a voice mocked, in my head.

She was meaner than I expected.

Don't go inside the house if he asks you. He just wants to do you in his parents' water bed.

I was looking around wildly then, to see where the voice was coming from. I thought she was behind me, but the voice had come from across the garage, on the other side of the car. So was she under it or crouching down against the door?

Just wait, she said. *You'll ruin everything.*

"No," I said. "I have a boyfriend."

"Whoa," Luke said at this, though I wasn't even talking to him.

I waited for the voice to return so I could find where she was hiding, and then when she kept silent I realized. That wasn't Abby. That voice was cruel the way Fiona Burke was cruel, and snide the way Fiona Burke used to be snide. That was Fiona's low whisper in my ear.

"Listen," Luke was saying, "if you do hear from her, no hard feelings, right? It's not like we were serious. She knew that."

My face must have said otherwise.

"She didn't?"

"She thought . . ." I started, wishing she'd speak up and tell me. "She thought maybe," I finished.

Luke shook his head. "Why doesn't she just call me herself? Why'd she send you?"

"Because I told her I'd help her," I said, and by saying it out loud, it was like I was declaring it. To him and everyone. To myself. To her and to Fiona Burke—I felt their held lungfuls of breath as they listened.

Then I wheeled the bike out of the garage and down the driveway toward my van without another word. Maybe I'd been wrong, I told myself. Maybe the bike *had* been blue.

— 16 —

I didn't end up wheeling Abby's blue Schwinn bicycle into the police station. I left it in my van parked outside and then I went in, to tell the police I had it.

The station was small, with a waiting room holding three chairs and an interior window in the wall, through which a receptionist sat reading.

I didn't see Officer Heaney or anyone else official-looking through the window, but I was told to sit tight and an officer would be with me very soon. I waited forty-two minutes. Then the receptionist went on break, apologizing for keeping me waiting, and an officer came up front to help me, leaving me sitting another eleven minutes while he ducked back in to take a phone call. During all the time I was waiting in the plastic chair in the front room I considered what this meant. If it was a sign that I should leave. If I was meant to hand over the bike to the police and tell them what I knew, wouldn't they have helped me when I first walked in?

I was about to get up, walk out, and drive away, when finally the officer came back to the window and asked what it was I wanted to talk to somebody about. He wasn't Officer Heaney, but he'd do. I dug through my pockets and my backpack searching for Abby's flyer, afraid I'd lost it, then remembering where I'd hidden it, in the inside zippered pouch. While the officer read the details on the Missing flyer, I felt something deep in my center rise in temperature, like a pinpoint of panic that would soon take over my whole body and come spewing out my mouth. Then it dawned on me what it was: not a sudden illness or something I ate, but the pendant I was wearing. The stone had gone hot as an iron against my bare skin. I lifted it out away from me, so it wouldn't burn me, hiding it in a ball inside my sweatshirt-shielded fist.

The officer handed back Abby's flyer through the window and said he did remember the girl from this summer. Vaguely. Some runaway. See, it says that right there on the flyer? Case Type: Endangered Runaway. Get that? *Runaway.* They can't go chasing every 17-year-old kid who runs away from home—do I have any idea how many there are out there? What a waste of time that would be? Of taxpayers' dollars? What a waste?

Within his words were the other things he was saying: how little this mattered to him, and how little this should matter to me. She'd be eighteen soon enough, besides, he added. And then there was really nothing they could do.

The officer loaded a website on the front desk's computer, angling the screen so I could see it—the missing children's database, a public record listing anyone who was under the age of eighteen when reported missing, on which I'd already found Abby's information. But he had a point to make. He entered these terms into the search field: current age: 17; sex: female. Then he scrolled through face after face and name after name, to show me. Here was a 17-year-old girl who had also run away. Another 17-year-old runaway. Another, another, another, all 17, all runaways. He kept clicking. Another 17-year-old, but her case was labeled "Endangered Missing," which meant she had disappeared under questionable circumstances. This next one, too. Some were missing, he admitted, but more—more than he'd sit there and count—had run away by their own choice. And they could always go home if they wanted.

The same number leaped out at me—17, 17, 17—pouncing and etching itself into my skin like a bloody needle in the midst of one of my mom's more intricate tattoos.

I was 17.

I was a girl.

Didn't we matter?

And the fact that I was also 17 and also a girl couldn't be all there was, but it was enough for me. It wasn't anything this police officer would ever be able to understand. This was meant for me only. A piece of information that was all mine.

"I'm sorry about your friend," he said, assuming that's what she was, and I didn't correct him. "Though I assure you, if she wants to be found, she'll turn up."

"But what if she *didn't* run away?" I asked. I told him about the bike—the same one mentioned right there on the Missing notice—and didn't they need it for evidence?

"I'm not sure why we would. Besides, this here says she's from New Jersey. Out-of-state."

Go, said the whispered voice close up to the blazing-hot lobe of my left ear. *Get out of there right now, you imbecile. Go.*

This time I knew right away it was Fiona. She knew I was about to mention the necklace, which made me wonder what else she knew. She'd keep insulting me until I left.

"Okay," I told the officer. "Thank you for your time. I understand." I grabbed Abby's flyer from off the desk and returned it to the hoodie's front pocket, where the touch of the pendant would keep it warm. I didn't look back. I was almost at the door.

"But maybe when I get a chance I'll look into it," he called through the window into the waiting room. My hand was on the knob and the door was coming open, and I knew he didn't mean it and that as soon as I walked out of the station he'd let himself forget. I glanced back at the window to be sure and noticed him looking up at the clock on the wall. "How old are you, miss? Shouldn't you be in school?"

"Winter break," I said, though technically it didn't start for another day.

"You sure about that? My daughter goes to Pinecliff Central, and she had school today, she—"

The door swung closed before he could finish. I was still here. I was still searching. I was the only one who seemed to care.

– 17 –

I didn't get far.

My eyes swam and then came into focus: the parking lot of the Friendly's. The square of blacktop divided by yellow lines. The gray concrete curb. The bumper of my van wedged against the curb. The sign on the plate-glass window advertising a three-course Christmas dinner special next week (was Christmas next week already?) for only $7.99. The cracks in the sidewalk. The faces in the cracks. Smiling faces at first and then mouths in the shape of screams.

I'd been on the sidewalk outside the Friendly's for I-couldn't-say-how-long. Something had come over me when I was leaving the police station and I'd had to pull over. It was the growing sense that I was being watched—and then it was the growing sense that whoever was watching, they were inside the van. They were in the bowels of the back, behind the bench seat. I'd opened the door when I put the bicycle in and I'd left it open too long when I was checking my phone and reading Jamie's text messages (six since that morning). I'd let them in. They knew I was looking for Abby—they'd heard everything I'd said.

This chain restaurant, this parking lot, was the nearest turnoff I'd seen. I'd barreled through the lot and I'd come to a stop and I'd opened the driver's side door and I'd leaped out, and it took much deep breathing and many minutes before I could open the two back doors at the tail end of the van. When I did I could hardly look, but I had to look, because I had to know—

All I'd found was Abby's borrowed bicycle inside.

I'd gotten myself all worked up over nothing.

Now I was sitting on the sidewalk, out under the cold, winter-white sky. I couldn't get back in the van just yet.

I was looking down at my knees, caked with ice and snow and with the salt kernels thrown out in winter so people wouldn't slip and fall in the ice and snow, and that was how I realized I must have fallen. I lifted my hands and saw that my palms, too, were caked with the mixture, pockmarked and dented from impact, discolored, almost grayed.

"Hey, you," I heard.

This voice was coming from behind me, to my left. I ignored it, of course, like I'd been ignoring Fiona Burke since we'd left the police station.

"Hey." The voice again. This was a girl's voice, I realized, the voice of a very young girl. "Hey. I'm talking to you." A clean, white toe nudged the scuffed steel toe of my combat boot. "Are you sick? Do you need me to get my mom?"

From the size of her tiny feet in those puffy white boots I knew she was far too young to even be a part of this. When I craned my neck to look up into her face, I saw I was right: This girl was nine or ten maybe, eleven at most. She was dry and clean and safe. She had years to go. Years and years.

The girl had many barrettes all over her head and just looking at them made my own head feel heavy. The weight of all those barrettes, if they were plated in steel like the kicking toes of my boots, that's what knowing all the things I knew felt like.

"I'm fine," I managed to answer her, finally.

"You threw up all over the sidewalk," the girl said, holding her nose.

I looked behind me, to my right. "Oh. I guess I did."

"Do you have germs?" she said. She took a step back. She moved comically slow in a white snowsuit decorated with little coiled demons awash in fire that I realized, upon blinking, were only goldfish. Orange goldfish were decorating her snowsuit, not demons.

"Do you?" she said again. "Have germs?"

"I might," I admitted.

"Gross," the girl said, wrinkling her nose. But she didn't move. She didn't seem to care if she caught my sickness.

I noticed that my van beside the curb was still idling; I'd left the engine on. The back doors were also open, showing the dark cavern inside. It seemed much larger than it should be, like a tunnel that didn't want you to see its end.

"Could you do me a favor?" I asked the girl. "Could you look inside there?"

"What?"

"My van. Could you look inside the van and tell me what you see?"

She started shrinking away from me. She must have had that special assembly in school about bad strangers wanting to snatch kids in their dirty, scary vans.

I had the terrifying feeling then that she'd be smart to play it safe and run, but she only hopped over to the van and peeked into the back. "Cool! A bike," she said.

"Anything else? Nothing else in there besides the bike?"

"No," she said. She looked back at me like I was a wacko. Still, she didn't run.

I began to worry for her. Where were her parents?

If she stayed with me for much longer, she really would catch it. She'd catch it off me and carry it around with her through elementary school and middle school and into high school. She'd carry it down the field during soccer matches, up to the top of the Empire State Building when she visited on a class trip, down hallways and in the pockets of her tightest jeans, and then her birthday would come, and she'd celebrate with friends, they'd have a party, and she'd fling herself around the room dancing, not having any idea of what's to come. She'd be 17, and by then she wouldn't remember any of this. She won't know what meeting me will have done to her.

I stood up all of a sudden and grabbed the handles of the back doors, closing up the van. "Go back inside," I told the girl.

Didn't she hear me?

"Go," I snapped, louder this time. "Get away from me. I mean it. Get out of here. Now. *Go*."

She leaped back as if I'd smacked her. Her face twisted like she was about to cry, but before she let me see, she whipped around and started running.

She was racing away, away from the gray, salted sidewalk, and away from me, into the warm and cheerful interior of the local Friendly's. Her mom was probably in there, her dad and siblings, too, and maybe a trademark Happy Ending Sundae would help her forget about this, and me.

I watched to be sure. When she was safely inside, I realized it was snowing. Snow falling on the roof of my van and on the pavement and in my hair and on my eyelashes and on my outstretched limbs. Fluffy white flakes of snow covering me just like they'd cover a dead body.

–18–

FIONA Burke *did* run away—there was never any question.

After she'd finished packing and making up her face, her bags strewn around the foyer and her lashes protruding from her eyelids in gnarled spikes, Fiona Burke made a phone call. Her voice softened as she spoke, turning simpler, slower, like she'd regressed to my age, or was mocking me by pretending so.

She kept assuring the man on the phone that everything was cool. She said *yes* a lot, like she wanted to agree with every single thing he said. She got very silent at one point and it sounded like the person on the other end was yelling at her. She stuttered, and said she was sorry, and after a while the yelling stopped and they were just talking and making plans for the night.

I felt her looking at me, where I was in the dining room in my My Little Pony pajamas, and then I heard her speak about me for the first time.

"The thing is," she told the man, "it's like . . . someone's gonna be here when you get to the house. Like, I'm not alone."

I held my tongue. While she talked, for a reason I didn't understand, she was making me stand in the corner, face mashed into the crook of the wall. If I opened my eyes from this position, all I could make out was her mother's dining-room wallpaper: a pattern of yellow blooms marching north in one mindless, orderly flock. They blurred to butter close-up. I couldn't see her as she spoke, but I could hear everything she said.

"No! Not my parents. I told you my dad's navy buddy had a fucking heart attack and they're in Baltimore for the fucking funeral. It's not them. It's . . . the kid who lives next door. I'm sort of watching her since her mom sort of had no one else to ask. But I'll just leave her here. I'm still going with you."

There was some arguing then. About me. About what I'd see and who I'd tell.

But then Fiona Burke hung up the phone and held still. Something in her face told me she didn't want to go where she promised she'd go. That man had been yelling at her, and she wanted to stay right here.

I thought she was about to say she'd changed her mind. Maybe she'd pull me out of the corner and she'd grab my hand and say we had to get out of the house before he got here—whoever he was—and I'd take her to hide in my bedroom next door. This was back when my mom let me have the pup tent in my room, set up at all times for carpet-camping, and Fiona

Burke and I would crawl in there and close the flap and I'd show her where I hid the leftover Halloween candy.

Maybe Fiona Burke spent a second thinking something like that, too. About running away from running away. But it was too late to change her mind. She'd set too much of it in motion.

Soon she was prancing over to me in the corner of the dining room, crouching so her wet-glossed lips had my ear.

"What am I going to do with you?" she said, singsong. "He didn't like it that you were here, Lauren. He didn't like it at all."

"Who's he?"

She ignored that. "And really, you're not supposed to be here. My stupid parents said yes to your stupid mom without asking me first, and I couldn't get out of it. This wasn't the plan."

I told her that I was sorry, deeply, as if I'd betrayed her.

Her hand whipped out and she shoved something hard and cold to the back of my neck, moving it up until it was wedged against the base of my skull. "Do you think I'd hurt you?" she said in a strange, helium voice. Her breathing quickened, and mine rushed to catch up.

I didn't answer, so she gave more pressure to the back of my neck, wedging in harder. I imagined the muzzle of a gun; I'd seen one in person at a friend's house once, and so that's what I pictured. His dad kept it in a box on a high shelf in the bedroom, and my friend had found a way to reach it by balancing on the dresser. But we hadn't taken it out of the box to see if it was loaded, and we hadn't played at killing each other, going *blam, blam!* with the steel against each other's temples and the writhing on the floor until we got tired and decided to be dead. I'd only touched it, with one finger, once, and all I remembered was that it had been this hard, and this cold.

Thinking of this, I may have begged her, please, not to, begged her, please, leave me alive, and she may have lost her bravado and cracked up laughing. She lowered her hand and all that was in it was a small Bic lighter.

She flicked it and brought up a tiny flame that matched the dyed sections of her hair. The color was indistinguishable up close, so for a moment it seemed her whole head had caught fire.

"God! What do you think I am, a monster?" she asked.

I shook my head as far as it would shake with me standing in the crook of the wall.

"Maybe I am," she said. "Maybe I should burn this whole house to the ground so that's what they'd find when they get home from the funeral. A pile of stinking ashes and their daughter gone."

She crooked her head at me, and she blinked, and I truly didn't know what she was capable of doing. Then she blinked again, and the flames shrunk away from her face, and I saw how scared she was. Petrified. She slipped the lighter into her jeans pocket that already contained the pendant, and she patted it, making sure it was there. Then she looked out the window at the driveway.

"When he gets here, you're not going to say a thing to him, are you?" she demanded.

"I'm not going to," I assured her.

"You'll stay here until your mom gets back. And you won't call anyone, and you won't do anything. What's she doing out so late anyways?"

"She's out dancing."

She scoffed. There was something in her tone that made me feel very small, smaller than I even was with her towering over me. "Oh, I know what she's doing. I think I know where she works. Your mom's not out *dancing*."

"She said . . ."

"You know what your mom's doing right now? She's grinding her tits into some perv's face."

I remember how strange a picture that made for me, with actions and objects I couldn't fathom at that age. And I would think back on this later, when my mom would tell me about her job at the club, and then when she quit that job and got an office job and went back to school, and I'd wish I had said something to defend her. But I'd never been able to stand up to Fiona Burke, not for all the time I'd known her, and especially not that night.

Besides, that was when the truck pulled up. First one man came banging into the house, and then there were two. Two men, and Fiona Burke had been expecting only one. The first was tall, and bigger than the width of two Fiona Burkes put together, and the other was quite short. I came up about to his mustache. This second surprise man, the short one, was the one who scared Fiona.

I was surprised, too. What surprised me was how much older they were. I knew Fiona Burke was 17, and I couldn't estimate the ages of adults—they all just seemed old to me—but these two men weren't in high school, I was sure of it. They were far older than that.

When she started carrying her bags out to the truck I realized the men were taking Fiona Burke away—she was voluntarily, assuredly going with them—but they were also taking more than just her. The little man was unhooking some paintings from the wall. And the big man was dismantling the stereo system.

With them occupied, Fiona returned to my corner.

"If my mom asks why, tell her I hate her," she hissed. "Tell her I hate her stupid guts, her and Dad both. Tell her I'm getting a ride to LA and I've got a job waiting for me and how's she like that? Tell her I'm never coming back, not ever."

I assured her I'd pass all this on to Mrs. Burke.

But Fiona Burke wasn't done. She'd been holding a lot inside, all those years since the Burkes had made her theirs. She wanted me to tell her adopted parents that they should have left her where she came from, and why'd they ever think she wanted to live in their stuffy old house with boring old strangers? And I think she would have kept on going if I hadn't stopped her.

"But *why*?" I asked.

I was the kind of kid who used to ask that a lot, to any small thing and any large thing, unwilling to leave anything unanswered. Maybe not much has changed since then.

Fiona Burke shook her head and rolled her eyes. “You’ll understand when you’re my age,” was all she said. So dismissive, like I’d never get it; I was just a kid.

I didn’t understand then—but I do now.

The little man approached. He’d taken everything he’d wanted from the house and entered the dining room with hands out and empty. Even so, Fiona Burke flinched at the sight of him, as if she knew what he was capable of doing with his bare hands.

He wasn’t saying anything. He was only looking. He was looking at me.

“What?” Fiona Burke said. She didn’t stand in front of me or block me with her body or anything, but she leaned ever so slightly in my direction to let her shadow cover me.

“How old is she?” the little man said to her, as if I didn’t understand the language.

“Nine,” I answered. A slight exaggeration. Fiona Burke probably had no idea how old I was anyway.

“She’s not going to tell on us,” she was saying. “She won’t call anyone or anything. I made her promise.”

“She knows my face,” the little man said. “She’s looking at me right now.”

“No, she’s not,” Fiona Burke said—though I was. I’d turned from the crook in the wall and was peeking up at him. His mustache made his upper lip appear to be rotting and his eyes were smaller than natural in his already small head.

While I was looking at him, he was looking at me.

“Maybe she should come along,” the little man said then in an odd voice, like there were unspoken things below the surface, murky and confusing things he couldn't wait to let out. His voice was betraying him.

"But what would we do with her?" Fiona Burke joked.

"Don't worry," he said in that voice again. "I could think up a few things."

She caught something in his expression and made a strange squeaking sound in her throat. A sound you'd emit only when alone, behind closed doors, where no one else could hear it. I heard it. So did he.

The little man laughed in response.

"She stays here," Fiona Burke said.

I didn't know then that she was speaking up for me. Protecting me. I didn't know a lot of things I know now.

The big man had returned, and there was a new sense of urgency, someone who'd called, somewhere they had to be. The little man became distracted by all of this and it was when his back was turned that Fiona Burke did what she did. She had me by the elbow, and then when I was too slow, she had both my arms and was dragging me out of the dining room and down the hall. She hissed into my ear to stay quiet and then she shoved me into a hall closet.

It was dark and thick with the heady scent of what I'd later discover was wool. The wool was from her parents' coats, decades' worth of coats, and there were pointy objects that were the bony prongs of her parents' umbrellas.

She'd jammed the lock from the outside, or she'd known that the knob would stick. I don't know. Either way, she'd locked me in.

I couldn't hear much of what happened outside the wall of coats that confined me in that dark, small space. When they were near the front door, mere steps from the coat closet, I could hear the little man's voice—it boomed bigger than you'd expect from his body—slithering under the door and through the layers of wool, causing a cool line of sweat to trickle anxiously beneath my pajama shirt and down my spine.

I would not scream to be let out of the closet, and I was afraid to try the knob again to see if it would turn. I wouldn't make a sound with him so close. Fiona Burke would come back for me when he wasn't looking and undo the lock to set me free. She'd do that before she went away in that truck with them. She would.

The little man was asking for me. "Where'd she go?" he was saying. "I didn't scare her away, did I? Call for her. Tell her I won't hurt her. Tell her to come back."

Fiona Burke refused. She must have been standing very close to the closet, but she didn't open it. We were there together, one thin slab of wood between us, like our hands were touching, palm to palm. I didn't understand then what he could have wanted from me. All I knew is she was determined not to let him find me.

"She ran," I heard her say through the door. "Out into the backyard, stupid kid. She'll come back when she gets cold—she's only got those pajamas on. Let's just go?"

"Oh, yeah? She's back there?" the little man said, and he must have made a move in the direction of the backyard because his voice got lower with distance. But then the big man spoke—he said very few words, but when he spoke everyone listened—and he was saying they had to leave.

I kept quiet. My mind was flashing on Fiona Burke's eyes, how wild they'd looked beneath the wings of shellacked black mascara as she hurried me out of the dining room. She'd been frightened of what could happen to me, and that's what frightened me.

At some point they left, drove away. At some point Fiona Burke said good-bye to the house where she was raised, turned her back on all of us, and took off.

She didn't leave a note. In a way, I guess I was the note.

Only, she'd stuffed me in the coat closet, and I was too short to reach the string that would turn the light on—and it was too dark for me to even see if there was a string.

I don't know if I could have saved her if I'd opened my mouth and told someone—her parents, the police, my mom, anyone—about the men she went with.

But—looking back on it now—I am sure of one thing. She'd saved me.

– 19 –

SPENDING the entirety of a night in a small, dark space ruins all understanding of time. A minute expands into an hour's worth of seconds. Air rebreathed is made of less and less air until you feel like you're choking on your own spit. The panic sets in and you think you'll never get out, that no one can hear because no one is there, that the hot, scratchy, heavy walls all around you will keep you forever, and when you hear someone yelling your name you don't know who it is at first. You don't recognize your own mother's voice; you can't imagine that you're safe now, that you'll be let out now, that there aren't two strange men and a cruel flame-haired girl crouching on the other side of that door waiting to take you away.

– 20 –

I don't know how many hours it was before the shock of light hit me and I could breathe air. I must have made a noise inside the coat closet because, soon, someone was pounding and I was pounding back and she was pulling and I was pushing and the door got unstuck and the light was in my face and she was there.

My mom enveloped me in her arms, frantic. The colorful pattern of prancing, dancing My Little Ponies had sweated onto my skin, and I'd been desperate enough to have to empty my bladder hours before, so I was sticky all over, smelling of sheep and urine, nearly blinded at the shock of light.

I chugged a glass of water, choking up most of it, and then when I found my voice I told my mom that Fiona Burke was the one who'd done this to me.

"Where is she?" she asked, seething. Her hands left me for a moment to ball into fists.

"Gone," I said. That's the only word I could think to call what had happened to my 17-year-old neighbor: She was *gone*.

"What do you mean, *gone*?" my mom said. She sparkled in a flurry of rage. I didn't realize at first that she still had on her work clothes, the kind of outfit she wore when she danced at the club, and that those sequins weren't the scaly, iridescent texture of her skin.

"Gone," I repeated, without embellishment. I meant *gone from the house*, *gone off somewhere with two creepy men I don't know,* but I think, from the way my mom ran around searching, she suspected that Fiona Burke had been hurt, from falling down a set of steep stairs, maybe—or on purpose, by hanging herself off the end of a rope.

Things must have happened after that involving my mom trying to reach the Burkes at the hotel where they were staying in Baltimore, and the police being called, and Fiona Burke's school picture—with the pearl earrings and the carefully clasped hands—showing up all over the news.

Mr. and Mrs. Burke may have at first wanted to believe she'd been abducted, that she'd never leave home by choice—but the police saw the truth without needing to do any digging. She'd taken her things from her room. Even without a good-bye note, they could see she'd run away.

The last words Fiona Burke had said to me were *Stay quiet, okay?* And I think I took that command too literally, as if something would happen if I spoke up or even uttered her name.

Keeping my mouth shut all those years meant swallowing information like little kids swallow LEGO pieces, which can have a way of growing like plastic teeth into your organs and never making their way back out. I would let the Burkes search for their daughter for years, blindly, having no idea what she said about them. Or about the two men and what they looked like. Or how I thought I knew where Fiona was headed—she'd said she was getting a ride to LA.

I choked it all down. When I heard her name on the car radio, I told no one. When the policewoman asked me, and when Mrs. Burke herself asked me, even when my mom asked me—which happened more than once—my mouth stayed wired shut. I revealed none of it.

– 21 –

THERE is one last piece that isn't technically a part of Fiona Burke's story, though at the time, in the way one memory can latch itself on to another memory and then forever after trail the first one, it felt that way to me. In my mind, the two events were connected.

This would have been weeks after Fiona Burke had run away, months even, though no more than a year. She hadn't tried to contact her parents, and we didn't yet know that she'd never reach out to them. She would never place a collect call from a pay phone and ask them to accept the charges. She would never open a free e-mail account to send an anonymous assurance that she was fine. There would be no blank postcard dropped in a mailbox in a city she was only passing through. No communication. No word.

Until the fire.

I woke in the middle of the night to the piercing scream of

the smoke detector, which somehow had been set off by the smoke coming off the house next door. My mom and I were afraid at first that the smoke was from inside our own house, and we looked for candles and ran to check the stove, but then we looked out the windows. Out there the smoke was thicker, a visible charge in the night, its source a ferocious spot of light over the dividing hedge between the Burkes' main house and ours.

The fire truck would arrive within minutes and the flames would be doused, damaging only their laundry room and the hallway between that and their kitchen. An electrical fire due to faulty wiring, it was said, not arson.

I knew different.

We watched for some minutes from the windows, my mom and me. Two firemen had forced themselves into the Burkes' house and pulled them out the door and off their grand front porch. The firemen wrapped the two hunched figures in wool blankets and made them stand at a distance from the smoking house, on the lawn.

Mrs. Burke was wearing slippers, but Mr. Burke's feet were bare. His pajama pants were too short, and I noticed his hairless, spindly legs and how he favored the left one. We watched them as they watched the east end of their house burn.

We were watching as the fireman went to talk to them. His words washed over Mrs. Burke, and we could see it in her face, how what he said took a very long time to settle, as if she were translating to herself so she could understand, and once she did she let out the cry. We heard it across the hedge that divided their paved driveway from our gravel one. The sound of it made me think of Fiona Burke, wondering if that's how Mrs. Burke sounded in Baltimore when she got the news that her daughter had gone missing.

We didn't hear a thing from Mr. Burke, but we watched him wobble on his bum leg, thin and pale as a sucked-clean toothpick. We were watching as the smoke thinned and no more flames could be made out and as the hoses left the whole side of the house sopping. And we were watching as Mrs. Burke's eyes traveled over the hedge to our house, perhaps involuntarily, remembering one disaster that had been connected with us and now connecting us to another.

"Should we go get them?" I said. "Ask if they want to come inside?"

But my mom had never forgiven them for the way their daughter had treated me that night, locking me in the coat closet. She hadn't known how to confront them, seeing as Fiona had disappeared, but she held it in, and didn't forget it.

"They'll be fine," she said. "The fire's out. You should go back to bed."

But she didn't move toward her bedroom, and I didn't move for mine. It had come true, what Fiona had threatened with her wet mouth shoved up against my ear. The fire she'd joked about setting in her parents' house? It had been set.

And though I didn't know how she'd done it from far away, I was convinced, then and all the more now, that she had. She'd tried to burn down their house, and she'd failed.

Years passed. Eight years. No more fires, and no letters,

and no phone calls. My mom and I stayed put in the carriage house because the Burkes never once raised our rent. They didn't adopt another kid. I grew too old to need a babysitter. I entered my junior year in the same high school Fiona Burke had once attended, and I dyed my hair black, the color hers would have been if she hadn't dyed it flame-red. I turned 17. And that's when a missing girl named Abby Sinclair would lure the ghost of Fiona Burke back here to Pinecliff. When the noise would wake the others.

And it's when I'd feel the first crack inside me, the fracture that started small, with one name, and then broke off into more names, and more names still, and left me gaping.

If I counted all the girls who ran away at the age of 17, starting with girls who lived close to me and then casting my net wider, spreading out along the East Coast in ever-growing circles, then adding girls who may have met more sinister fates, who didn't go by choice, whose bodies still had not been found, I'd be nowhere. There'd simply be too many.

Which terrified me.

To know a girl was one, I had to sense it. Something would compel me to stop over a certain page online or in the newspaper microfiche in the library. There'd be a humming in my ears, a chorus strengthened by a new, added voice. Then the warmth, below my heart, gaining heat until I had to take off the pendant or else it would burn me and leave a lopsided almost-circle of a mark. The edges of the room would swim with shadows, and those shadows had arms and legs and mouths that opened. They had shoulder blades and they had elbows and they had knees. They came out when I discovered another, to crane their shadowy necks around corners, to see who it might be.

This was how I found Natalie Montesano, 17, of Edgehaven, Vermont, missing for the last seven years. Or, I should say, this was how she found me.

ICE STORM WREAKS HAVOC ON MOUNTAIN ROADS; LOCAL GIRL, 17, MISSING

Jan. 3, 2006—EDGEHAVEN—Friday's heavy snow turned to ice on Saturday and left treacherous driving conditions throughout the high-elevation mountain roads. There were reports of power outages across the county. In addition, in connection to a car accident on Plateau Road late Saturday, a female Edgehaven Central High School senior, 17, was reported missing.

Witnesses say the girl had been a passenger in a car that collided with the guardrail, but she could not be located in the wreckage. "We can't help but hope someone came along and pulled her from the car. But she hasn't been checked into any local hospital and her family hasn't heard a word," Sheriff Arnold F. Wymes said in a statement to the public on Monday. "If she wandered out on her own . . . it's not likely she'd have survived the elements." A search is still under way.

The public is asked to report any information to the Edgehaven Police Department. The northern pass of Plateau Road is closed to nonemergency traffic until further notice.

– 22 –

THE new girl, Natalie, had inherited the eyes. The ones on her mother's side, paler than a pair of eyes should be. They looked to be coated in a thick layer of ice, and only if you chipped through would you find the person they belonged to, the girl shivering beneath.

These eyes were exactly like her mother's, who was serving two consecutive life sentences at a women's correctional facility four hours away, and would never get out, not in her lifetime.

Natalie had not once gone to visit the prison to look into the frigid eyes of the woman responsible for bringing her into the world. Even if those eyes would be held back behind a wall of clouded glass lathered on both sides by the links of the metal cage that encased it. Natalie was afraid it would be like looking off into the far distance, into a future she didn't want to see. Like mother like daughter, people always said.

They assumed, but they should have asked, because looks are deceiving sometimes. Eyes can be.

I first saw Natalie's eyes for myself on a cold January morning while I was combing out the rat's nest of my hair. That was the first day of the new semester, and I had to get to school.

I was looking in the mirror, trying to get the comb in and the knots out, but the knots had caught themselves on the teeth of the comb, getting more tangled the more I tried to pull it through.

I'd had the dream again in the night. Fiona Burke hadn't been there. I didn't see Abby, either. But there'd been someone in the smoky house with me, up a set of stairs, around a corner, a shadow that leaked out from the other shadows, reaching out one beckoning, outstretched hand.

I'd woken in my bed as if I'd spent the night clawing my way up a riverbank—drenched through my clothes, muscles sore, hair tangled in sweat—though the dream had been very dry. Dry and hot, as if somewhere the fire was still burning.

I took one last look at my tangled head in the mirror and decided to do something about it. With the comb still wedged in, I found the scissors, the good ones not made for cutting paper, and I just started chopping around the comb, snipping shorter than I meant to, and then needing to cut shorter still to make up for a crooked spot. The haircut was DIY, it was daring, and it brought out my eyes.

Someone else's eyes.

I flinched. Something had happened to my face. The mirror was showing a second face projected over my own. Her face hovered, lit up like a round and glowing moon.

I noticed a nose shorter than my nose, thicker eyebrows than mine, and arching far higher than mine could arch, the straight line of the mouth, just like in the picture, and the eyes, mostly the eyes, pale and unsettling and absolutely recognizable from that photo I'd found of her, the one used in some of the newspaper articles. Eyes so cold, they could cut your throat.

My hand lost its grip on the scissors and then we were watching them fall into the sink, the girl and I, blades spread open, and then a mouth also opened—my mouth, hidden behind the girl's—and a sound emerged, startling us both.

I guess I'd yelled something, because my mom came running and was soon in the doorway, one leg of her black-patterned tights on and the other dangling from her hip like a shriveled extra limb. She wore her usual button-down work shirt to cover most of her tattoos, but the buttons were gaping open to show the bare, perfectly clear skin of her chest. She had no tattoos there, so she seemed even more naked.

She buttoned her shirt quickly and said, "Way to give me a heart attack, Lauren! I thought you slipped in the tub."

I shook my head and waited, waited for her to see the face in the mirror. Natalie's face.

All she noticed was the haircut. "Wow," she said. "I mean that: *wow*. Wanted something different for your first day back at school, huh?"

I was still waiting.

She touched my hair and fluffed it out at one side. She clucked her tongue, cocked her head, then smiled. "I love it," she said. "It's killer. I hope you don't hate it, because it'll take years to grow the length back. Is that why you screamed?"

She didn't see the face.

"I saw . . ." My arm, threatening to give me up, was already pointing at the mirror. I *saw*, past tense, and *was still seeing* someone else's face. I was wearing a mask made out of her skin and features and I couldn't get it to come off.

". . . nothing," I finished. "I thought I saw something, but it was nothing."

"You okay?" my mom asked.

I turned back to the mirror and realized she was gone. The new girl, Natalie Montesano, gone as she was in real life. The face staring back from the glass was my own face—and, because my reflection was clean, I saw the deep and shocking truth of what I looked like: I'd given myself a stupendously unattractive haircut.

My mom had asked if I was okay and, for the first time, I answered her honestly. "I don't know."

Her gaze held mine in the mirror. "What is it?" she asked my reflection, as if it would be easier to talk to than to flesh-and-blood me. And, you know, maybe it would have been. Maybe my mirror-self could have told her about the dreams, still smoking in the backmost rooms of my mind, or about the voice that sometimes sounded so much like a girl I knew a long time ago, if that could even be possible, the voice that called me names and needled at me to not tell my mom a thing. The voice that stayed hushed now, listening.

Maybe my reflection could have told her that a wriggling

thought was dislodging itself in my mind as we stood in the morning-lit bathroom, and this new thought was telling me that if I opened the shower curtain and looked in the tub I'd find one of them: Fiona. Or Abby. Or Natalie. Or, worse, all three of them together, a tangle of shadowy legs and vapory arms, a huddle of heat and smoke and the dream's deafening darkness. I'd pull open that shower curtain and show my mom and she'd be the one to scream.

Of course I wouldn't tell my mom. Once you tuck one secret inside yourself, digging out a little pocket to hold it, you'll find the pocket can be stretched to fit another. And another, and another . . . until you've got yourself a whole collection.

So, instead, I searched for an excuse and found a good one: "Jamie and me," I said. "I think we're over."

She made a noncommittal noise in the back of her throat; I knew she liked Jamie, but all her loyalties had to be with me, since I was her daughter. "I figured," she said. "I haven't seen him around in a while. I knew you'd tell me when you were ready to tell me. So you're nervous about seeing him in school today, right?"

I shrugged.

"All right," she said. "We don't have to talk about it. Just tell me one thing. Should I be mad at him? Did he do something I should know about?"

"No," I admitted. "It's all me."

She kept the judgment off her face, a skill she wouldn't even need to practice for when she finished her psychology degree and became a therapist or a school counselor or whatever she decided to do after graduation. She stepped closer to me and reached out an arm to touch the nape of my neck, playing with the chopped pieces of hair back there. "Want me to even out the back a little for you?"

I nodded and let her keep touching me, even though every finger on my scalp and every brush against my neck felt wrong all of a sudden, weird. It wasn't so much her. Again, it was me. All me. My skin was tightening against intrusions. My body was pulling in on itself like a knot tied over a knot tied over a knot that would never come undone.

It took my mom another ten minutes to fix my haircut, since she insisted on straightening out the sides and finessing the front. By the time she left the bathroom, my hair looked far more stylish than I felt, like I'd gone and gotten it cut on purpose for the first day back from winter break. But beneath the hair, the skin of my face had hardened to ice. I was alone again. At last.

I leaped across the bathroom and did the expected. It's what you see in the movies when the heroine fears someone is hiding behind the closed shower curtain and pulls it aside in a panicked flurry . . . only to reveal an empty tub and no serial killer lurking with a glinting knife from the kitchen. The heroine will sigh in relief. She'll laugh at her silly, overactive imagination, leave the room unharmed, and the scene will end.

But the difference was this: When I pulled aside the shower curtain, the tub wasn't empty. Fiona Burke leaned against the far wall, her legs straddling the faucet, her glossy mouth in a small smirk. Abby Sinclair's feet—one muddied and bare, one in a mangled flip-flop—were dirtying up the white bottom of the tub. And the newest girl, Natalie Montesano, was hiding behind a second curtain, but this one was made of her long hair.

I saw them for an extended moment, unable to react, as if my mind had been shoved full of socks. Then I blinked and the tub was empty and clean and the lost girls were gone and my mom was calling from the kitchen that I'd have to eat breakfast, now, or I'd be late for school.

– 23 –

I saw Jamie when he got to school, but he didn't see me. I had AP Lit first period, but when I caught a glimpse of Jamie's jacket—that sludge-green peacoat I gave him—and his dark mop of hair coming around the corner of the social-studies hallway, I took off up the stairs.

Seeing him, something caught in my throat. Regret maybe. Or confusion. I'd told my mom it was over, but we'd never officially broken up—at least, Jamie didn't know I'd made it official.

Needing to get away from him, I made my way up the north stairwell—past another junior, who said, "Lauren, what happened to your hair?" and another who said, "It looks awesome!"—and into the safety of the north bathroom, in the hallway near the art classrooms, where I could close myself into a stall and breathe.

When I finally emerged and went to wash my hands, I realized I'd been followed. I was alone in the girls' room, or thought I was alone, when I heard this:

I didn't mean to do it.

That's what I thought she said. Really what I heard were those whispered words slurred into one long word:

Ididntmeantodoit.

I doubled back. I checked all the stalls until I came to the third one from the right, the only one that had its door fully closed. I pushed on this door and it didn't swing open; it was locked from the inside. Most stalls in our school bathrooms didn't lock anymore. The stall doors had to be held in place while someone was inside with an outstretched leg or a wildly reaching hand.

Here I was now, outside an impossibly locked stall door, reaching to open it.

The stall was as green as a lime left to grow mold in a fridge drawer. It was cold, not warm.

"Hello?" I said against it.

What I heard was . . . a hiss. The hissing wasn't her breathing. I knew it was only the old radiators against the far wall, the spit of the steam heat.

I tried to push the stall door again, but it held in place. I bent down, but no feet poked out below.

I climbed the toilet in the neighboring stall and balanced up on the point of one toe, bracing myself against the shared wall, to dangle over. No one was hiding inside, though the toilet looked stopped up with paper. I assumed the stall was only locked because the toilet was out of order.

The last bell rang, meaning class had started already, and I should have been in my chair getting ready to discourse on Shakespeare. I hopped off the toilet and grabbed the backpack I'd left on the sink. I was almost at the exit when I heard the voice again. Heard it distinctly. Heard it in my ears and heard its echo through my bones.

Lauren, wait.

I did. The bell stopped ringing. Again I found myself edging closer to the third stall from the right.

"Natalie?" I said softly. "Is that you?"

It was then that she knocked in response. Her knuckles rapped from the inside of the stall in quick succession.

Even though I'd willed it to happen, it startled me. I jumped backward and almost took out a sink.

She was in that stall—or something was. An entity without visible feet was trying to communicate with me. To let me know she didn't mean to do . . . whatever it was she did.

I could sense her inside, willing me closer. I didn't speak, and she didn't speak, and when I took two steps in her direction, a foot could be seen dropping down, finding floor. A scuffed snow boot, once pale blue but dirtied and streaked with soot. A second boot followed, more blackened than the first.

Time distended into one long, unbreakable moment that broke anyway when the girls' room door banged open, slamming against the wall, and a group of three freshmen clattered in, crowding me.

At the same time, the door, third from the right, slowly swung itself open, creaking as it went, revealing an empty stall. No soot-covered snow boots. No girl.

The freshmen tittered a little, bowing their heads and not making eye contact—as freshmen do around upperclassmen and I don't even know why—and then one of them got brave and spoke up. She was the smallest of the three, brown glowing skin and shiny dark hair held tight against her head with two yellow clips, and she said, "You cut off all your hair." She flushed when I turned and looked at her, but still stared at my head.

"Rain!" one of her friends said, admonishing her.

"I like it," Rain said, ignoring her two friends but talking so fast it could barely be made out. "I mean it brings out your eyes or, I don't know, something."

"Thanks," I said. This was the same girl who'd bothered me in the library, but now I had my eyes on the stall. I had my heart lodged in my throat and a whisper of a voice in my ear. The voice wasn't Fiona Burke's; it didn't snap at me, it wasn't cruel. And it wasn't Abby—she was staying quiet, giving this new girl a turn to speak. It was Natalie Montesano, whose face had lodged itself over mine just that morning. I was hearing voices, seeing phantom feet. I didn't care what some freshman thought of my haircut.

"I'm Rain," she said patiently. "We used to be on the same bus? You look—"

"You should go," I said. I almost growled it, and I don't know why it came out that way, like I was one of those bullies who'd demand lunch money or an iPhone and humiliate someone simply because she was younger than me. I fit the part, maybe today, with my asymmetrical haircut that toughened up the angles of my face and my red eyes from the thrashing I'd done in my sleep and the insistence, the deep *need*, to be alone again because someone was trying to tell me something important.

"Oh, okay," Rain said, lowering her head.

"The sink's broken in the art room, so we just needed to fill this up," another freshman said, and I noticed now that she was carrying a bucket. "Ms. Raicht said we could. She told us to come in here. She said . . ."

"Just do it," I said, like I ruled the girls' room and commanded the sinks, "and hurry up."

They filled the bucket quickly and were heading out the door when Rain turned back and held it open, pausing to say this to me: "Are you feeling okay? You look like you've seen a ghost or something."

I looked her in the eyes for the first time and wondered if she might be able to see the girl in the stall, too. If I pointed her out.

Then she said, "I had the flu over break and I was so dizzy and I puked and everything. Do you need me to take you to the nurse?"

I was about to tell her I was fine and she should leave me alone when a person shoved past her into the bathroom and said, "Someone said you were up here. Nice haircut."

Jamie walked in and leaned up against the far sink.

"You're not allowed in here," Rain said to him. "You'll get in trouble."

Jamie glanced at her, then said to me: "Who is this girl?"

"Nobody." It was true. She wasn't even close to sixteen yet, let alone 17, so I didn't have to bother about worrying over her. I was staring right at her and blanking on her name.

It took her a few moments to sense that she should leave. The door slammed closed, and Jamie stepped closer, as if we were alone, but we weren't. It was impossible now to be alone with me because I was always being followed. He stepped close to me, and then I stepped away, and I think that's when it began to dawn on him.

"Didn't you see me downstairs?" he asked.

"Yeah," I admitted, not able to keep it up anymore, not now that the visions were multiplying, now that there were three girls.

"So you're avoiding me?"

I shrugged. I felt my shoulders make the motion, and I didn't do a thing to stop them.

"What's gotten into you?" he said, just coming out with it. "Are you into someone else? Is that it? Who is it?"

"It's no one. It's not that."

"So what is it then?" I now realized we were having "the talk," and that I wasn't going to get away with avoiding it today.

He'd retreated back to lean against the sinks. His arms

were crossed over his narrow chest and his thick, dark hair was curling down over one of his eyes. He didn't reach up to move it away.

I didn't want to let myself keep looking at him—like I'd given up that right—so I dropped my gaze and thought and thought of what to say. There was a drain in the middle of the tiled floor that I hadn't noticed before and my eyes caught on it. Was that how Natalie had entered the room? And was that the exit she'd taken to leave? Could the girls travel through the pipes of the school? Were they anywhere, and everywhere, able to find me wherever I went, no matter if I wanted them to or not?

"Lauren," Jamie said. "You owe me this. You know you do. Just say it. I can take it."

He was right: I did owe him an explanation. It was more than just that we'd gotten physical together and that made all of this so much more serious. And with seriousness comes the lowering of the walls, and with the lowering of the walls comes the nakedness, and with the nakedness comes the connection and the fear. Both of us had done things we'd never done with anyone else before—at least that's what *he* said; I know I was telling the truth—not to mention the talking and all the secrets spilled after, like when we'd lie in bed together, under the covers, at his house or my house, when no one else was home.

He told me how his dad used to hit him until one day, when he was thirteen, he hit him back and got lucky with his aim and bloodied his lip. I told him how my dad disappeared when I was three and a few years ago we thought he was in a homeless shelter down in Texas, but when we called to talk to him he wouldn't come to the phone. Jamie told me how he used to think of suicide sometimes, when he was reading a lot of Camus. I told him how I never once thought of suicide, but I knew my mom had, before I was born, and knowing I was the one keeping her alive and happy made me more afraid to die than anything ever could. Jamie and I simply told each other a lot of things. And I guess that once you've gone that far with someone, once you've let him in, in all the ways a person can be let in, you should say why you don't want to see him anymore. You should *know* why, yourself.

I didn't, but I tried to explain.

"It's me. It's me and it's not me. There's more of me than you know. There's more, and I can't tell you, I can't say. There are things . . . There are people." I got the distinct feeling I was saying too much. It's true that Jamie knew a lot about me, but he didn't know everything. I'd never told him about Fiona Burke running away all those years ago. And, right then, I was relieved I hadn't. She wouldn't want him to know.

"Wait, so you're saying I don't know you? Are you *serious?*" He'd heard only part of what I'd said.

"You used to. You don't anymore."

"You're not making sense."

I agreed. It felt like we were having two separate conversations, that he was hearing things my mouth wasn't saying, and I was saying things his ears couldn't hear.

Then I remembered the phone call he'd taken when we were at the Lady-of-the-Pines Summer Camp that night. He was acting like all of this was my fault, but was it? Who was the guilty one here?

"Maybe I should ask *you* if there's someone else?" I said. "If there was, would you tell me?"

"No," he said, and hearing that answer felt like a slap. Then he clarified. "There's no one else." He added this last bit without looking at me: "But it sounds like you want me to get with someone else."

I couldn't blame him if he did. I wasn't fit for consumption. I was defective. I was about to melt down that drain and share the pipes with the only people who understood me. The girls.

I don't know what I wanted him to do: pull me into his arms, maybe, and say it didn't matter. Sense there was someone in the stall and not be scared away by it.

He did none of those things. You see, Jamie Rossi was great. He was kind. He was really, really into me, or at least he used to be. But he was also a pretty typical 17-year-old boy, and you can't expect so much from them.

"Whatever you want," he said, his eyes hardening. "I guess we're broken up then." He turned for the door, and I thought he was about to leave; then he turned back.

"That's mine. That hoodie you're wearing. Take it off."

"You're kidding."

He waited, and the expression on his face said it all. It was more a lack of expression, an iron door behind which he'd packed all his emotions; I'd never get close to them again since I wasn't strong enough to lift that door. He absolutely was not kidding.

"C'mon," he said. "You made me late to class already. Just give it so I can go."

I unzipped the red hoodie, then pulled it off, arm by arm. Underneath I wore only a T-shirt of the thinnest cotton, and it was January, and my nipples turned to pebbles and the goose-flesh on my arms popped up, and surely he'd see this and let me hang on to the hoodie for the rest of the day.

Nope.

I held it out to him, dangling it in the open space between us. He closed the gap, tore it out of my hand, and left.

Natalie, upon hearing the door slam, dropped her feet down off the toilet and came out of the stall. She made me cough, and she made my eyes tear up, and I couldn't look at her, not even in the mirror, and there was a lump in my throat so I couldn't speak.

She didn't touch me, because I don't think a ghost can touch a person. But she stood very, very close to me so her whisper teased at the lobe of my ear:

You don't need him, she said, and I knew just what she'd say next. *You have us.*

-24-

NATALIE wondered what else she'd inherited from her mother, beyond the physical characteristics most kids inherit through the curse of DNA: eye color, hair texture, bumps on the nose, extra weight around the hips. Did she carry something else of her mom's, that raging flare buried and faintly glowing somewhere in her, the one that made her mother sneak the blade from the kitchen and plunge it, without warning, into the snoring chest of that man in her bed?

Maybe this kind of calculated rage was genetic. It could be that Natalie had this trait just as she had anything else.

You have your mother's eyes.

You have your mother's skill with a carving knife.

Natalie feared it could snap on at any moment. It could come crashing down on her like the ice storm that was her fate. Coating her eyes and her tongue and crusting deep beneath her fingernails. Turning her a color she'd never been before. Making her do terrible things.

But I didn't sense that in her—and I'm sure I would have, traveling through her wants and thoughts and aches and regrets and wonderings as I did, once she let me in. I slid on her consciousness like trying on a borrowed dress. There was nothing wrong with that dress, even if it didn't fit me exactly.

I didn't think she'd come to hurt me. I knew all she wanted was to talk.

To tell me.

She told me everything up until the moment she disappeared.

The before, I could see and experience and mull over. And the during—the accident, the car sliding circles on the ice and crashing sideways into the guardrail, that slice of fast-moving time that came so suddenly—that, I could play back in slow motion. Pause and hover over. Investigate. It was only the after that I couldn't guess at, couldn't pierce a hole through.

Probably because she had a hard time seeing it, too.

She told me about Lila, who was hosting the party in her father's finished basement. She told me how none of this would have happened if not for Lila's party, one Natalie wasn't even technically invited to, seeing as she and Lila weren't what could be called friends. She'd tagged along to the party anyway because of some boy. If she hadn't met that boy when she'd served him a burger and fries at Murray's, where she waited tables two days a week, if he hadn't grabbed ahold of her wrist when she'd walked by his booth and slipped the napkin onto her tray, the one where he'd written, in sloppy boy-handwriting—*Babe you are hot. when you get off work want to go to party later? let me know*—and signed with his name (Paul), then she wouldn't be haunting me in bathrooms and whispering her story in my ears. She'd be back home, alive, and I wouldn't know her.

She wanted me to get a sense of how it was, up where she lived. How little there was to do up there. How boring it was, especially in winter, if you couldn't afford to ski. So she may have despised Lila—in the locker room after phys ed she'd heard the girl call her a psychopath like her psychopath mother, and in the hallway out of sight of the teachers, Lila had let Natalie know how she felt about psychopaths with psychopath mothers. The girl had claws.

But she'd go to her party. Where else was there to go?

The drive up the mountain was uneventful. When they'd started the climb up the mountain pass, it hadn't even begun snowing yet. But by the time they were crawling to the top, searching out the marker for Lila's parents' driveway, the sky ahead was shrouded in a thick white sheet.

Since the guy who'd invited her was driving—this was his old '65 Mustang coupe, oily and black in the night—she'd sat in the front and could ignore the looks from his friends. They were townies like her, and they'd all heard the stories of her mother.

But Paul, who was driving, wasn't from around there, so he had no idea.

There wasn't a reason for a party, except that Lila's father was letting them use his finished basement. That's why everyone drove up to the highest heights of Plateau Road when a snowstorm was expected. Lila's house was at the tiptop of the mountain, down a squirrelly dirt driveway that fractured from the main road, so that cars had to be parked out on the road itself, making those who came in sneakers have to ice-skate their way to the front door. But her father had a fully stocked bar and a billiards table in the carpeted lower level of the house. And the soundproof door at the top of the stairs locked from the inside, so her parents couldn't check the booze supply till morning.

It was Tim, the hippie, who brought the pills. And it was Tim the hippie who insisted on the orange juice, saying you could enhance the roll on vitamin C. It was Jeannette who said there was a store close by, halfway down the road. It was Paul who volunteered to drive.

And that's how Paul and Tim and Jeannette and Natalie had all gone back out for the car. And this was also how Natalie slipped on the ice that was now falling from the sky and grabbed for the first solid object, the hood of the car, and that's how the zipper of her coat caused a nick in the paint.

Paul let her in the car, but he made her sit in back this time.

They were on the road when the drug kicked in, on a narrow lane skirting the edge of the mountain, blinded by shooting snow. The white battering the hood was the same white flitting into the sky and the same white slapping the windshield. All was white.

You can't know how long it'll take to trickle into your system, Tim had told them, but it's not instantaneous, and they probably had a good half hour, so it'll be a smooth ride in, so gentle you won't know until—

Jeannette smiled and said she felt it right now. Shit, man—she felt it.

Paul, the one driving, slowed to a crawl. He spoke over his shoulder to Natalie, who was in the backseat behind him, forgetting that she'd nicked the paint job on his car now, saying, "Whoa, you feel that?" like they shared the same body and were feeling the same things.

She told him she did. She told everyone in the car that she felt it. In fact, she felt other sensations instead. Like how cold it was, so cold since Paul hadn't let the car warm up before shifting it into drive, and colder still because Paul had the window cracked. Also she felt a climbing ache in her head, probably from the overpowering scent of gasoline. Was the car's gas tank leaking?

None of this was an effect of the drug. She was completely sober.

What no one knew was that Natalie had pocketed the pill Tim had given her. She didn't know, and never would get to, what it felt like to "roll," as Tim called it, on a white winter's night while driving.

They didn't know she was faking. The snow seemed funny to Jeannette, so Natalie pretended it was funny to her, too. Tim was mesmerized by the seat vinyl, how soft it was, how beautiful, so Natalie spent a long moment contemplating its perfectly smooth skin.

Paul kept watching her instead of the road, and she wanted to tell him to keep a lookout for other cars and for patches of ice and swift turns that would veer them off the side of the mountain.

Also, she wanted to ask, haven't they driven far enough? Wasn't the store supposed to be just down the road?

But if she did that, she'd reveal she'd only pretended to swallow the pill. That she'd lied.

It was only that she didn't want to lose control. She didn't want to have no sense of what was real or unreal, to think everything was wonderful when it actually wasn't wonderful, which was what Tim had told everyone who hadn't done it before to expect after the chemical seeped into their bloodstreams.

Everything Tim had described was the last thing Natalie would have ever wanted, especially knowing she wasn't among friends.

To lose control?

To not know what was real?

That would be too much like looking down at her hands and seeing they'd become her mother's hands. Like looking into the mirror, as Natalie did every single day since the two consecutive life sentences were decided, and gazing into the eyes of a woman who could plunge a knife into a man's stomach forty-seven times and then bag him up with his gym socks and his tennis racket and leave him at his wife's door to be discovered when she went out to get the newspaper Sunday morning.

Natalie didn't, couldn't be sure, what she was capable of, having this woman for a mother, and so she could never let go the way the others could. She'd never get so inebriated she'd climb atop the bar in a basement rec room and pitch herself face-first into the arms of whoever would catch her, like Lila had before the orange-juice run.

And yet somehow, sober, Natalie had gotten herself talked into going for a ride in Paul's Mustang. And she was sober when Jeannette turned to her in the backseat of the moving car and said, as if she'd only just noticed her, "Natalie Montesano? Natalie, is that you?" Jeannette's pupils had grown to two black nickels, gargantuan against the shrinking sea of her irises. She wasn't slurring; she was talking as if she didn't know how to make full use of her mouth. "Wait." She seemed confused. "Wait. *Why* don't we like you?"

And that was all it took. The fine feeling, the open mind, the sense of adventure in agreeing to go on the drive in the snowy night, it all left Natalie. And good riddance. In its place came disdain. Pulsed through with rage. Woven with hate.

Maybe there was a piece of her mother inside her after all. It wouldn't cause her to grab a sharpened object and plunge it into the closest chest—three hearts to choose from in this car. It had always been subtler, inside Natalie. It made her not care. Not about herself, and not about anyone else.

She didn't care if they all died on this road tonight.

When she did it, it was without thinking, and it was also as if she'd been premeditating it for years: She reached her arm forward into the front seat and she said, "Watch out for that car!"

There was no other car. There was only the car they were in, which shuddered when the brakes were jammed, and then slid. Soon the old Mustang was careening across the ice, not going straight and not going sideways, and there was the railing at the road's edge, and there was the space ahead of it, filled only with air and emptied of trees.

There was this moment before the car made impact, so of course she remembered it, where she saw everything that was happening and was about to happen and understood it in a way she didn't know life could be understood.

Then she saw the guardrail come for them—and beyond that, the gaping edge of the mountain—and this was when she screamed. She screamed the way the man's wife did when she found the bag with the body, the way a madwoman would scream when she tore open the guts of a lying, two-timing man. She screamed, and then the car jolted to a stop.

She showed me how she screamed, and my ears rang for days.

– 25 –

NATALIE'S story doesn't end there, with the accident. There was what came after.

If anyone could have been on that mountain to see the smashed black Mustang, if they'd been peering in through the cracked windshield to where Natalie lay in the backseat, they would have wondered what might happen to her. Would any of the kids who'd been in the car come back for her, and why hadn't anyone tried to wake her first before taking off?

There had been all that snow as the night went on, but now ice cascaded from the dark heavens in whipping, slapping sheets. Anyone would have hoped, as Natalie would have hoped had she been fully conscious, that they wouldn't just abandon her. The girl, Jeannette, did say they'd go get help.

To stay put.

To be okay, okay?

To hang on. They'd be back.

But Paul did not come back. Tim did not come back. Jeannette did not come back, either, even though she was the one who said they would. They climbed out of the totaled car and slipped into the storm, retreating on foot to Lila's house, where they could call for help.

It could be that they ran through the ice as fast as they could. Maybe leaving her behind was all they could think to do, under the circumstances, with the drug in their systems and no signal on any of their cell phones. It could be that they did care, that they did try, that some obstacle they couldn't control was what kept them away and kept the accident from being reported for so long.

Or it could be that they knew what Natalie had longed for, recognized that burning-cold part of her that made the offhanded wish and then watched it happen—and they turned their backs because of it. Why they never came back for her is not the part of the story I know.

What I do know is that she was unconscious for a long time. Then, when she woke up, she was simply confused.

She emerged from what felt like a deep sleep, pieces of glass embedded all over her body. Then she was crawling through the shattered windshield and calling out for someone, anyone, on the vacant road. Discovering there was no one. The wind whipping through her hair as she got to her feet. The crunch of ice under her feet as she started walking. And nothing after that. No trace of her. No trail. No girl.

– 26 –

THE house in my dream howled with wind. The wind blared through broken windows; the drapes flapped and slapped at soot-stained walls.

I was aware of some things, like time. Like I knew it was January in my waking life, so maybe it was also January in the dream. It could be that the dream lived alongside me, mirroring the weather and holidays, that as I moved ahead through life, so did the dream.

But if that was true, the embers from the fire would have gone dark by now.

If time was the same in here, Fiona Burke would have grown older. All the girls would have. From the newspaper stories I read about her, I knew that Natalie Montesano would have been twenty-four.

Natalie found me before I could find her. She was on the second floor, pale eyes peeking from between the shrunken black sticks of kindling that had once been the banister and, from behind that, all her hair. She wanted me to come up, and I wanted her to come down, so we met, instead, in the middle.

If I'd had my wits about me—if in the dream I kept my wits—I would have asked her why she was following me. Was there something she wanted me to do? Is that why she kept visiting?

But the gum in my brain could only function enough to get me close to her. Close enough to hear her speak.

I didn't mean to do it, she said. And again. *I didn't mean to do it.* Sometimes she said the same thing so many times, I'd lose count.

There was no working electricity in the house, so we hovered on the delicate stairs in the darkness.

They never found me, did they? Natalie asked, and the way she said it, resigned to the wind in her face, to the darkness thick with smoke, made me realize she never expected them to find her. Not ever.

"No," I said. "Do you need me to—do you want me to . . . call someone? Do something?"

She tilted her head, and I sensed her cold eyes go dim. *What could you do?* she said. I should not have even asked such a ridiculous question.

All she wished, if she could have a wish, if somewhere outside this limbo a wish from a girl like her could be plucked from the darkness and granted, she'd want them to know she hadn't meant to cause the accident. That she was sorry. That she would take it back if she could.

It was here that the smoke of the dream seemed to clear and her hair parted and I could see her face for the first time since it appeared in my bathroom mirror. What I saw was something different, because in here, in this house, she was her true self. Her cheeks were still punctured from the windshield glass, causing her face to alternately bleed and sparkle. It was lovely and terrible at the same time.

She turned her back and walked the rest of the way up the stairs. My eyes were adjusting to the lack of light and I saw for the first time that she had impossibly long hair, hair that had never known a pair of scissors in its lifetime, plain and stick-straight and parted down the middle. And for a moment all she was out of the darkness was hair, and all I was in the darkness was another person who'd done nothing to help her.

She turned in a cloud of frizz.

It's too late, she said, *for me.* The frizz alighted, and the glass shards in her cheeks shimmered, and the two sharp needles piercing through it were her cold eyes. *But it's not too late . . . for her.*

– 27 –

NOT too late for *her*. Something told me this had to mean Abby Sinclair.

I'd seen Fiona Burke in the house, and now I'd seen Natalie in the house, and on my way out and into consciousness, before the dream sifted away like a haze of smoke tends to do, I caught sight of another figure. This one stood statue-still, her back to an ash-gray wall.

No, not Abby—and no matter how much her disappearance itched at me, tugging and not letting go, she wasn't the only girl who wanted me to have her story. That's the thing I'd soon discover: There were more. So many more.

There were more lost girls out there than I'd ever imagined, and now they knew where to find me. Their whispers came from the shadows, the sound of so many voices more static than song.

MISSING

SHYANN JOHNSTON

CASE TYPE: Endangered Runaway

DOB: November 10, 1994

MISSING: January 30, 2012

AGE NOW: 18

SEX: Female

RACE: African American

HAIR: Black

EYES: Brown

HEIGHT: 5'6" (168 cm)

WEIGHT: 153 lbs (69 kg)

MISSING FROM: Newark, NJ, United States

CIRCUMSTANCES: Shyann was last seen leaving school on January 30, 2012, when she was 17 years old. She has a chicken pox scar under her right eye. She is believed to have stayed in the local area.

ANYONE HAVING INFORMATION SHOULD CONTACT

Newark Police Department (New Jersey) 1-973-555-8297

– 28 –

THEY called her names. They called her ugly names, and stupid names; any cruel name they could think of, and there were many. It didn't matter what names they called Shyann—there was no logic to it. Like, when she gained that weight over the summer they called her Shamu, and then she went and lost all the weight, and they still called her Shamu. They had no imagination.

For every name she'd been called by the age of 17, Shyann Johnston could have forged a fake ID for every sleazy bar in the city and gotten her drink on, even though she'd never tasted beer and she probably wouldn't like it. She could have left, too. She could've collected enough passports to travel the world a dozen times over, escaping so far from her neighborhood she'd never have to go back, not to finish out high school, not to attend her graduation, not to carry her stuff out of her mom and dad's and cart it to somewhere new. She wished she could do that, but she was stuck there, with these kids she hated because they hated her. These kids who made her life a living nightmare, who followed her around sometimes, in school and after school let out, trailing her down the street, across the crosswalk, pelting her with whatever they had in their pockets when she came down the steps of the library or out of that grocery place on the corner with a bag of food in her arms. Her tormentors.

There were enough bad names swirling through her mind that some mornings she looked in a mirror and saw what they saw. How could she not?

She believed the bad things more than she knew she should. She took in those words and let them burrow. Let them bat back and forth inside her brain. She began to think she'd never be able to spit them out, even if her mom and dad and the anti-bullying counselor assigned to talk to her fourth period told her none of it was true and building some self-esteem was how to fight back.

Bullcrap, Shyann thought. Maybe she should fight back by blasting them in the face with the gun her dad hid behind his porno collection. But she hated guns, and she didn't want to go sifting through her dad's personal items, besides, so she fought back by using the most anti-violent method she knew. She turned tail and she ran away.

It was soon after I first read about Shyann that she reached out to me to confirm it. To show she was one of the girls.

All I got at first was her voice on my cell phone. The blur of her body and the shriek of her voice saying, *Leave me alone. Stop it already. Stop.*

It came from an unidentified caller that said only "New Jersey." There were no words in the message, but a video was attached.

It was a Monday, lunch period in the cafeteria. And when the text message came up on my phone, when I saw there was a video, I had a feeling, a sense that I was coming into contact with another girl. I stood up, holding the phone close to me so no one could see what was on the screen. "You can't have that out, it'll get confiscated," I heard one of my friends say.

I rushed through the caf, almost knocking over some kid, causing him to drop his tray. I'd reached the edge of the room and I was pushing through the double doors and I was out in the hall and then, finally, finally, I was alone and could hit Play.

Leave me alone, I heard first, coming out my phone's speaker. *Stop it already. Stop it. Stop.*

The camerawork was shaky, the picture distorted. I couldn't tell who was talking except that it sounded like a girl. The frame showed ground covered in gray, murky snow. It showed two running feet. It focused in, for just a moment, on those feet: a pair of sneakers in the snow. The laces were yellow, which seemed wrong somehow, too cheerful. One set of laces was undone, trailing.

Here, the camera zoomed out, and the video exploded with laughter. A whole group of them out of view, an anonymous herd hidden where I couldn't see.

They were taunting her. Calling her names. And now I could see her, all of her, better than I could before. She was cowering under her hair, then trying to run away down an urban sidewalk patched with ice and trash bags left on the curb and low, dirty drifts of snow. Tripping over her shoelaces and trying to run.

The camera lens pointed down for some seconds, at the ground, like the owner of the phone—a guy, his voice was the loudest—was checking to make sure it was still recording. It showed the world crooked and almost upside down, as if this patch of pitted sidewalk were really sky, but then it raised up again in a great blur of motion. He was running now, running with the phone in hand. When he stopped, the image stopped, too. It jittered and held in place, moving in to show a brick wall.

A girl was standing against it, shielding her face from view. This was Shyann.

The last few seconds took a wild zoom in on her face and held there, so I could see her: dark skin, big bright eyes, hair gone white from all the snow and ice thrown in it.

Then, before the video came to a stop, she took off. Left the brick wall and bolted off where the camera couldn't find her. At this, the video cut out.

She'd sent me this video to show me her troubles. So she didn't have to put it all into words first. So I'd know why.

A teacher was passing by, and I didn't think fast enough to hide the phone. "Where are you supposed to be, Miss Woodman?" she asked, then noticed it. "No phones out during school hours, you know that." Then there was her hand, the long, bony fingers wrapping themselves around my cell phone and detaching it from me.

"Hey, that was important," I said, reaching for it, but she shook her head and told me to get to wherever it was I was supposed to be this period, *that* was what was important.

I stared at her for a moment. I'd been living for weeks in two places at once: here. And there, where they were. This teacher—what did she teach, some slack class like health?—she had no idea what was important, or where I most needed to be.

— — —

When I got my phone back from the vice principal's office after last bell, the video of Shyann Johnston was gone. The only proof I had that the video did come to me, that my phone had caught the electric charge of her first contact, was the blinking light and the message that said: UNABLE TO DOWNLOAD. ERROR.

–29–

JANUARY was bringing the most snow the Hudson Valley had seen in close to ten years. It also brought more of those dreams.

The dreams didn't fit with the falling snow. They were hot instead of cold, made of smoke that steamed my lungs and warmed my skin. But it was that night when the dream became somehow even hotter, so real that I burst out of my bedroom gasping, my arms wildly waving away the smoke, that I became aware of my mom, saying I'd been sleepwalking, saying with a sigh, "Go back to bed, babe," like this had happened before.

I returned to my room to find her. Shyann Johnston. This time, not a blur on the miniature screen of my cell phone. Not an error message. This time for real.

It shocked me even though I should have been expecting her visit. I didn't scream.

I waited until I couldn't hear my mom anymore. I held still by the door, my hand unable to come off the knob where I'd hung all my bras, sifting through the underwire while I waited for my mom to get back to her room. It took some minutes. All the while *she* breathed in and out, quick breaths, like she was more scared than I was.

I couldn't make out her features in the darkness, but she seemed cold from the way she shivered—and her lips, from what I could see of them, seemed tinged blue.

I wondered how long she'd been sitting there. The whole time I slept? Or had she followed me out of the dream minutes before?

I sat on the edge of my bed, across from the seat she'd chosen. My heart could be felt in my throat, its jogged beating made from the natural instinct to panic at this impossible sight in my room. But also questions, rattling with questions. And the questions won.

"Was that you?" I made myself ask. "On my phone?"

Her bluish lips pulled into something of a sad smile, which I took as an answer.

Abby and Natalie had both let me into their minds straightaway, and Fiona Burke had my mind for the taking. But Shyann didn't trust me enough at first. She probably thought I'd make fun of her for what I saw in there, call her one of those names.

Didn't you see me? she said. *I saw you.*

I knew she didn't mean here, in my desk chair, where the outline of her was sitting in the dark, my bathrobe folded over the back of the chair and my school papers scattered across the desk. She meant somewhere else, that place where I'd been before I found myself sleepwalking, the charred space of the recurring dream. That's where she actually was—in the house, with the others. That's where she now had to stay.

I admitted I had seen her. That had been her, standing against the wall. In the dream as in the video; in the video as in the dream.

"Why are you here? What do you want from me?" I asked, and then before I could hear her answer, my mom was back, knocking on my door and wanting to know who was I talking to, was I on the phone? And I was turning away from the desk chair, turning away from the outline of the girl in the staticky darkness, and calling through the door to my mom to say I was fine. My mom asked if it was Jamie, and I said yeah, because he'd be as good an excuse as any. I just didn't want her opening my door.

"Aren't you two . . . I thought you said it was over," my mom said through the door.

"We're only talking, Mom."

My mom did open the door, and in those first few seconds I thought for sure she'd see it. The ghost. The girl. Then she'd know.

She leaned her head in and I noticed her spot my phone—it was off, sitting on my dresser all the way across the room, where I couldn't have just been talking on it. She saw that, but she didn't see Shyann. "You okay?" she said.

"I'm fine."

If she knew something, if she could sense something, she would've stayed. But she only said good night again and closed my door.

I looked back, and the desk chair held only my bathrobe, the dark air shimmering as if my eyes were still adjusting, drawing shapes of a girl who wasn't there anymore, who'd run off, who'd gone. My mom had scared her away.

I was alone, and I felt it. There wasn't even a breath in my ear.

What did Shyann want from me? Only this. Only to tell me her story and be heard.

– 30 –

SHYANN'S parents had reported her missing at the end of January about a year ago, saying she'd run away. "Teen Flees from Neighborhood Bullies," stories online said. "Bullied Teen Still Not Found." The bullying "experts" were called in, the ones who liked to get gussied up for TV talk shows to denounce the epidemic sweeping our schools, made worse by social networking and technologies like camera phones.

Shyann's school principal was interviewed, and some teachers. There was one girl who spoke on camera, acting as if she had no idea what had been done to Shyann. "Don't really know what happened to that girl," she told Channel 4 and Channel 11. "Nobody was messing with her. Why'd she run off for no reason?" She smiled a carefully calculated smile, and I wanted to reach my arm into the screen and punch her in the face.

No one but me knew what had happened to Shyann.

If Shyann could have planned better, she wouldn't have gone in winter. New Jersey in late January was full of frigid gusts of wind, the kind that swept up your pant legs, and strung out tears from your eyes. Snow in the city limits quickly turned gray; maybe it even came down from the sky that color. It could be that it was only white in other towns and in storybooks, and in the cotton-candy fluff they pumped out for holiday movies. Here, there were gray patches on the sidewalks, the ice making the pavement so slick someone could slip and fall if she tried to run.

If it had been warmer—if Shyann could have held on through the winter, kept her head down, didn't let herself care so much what they all said about her—she would have gone in spring, when the city warmed but before the humidity got the whole area in its clutches. There were ragged plots of land behind some of the row houses in her neighborhood, and if a person didn't have the money to hop a train and leave, a person could survive there without being detected. If she were smart about it.

The brush was thickly grown over the fences, and the trees gave shade. No one in their right mind went back there—no one besides dealers, who went in there to hide stashes, or bums, who went in there to sleep—but she could see herself in one of those vacant lots, building a tree house out of vines and old plywood, tires and netting, completely concealed from anyone down on the ground.

Maybe sometimes a couple from the neighborhood would slip in past the fences to hook up, but they'd get it done and be out fast enough. Cops didn't go back there. Feral dogs did, and scruffy cats without collars, but she'd just kick them down when they climbed her tree.

She'd descend from her perch in the branches only at night, to scrounge for food. When she slept, in her tree house hidden in the middle of her city, she'd open her eyes to see a blanket of stars. No one could take that view from her. Out there was an entire universe, proof that there was life outside this one, and every night she'd have a reminder.

She would have gone in spring, if she could have waited.

She couldn't wait.

Shyann did have her reasons, and they weren't secret. She'd left her parents a note:

CANNOT take this anymore!
What is it going to take to make u listen!
I am NOT going back to that school!

But the note wasn't found for four and a half days, because her little brother balled it up inside his toy dump truck. It wasn't until the toy tipped over, spilling its contents, that Shyann's mother recognized her handwriting and unballed the note to finally see what her daughter had said.

Truth was, Shyann watched her family's windows for hours before she left the confines of the backyard. Out there, where the trash cans were stored, there was a shed that the superintendent never used. Shyann spent her first night inside this shed. She bundled up, keeping a hole uncovered for her two eyes and nothing more, and every once in a while she'd stand and peek outside the shed to her parents' second-floor windows. They had no idea she was so close. Her mom could have called her name out the window and she would have been startled enough to bolt up and say, "Yes, ma'am?"

Her second night away, she abandoned the shed. It was too close, and now that she'd stayed out a whole night, she was getting anxious about the consequences of coming back. Part of her did want to go home, but when she stepped nearer to the trash cans, she heard voices she recognized, from those kids who lived on her block. She imagined what they'd throw at her, like the bottle that one time. Like trash in the street. Like brightly colored pellets of candy, small and rock-hard as hailstones. When held in hot, grimy fists they sweated off some of their coating, so you could see the impact of them on her clothes as if she'd been out playing paintball. Orange, brown, blue, green, red; the darkest spots where she was hardest hit.

She was about to come out, but she heard those voices. And she knew that if she left her hiding place, if she went home and returned to school, she'd get worse things thrown at her. Far worse. And then she'd topple. They could dump all they wanted on her, the contents of whole trash cans even, and she'd just lie there, and let herself be buried, and that would be the end of Shyann.

That was why she couldn't ever go back.

After the first night in the shed, she spent one night in an old warehouse, and the night after that in a condemned house where the padlocks had been ripped from the doorjamb so anyone or anything could get in. Her fantasy of spending her last months before she turned eighteen in the wilds of a vacant lot, sleeping nights high up in a thick oak tree where nothing could bother her—that fantasy fell to pieces once she'd experienced the cold.

She was constantly shivering, in dark places where the electric and heat didn't work because the city had shut it off. She tried to keep warm, but the winter nights were long, longer than she'd expected. She didn't know how many nights she'd be able to last.

The last thing she remembered was something of a dream. Her eyes were closing, and the cold had gone deep into her bones, and she felt like she could hear the whole city talking about her. But they weren't taunting—this time they were saying nice things. The mayor would lock them up if they didn't.

All the girls at school, on camera, they were going: "Shyann, please come home, we're so sorry. We're saving you a seat at lunch." And the guys on her block, they were going: "We only said you're ugly 'cause we want to get with you, Shyann. Didn't you know? We thought you knew."

Teachers were praising her, coming up to the microphone one by one. Mr. Wallace said how wrong he was for blaming her for the candy dropped under her desk and giving her detention for eating in class. Ms. Taylor, who led the grueling warm-ups in gym, swore on the spot that Shyann would never have to do extra sit-ups for being slow with the laps again. And Ms. Atkins, the nasty English teacher, publicly announced that she was taking back all the Fs and awarding Shyann an A.

Stuff like that. Stuff like her parents saying all this was too little, too late, and they'd homeschool her to graduate. And they'd buy her a car. And she'd find it when she came home—all shiny and blue, wrapped in a bow like on commercials.

She was too cold to move. Too cold to get up and see if this had all come true, but she could picture herself doing it. She could see herself slipping into that sparkling blue thing—hers, all hers—and driving far, far away.

– 31 –

I looked it up to be sure. They still hadn't found Shyann's body—at least, there was no funeral announcement, no search party scouring the vacant lots of the city, paying careful attention to private hideaways and the climbing branches of tall trees. They hadn't found her, just like with Natalie on that mountain road two states away. And with Fiona, down whatever road she took, wherever she landed aside from back here with me. None of the girls I saw in the house had been found.

There were more stories still to be told. More girls, their voices rising, their Missing flyers entering my collection. My memory expanding now to hold all of their names.

–32–

ISABETH

Isabeth got in the car. Didn't she know a girl alone should never get in the strange car when it pulls up alongside her, when the man calls out asking if she needs a ride, when even after she says no, he keeps tailing her, keeps asking?

She knew.

On any other day, she wouldn't have accepted the ride. But what she wanted her family and friends to know, what she hoped they'd only understand, had they been there, was how the rainstorm had caught her unaware when she was walking home from school. How the burst of showers came from out of nowhere and how, within seconds, she was soaked. And that's when the car pulled up behind her.

At first she ignored him. Then he pulled the car closer, and she happened to take a peek and realized—a glimmer of relief—that it was only someone she knew. Well, sort of. The man's face was familiar; he was from around the neighborhood. He knew her dad, or was it her brothers? He worked in a store in town, or was he a member of her church? Either way, she'd seen him before, somewhere.

"Need a ride?" this man, technically not a stranger, called.

She hesitated.

"Come on, get in out of the rain," he said.

Isabeth nodded, and within moments she was depositing her schoolbooks in the backseat. She was climbing into the front seat. She was closing the car door.

Only then did she waver. She hadn't done the wrong thing, had she? Did she really know this man? Should she ask his name to be sure? Would that be rude? That would be. *So* rude. She didn't want to be rude. That's what she was thinking moments before she realized the door had been locked automatically.

Isabeth had done everything she was told to do for the past 17 years: She had studied. She had washed the dishes. She had kept her legs closed. She had stayed off the Internet past ten o'clock. She had joined her family for church every Sunday. She had eaten her vegetables. She had, once or twice, helped an old lady cross a street. She had never once rolled up the waistband of her school-uniform skirt to show more leg.

She'd done so many things right, and one thing wrong. She shouldn't have gotten in that car.

Isabeth Valdes: Gone 2010 from Binghamton, New York. Age 17.

— — —

MADISON

Madison was going to be a model. She'd been told she should model all her life, like randomly when she was out shopping for a cute new outfit at the mall or sucking on the straw of her iced, sugar-free, skim-milk chai latte at the coffee place or just minding her own business walking down the street. She figured it was only a matter of time before someone plucked her from the great big nothing that was her life and plastered her face on a billboard and made her into Something. She figured heading to New York would only bring her into Somethingness that much faster.

She met the photographer online, or talked to him anyway. He said he'd do her portfolio for free, and he had the lights set up in his apartment and everything.

So Madison spent the entire six-hour ride practicing her posing face in the bus window. She had an expression she was trying to perfect, half serious, half sweet, lips pursed, eyebrows lifted, chin held high. She knew the photographer would love her for it.

Madison Waller: Gone 2013 from Keene, New Hampshire. Age 17.

— — —

EDEN

Eden simply wanted a taco. She was the one who saw the roadside stand at the edge of nowhere and begged her friends to stop. She was the one who raced out of the car before anyone else did. The light was falling, and picnic tables were empty, and all she knew was that the roadside stand said TACOS and she needed one, right now. The rickety shack was covered in hand-painted signs like that. One said STRAWBERRIES and another said BLUEBERRIES. And the biggest of them all said JEWELRY / PIE / WOVEN RUGS / CIGARS. Though the place was ready to close up shop, Eden talked them into serving her and her friends some tacos slathered in cheese and sour cream and pico de gallo and heaps of guac. But by the time she and her friends were finished eating, the place was closed and dark and there was nowhere to use the bathroom before they got back on the road, so Eden had to make use of the weeds.

The last thing Eden's friends heard her say before she trampled off into the darkness beyond the picnic tables was, "Back in a sec! Gotta pee."

Eden DeMarco: Gone 2011 from Fairborn, Ohio. Age 17.

— — —

YOON-MI AND MAURA

Yoon-mi said she knew the minute she walked into the gymnasium for early pep-squad practice. She knew as she stretched and as, across the gym, the last phys ed class of the day counted off into teams. She knew as the class spread out to start dodgeball, getting ever closer to where they were practicing. And she knew as she stood up to learn the new cheer. She knew when she felt the smack of impact as the ball hit her square in the face. She knew as she fell backward, and she knew as she lay there, staring up at the ridiculously tall ceiling, where caught in the rafters was a lone silver balloon from the formal the month before. She'd gone to that dance with a boy, even though she secretly liked girls. What she knew is that something significant would happen today.

The feeling took shape and grew eyes and a mouth and a face, turning into this girl, this fellow junior named Maura.

"I'm so freaking sorry!" Maura was going. "I didn't mean to get you in the face!"

And there were more people surrounding them—the gym teacher, the other juniors in last-period gym, and the girls on the pep squad, a crowd of heads and hands—but Yoon-mi focused in on one of them.

Maura Morris, who'd moved here from Canada last year.

Her future girlfriend who'd just clocked her in the face during dodgeball.

Maura, on the other hand, didn't know a thing when she walked into PE that day. Not even when she smacked the beautiful pep-squad girl in the face with a speeding dodgeball. Yoon-mi Hyun, the girl to whom she gave two black eyes—little did Maura know that, within a week, she'd become her first girlfriend.

The mystery wasn't how they fell in love—that was quick; that was easy—it was what happened once they went public. Their families' reactions. The kids at school. When Maura suggested they could run off together and start a new life up in Canada, she'd only said it offhand. A little wishful thinking, a silly dream. She didn't expect Yoon-mi to show up at her house with her bags that very night and say, "Let's go."

Yoon-mi Hyun and Maura Morris: Gone 2007 from Milford, Pennsylvania. Both age 17.

— — —

KENDRA

Kendra ran to the edge of the cliff and waved to all her friends. "Guys, guys!" she called. "I'm gonna do it. Watch!"

Kendra had seen the guys jump the cliffs before—one of the guys would take a running leap to clear the outcropping of rocks and cannonball into the bright blue basin of water below. The splash would be terrific. Then there'd be those heart-pounding moments after the jumper went in, when he was so deep no trace of him could be made out, and then, just when some coward was thinking of dialing 911, the surface of the lake would shatter.

The jumper would surface, whooping and yelling, and the next guy would get in line to see if he could make a bigger splash.

None of Kendra's friends had ever jumped off this particular cliff—the highest point above the lake—and she knew they were too chickenshit to try. She'd be legend.

She powered through the run, took the leap, and her body set sail. Gravity took hold and air rushed around her as she started to fall. It sang her name.

When she hit water, she didn't expect it to sting so much. She'd fallen sideways, and the impact was a surprise, and the cool temperature of the water was also a surprise, and she was sinking fast, going deeper than she knew the lake could go.

Traces of foam surrounded her, forming a tunnel that seemed to bury her in the wet and sopping center of the Earth.

She looked up and up, and up and up some more. That pinpoint of golden light at the highest height of the blue above her was the sun, she knew, casting down over the water. All she had to do was swim up to reach it.

How far could it be?

Kendra Howard: Gone 2012, from Greenwich, Connecticut. Age 17.

-33-

EVERY night it seemed I was out on the cracked sidewalk again, feeling that distinctive pinch of smoke in my throat as I approached the front gate. I was climbing the stairs and ignoring the bell—because there's no need to ring a doorbell in a place that's like home—and going in. I always went in.

The house was brighter, the flames having caught the drapes and only beginning to dance in delight across the vaulted ceilings.

I didn't know if this was a new fire, set from a flick of Fiona Burke's lighter, or if time had woven in on itself and the remnants of fire I saw on nights before this were meant to become this one, this fire that still had a chance to build and rage.

Still, the flames didn't hurt us. We lived with them like we would the quirks of any ordinary house, the way my mom and I constantly catch our socks and pant hems on the loose nail in the floorboard in the upstairs hallway, but we've never bothered getting it fixed.

The house was getting crowded now as each new girl arrived. Voices coasted down corridors and stairways, echoing so it sounded like they were repeating ever after the same things.

Two of the newest girls were moving in. They wanted to share a room, since they came here together, and they didn't want to spend a night apart.

I met them on the stairs outside and noticed they were holding hands.

What is this place? Yoon-mi asked me as she eyed the door. Yoon-mi wore a hat that hid her long hair, so she seemed made of only two bright brown eyes.

Beside her, Maura wore her own hair tightly tied back, pulling sharply at the skin of her scalp. Only when they were alone did she take down her hair. She whispered something and then Yoon-mi asked that question also, for the both of them.

Why are we here?

"It's where you live now," my dream-self told them, holding open the door so they could join the others. Once they made it through, I pushed the door closed. And I wondered: They wouldn't get out, would they? Now that they were here, they were as good as stuck and I couldn't do a thing to stop it.

They must have read the curse of this place from off my face. Maybe they thought I was the one who'd manufactured their doom, who commanded this house and kept them bound here. I expected them to fight me, claw at my arms and try to push open the door to get out onto the ashy street, but they didn't seem too upset so long as it was both of them on the same side of that door.

There was one girl, though, who couldn't accept it—the curse of what being in this house meant for her fate. For her plans.

Whenever I saw Madison, she was trying to find a way out. The house had many windows, some with no glass left in the frames so it should be easy to jump through and hit the sidewalk running, but none of the girls could leave through the windows or even the front door. If they could make it to the rooftop, if the crumbling stairs didn't cave in on the way up, they still couldn't take a flying leap to reach the bottom. Something always stopped them.

Still, Madison had tried every one of the exits. She's got someone to meet, she'd go around saying. That photographer. It was really all she talked about—how she had to leave and get back to his place, how they never did get around to finishing the pictures for her portfolio.

Madison hated that I could simply come and go and she couldn't, so she tried to block the door to keep me with her. It was only fair, she told me. It's not like anyone would want to take *my* picture, with my choppy haircut and my ugly boy boots and my face, which was okay, she conceded, but nothing special.

She held her leg across, her back wedged against the frame. She was tall, and her legs were quite long. Her top leg was propped up just high enough that I couldn't hop over. Her bottom leg was propped lower, so I couldn't crawl under. She wouldn't budge.

Why do you think you keep coming back here, Lauren? she asked me. She spoke as if she were only curious, but I could see on her face it wasn't that.

She wanted me to stay this night and the next. She wanted me here all nights, and it wasn't because she liked my company. It was only that if she had to be here, she wanted me to have to stay, too.

One night you'll come back and you won't be able to get out again, she said.

There was a threat in her words, something unspoken. All the girls had that unsaid question in their eyes when they looked at me. I was in danger, too, wasn't I? Because why else did I know about this place, and them—why else was I here like they were?

Madison was very blond in the dream, even more so than in the pictures posted all over her online profiles. It was like a fire was still burning somewhere, or flashbulbs were dancing in her hair.

One night you won't be able to get out, she said again. Then she adjusted her leg, lowering it a smidge, and in that quick moment, I leaped over her shin and darted out the door. She called after me as I made it down the front stairs and into the street, *I'm the one he wants to take pictures of. Not you.*

I always did make it out, every time. And though the voices stayed with me, snippets of the things they said (*You should've seen me jump, man,* Kendra was going, *you should've seen me.* Or Isabeth, more quietly, *I should have walked. It was only rain. I should have just walked home.)* cascaded through my head like little lullabies sometimes, other times like cymbals crashing.

These girls were here inside the house and they couldn't get out—and maybe, no matter how much it pained me, this meant they were dead.

But there was one girl who hadn't set foot in the house yet. I'd looked, and I still couldn't see her. She'd reached out to me, and it wasn't to keep ahold of her story, to record it when no one else was listening, to hear her confessions, her regrets. To know her like no one else on the outside could. There had to be another reason.

She was different, wasn't she? She was the one I could keep from ending up here. Maybe even save.

-34-

On Thu, Jan 17, 2013, at 10:03 AM, Cassidy Delrio <Cassidy.Delrio@wnju.edu> wrote:

Lauren,

Sorry it took me a little while to write you back. Yeah, if you're around campus and you want to get coffee or whatever just let me know. I get out of econ at 2:40, then I have anthro at 4:10, so if you could meet me at like 3? Sorry about your friend. She was sweet. I really don't know why she ran away, none of us counselors did. Sucks you haven't heard from her, for real. But if that's not a bummer and you still want to come by and talk about it, that's cool. I have an hour to kill.

Cass

—35—

I was in math class when the message from Abby's camp counselor came through on my phone. Which meant I had to leave. Right then. I couldn't think about sines or cosines or try and fail to find the hypotenuse on the triangle when I knew I could meet her today, if only I could leave school and drive down there.

I raised my hand, and Ms. Torres said couldn't I wait until the bell rings? I assured her I'd be quick even though I wouldn't be, because it won't matter, will it? Trigonometry, after you're gone.

Jamie was sitting a few rows behind me in class, and his eyes followed me to the door. When I closed it and gave one last backward glance through the window slit, he was still staring. Glaring actually. He knew I wasn't planning on coming back—but he wasn't trying to stop me from leaving.

I grabbed my coat from my locker and then headed for the

main hallway, the closest way out. The lockers in this hallway were red, and the floors were checkered in black-and-white, making the exit bob and swim out there in the far distance. I could see down the long corridor into the sunlight beyond: the south parking lot, unguarded, the gleaming windshield of my van. There was more I needed to find out about Abby, and I felt drawn to talk to this Cassidy girl, to someone who'd been there with her that summer. There was more, and I could learn what it was . . .

If I could just get myself out of this building.

"The bathrooms are that way," a voice said. "I mean, if you're using that hall pass for what I think you're using it for."

I paused in the empty hallway and looked back. Around the corner, braced by a wall of teal-painted lockers, stood a tall girl. A real one.

I blanked on her name for a moment, like I barely even knew her, and then it came to me: Deena Douglas. Deena of the fake eyelashes and the smoky voice, of the boyfriend who was six years older and the habit of sucking her thumb when she slept and then denying it when she woke, even when it was sticky with saliva and still hooked in her mouth. Deena was a senior and—I remembered, as if I were looking back on a life I'd abandoned on the highway, gaining distance and watching it shrink—at one time, she was the closest thing I had to a best friend.

I hadn't been thinking much about Deena lately because I didn't need to. She wasn't one of them. Besides, she was older than me. She'd turn eighteen soon, and none of this would even touch her.

She had no laminated hall pass in her possession, as far as I could tell, and yet she didn't seem in any rush to get to a particular class. I couldn't recall the last time I'd had an actual conversation with her.

She must have been thinking the same thing, because she began to carry on a two-way conversation, doing both her voice and mine. "How are you, Dee? Awesome, thanks for asking. I'm so sorry I forgot, isn't it your birthday this week? Oh, no worries, Lauren, I know you love me. Things with Karl still on? Oh, yeah, thanks for caring, I know you never liked him. Hey, speaking of, heard you dumped Jamie. What's up with *that*?"

She stopped with the voices then and raised an eyebrow, waiting for my answer.

"I can't talk about this now, Deena, I'm sorry. There's someone . . . There's somewhere I've got to be."

"Jamie's right," she said. "You've changed, and it's more than just the hair."

The awkwardness between us wasn't entirely about her boyfriend, Karl, though it would be nice to say it was. Truth was, I'd done this. I'd pushed her away. It was frighteningly easy to do that with people. I couldn't pinpoint when I started pushing—but I guess it would have been around the time I found Abby's flyer. My friendship with Deena could have been halfway to Montana by now and I wouldn't know it.

"So are you coming to my party, or what? At Karl's house, remember? Or, let me guess. You're planning to bail."

"I said I'd go," I told her, though I'd forgotten about all

her plans for her eighteenth birthday party, including details about it being at Karl's house and if I was supposed to come help her set up or anything.

I was going to ask, but then I caught sight of her at the far-off door glimmering in the distance. Not Deena; Deena didn't have anything to do with this. It was Abby at the end of the black-and-white-checkered hallway, Abby holding the door open straight into the sun. Or it was a vision of Abby. Ghosts can't hold open doors.

Did she know I'd gotten in touch with someone from Lady-of-the-Pines? And that I was headed down to see her now? Is that why she'd come out?

Abby was wearing what she always wore; I'd never seen her in anything else: her Lady-of-the-Pines T-shirt with COUNSELOR-IN-TRAINING above her heart—it was pasted to her skin and dotted with flecks of mud. The shorts with the racing stripes. The leaves and twigs and muck matted into her hair that, from this distance, seemed woven into a headdress, as if she were modeling some new girl-run-over-by-a-car look in the fashion pages of *Vogue*. I couldn't see her feet to make out if she had on the one flip-flop.

"*What* are you looking at?" Deena asked. "Mr. Floris is taking the rest of the year off—I heard he had a stroke. We're good."

My eyes left the open door where Abby was waiting and went to Deena, who was much closer. I'd really liked her once. I'd liked being her friend. I remembered this in an absent way, like how a long time ago I used to enjoy pooling sand into newly dug holes on the playground when I was, like, five. Right now, I needed to get rid of her.

"You're cutting class, right?" I asked her.

She lifted her chin, proud. "Spanish."

I held up the hall pass. "Want this? In case you get stopped?"

We both knew that, without a pass, getting caught in the hallway during a class period would get you detention. Making a run for it once a hall monitor spotted you would get you ISS, or in-school suspension. I don't know what never coming back would get you. The chance to never come back?

She shrugged, and I handed over the pass. As our fingers touched on the laminated plastic, there was a charge of life running from her into me. Deena would keep living to see this birthday and the ones that came after. I didn't know what her life would be—maybe that creepy Karl dude would make her happy one day with baby Karls. Or maybe they'd forgo the offspring and take up a life of robbing liquor stores instead. But whatever choices she made, whatever mistakes, she'd live them. She'd go on. It wasn't in Deena Douglas's fate to disappear.

I drew back my hand and shook the feeling out of it. From around the corner, two approaching teachers could be heard talking.

Deena perked up; she loved taunting the teachers. She whispered, "You go. Make a run for it. I'll be loud, cause a diversion. They won't have any idea."

She winked at me and then began stomping off toward the

teachers, rattling lockers as she went. She turned the corner and I couldn't see her anymore, but I could hear her. I could hear her even when I reached the end of the corridor, where there was no vision of Abby waiting, but there was an exit door propped open with a cinder block into the dazzlingly white winter's day.

The south parking lot, once I reached it, was drenched in the kind of bright light that always seems artificial. Anyone looking out the school's south windows was sure to see me. I spotted my trig teacher at the head of class as I drove for the exit and, in a row in the middle of the classroom, the back of Jamie's head. Ms. Torres had mapped out a problem on the whiteboard, and at the exact moment I drove past her window, she looked up, straight at me, and revealed the answer.

–36–

THE girl who had been counselor to Abby Sinclair's counselor-in-training was in the coffee shop between classes as she said she would be—she just didn't know how long I'd driven to get to her university's campus, and that I wasn't actually "in the neighborhood" that week as I'd said. In fact, I'd never been down to that part of New Jersey before in my life.

Cassidy Delrio—Cass, as she seemed to want me to call her—was a college sophomore and a sorority girl. She had Greek letters emblazoned on every item of clothing, even her socks. When Abby's name came up, her face darkened.

At first, I thought, because she must have felt it—the spiraling of Abby's fate down that road through the pines and what it must mean for everything that came after. Maybe she could see Abby when I couldn't anymore, and hadn't since that glance of her in the doorway at school. Maybe I wasn't the only person alive who knew that something was taking these girls and that Abby, out of all of them, could be grabbed back before she was made to stay there forever.

But no. Cass's face had darkened for two reasons: The barista hadn't made her mocha with soy, as she'd asked specifically. And because Abby had made her look bad. No other counselor in the history of Lady-of-the-Pines Summer Camp for Girls had one of her trainees flee in the night like that. And Cass knew this because she was a legacy. Three generations of Delrios had traveled up to that patch of wilderness and rowed those canoes. Not to mention, she herself had been going to Lady-of-the-Pines since she was nine. No way would she get hired back next summer because of what Abby did to her.

"Listen," Cass said, "the thing about Abby is really pretty simple." She leaned in, and I felt my breath catch. I noticed how perfectly straight and smooth her hair was and how vacant her eyes were and I wondered what she'd been holding in for all these months. "Abby wanted to go home, so she went home," Cass said. "She hated camp, so she left."

She waited for me to respond to this.

"That's what you think?" I asked. (Though I believed she was right about one part: Abby did despise the place—the way it made her itch, no matter what she sat on; the way it smelled, eternally damp like a flood had just washed through; and the way it was so far away from anything interesting. That is, until she met Luke.)

"What the hell was I supposed to do?" Cass said. "Run after her, beg her to stay? Say pretty please?"

"But you know she didn't go home . . ." I said. "Don't you?"

"Well, yeah, I know that *now*. But I didn't know that *then*."

She was sipping on her mocha even though it had cow's milk in it; I watched as the brown-tinged foam gathered at the corners of her painted lips and I almost motioned for her to get a napkin and dab it off—then I didn't. I had plain coffee with plain sugar and plain milk, and I took a chug of that.

"What? I'm wrong?" she said.

"I don't think she ran away," I said. "That's why I'm here."

"So she really hasn't called you or e-mailed or texted or anything? Not any of her friends?"

I shook my head—I'd counted myself among Abby's friends, and Cass hadn't yet questioned it.

"I guess that *is* weird," she conceded. "Abby was always going on and on about all her friends."

I wanted to ask their names—so I could track them down, too—but then she started shaking her head, and I felt the shift coming. I felt the turn before she even went there herself.

"But?" I said, helping her along.

"But yeah," she said. "I mean, she didn't take her bags."

"See? She left all her stuff, right? Wouldn't she have taken her things if she ran away?"

She nodded, then shrugged. "Not if she got the chance to go, like, out of the blue or something. A ride. That's what we figured. I mean, it's not like she didn't have *anything* with her. She had her wallet—this hideous plastic purple thing she kept stuffed with pictures and random crap. That thing was so big, she needed, like, a whole purse to carry it. So if she had her wallet, she probably had her purse, too. Why come back and get the rest of her junk if she had all that?"

"I don't know . . ." I said.

It was here that her eyes began to glow with something sick and warm coming up to the surface. She'd kept it down all this time and now I guess my questions about Abby worked to put it into words in a way she wasn't able to before.

"Do you think he killed her?" she said suddenly, and it was so much worse than I thought.

She was nineteen or twenty by now; she'd stick around. Right then I hated her for that, and more still for what she said. For not caring. For not noticing. For not doing a thing.

No wonder Abby had reached out to me.

"He, who?" I said from between my teeth.

"He, whoever. Whatever freak of nature found her in the woods and murdered her."

"Wait, what do you mean? Did you see anyone in the woods?"

"No. Of course not. I'm just assuming."

It wasn't something I was going to assume. Some of the girls I'd seen lately in the house had met terrible fates before they walked up to the front door—it could be told through their eyes and in the way, sometimes, parts of their bodies would go all pins and needles like they hadn't gotten used to having legs again. Or the way the smoke would flow through their guts like a magic trick, a sad one, without scarves.

It was all in the patches of the stories we skipped over, the unspoken ends. Isabeth. Eden. Shyann, even, maybe. I ached for them.

But wouldn't I have known if something like that had happened to Abby, out of all the girls?

"What was that movie where they put the girl's head in a box?" Cass was saying now. "You know what I'm talking about, right? That movie? There was this box, and they look in it and there's her head?"

I didn't know the movie and hoped I never would. I left Cass quicker than I meant to, especially after driving all the way there.

Talking to Abby's camp counselor had given me nothing. Worse than nothing: She'd drawn a detailed enough image that felt more real than the real thing. I didn't want to think anymore about what she'd said, didn't want to picture it.

This visit to the coffee shop was what propelled me down to New Jersey, but there was another place I could try in another part of the state. I had the address. I still had questions. And though I didn't know how to make sense of it, I couldn't let myself believe she was dead.

– 37 –

"SHE ran off," Abby's grandmother said when I asked her. "That's it. That's the story. You drove yourself all the way here to hear that."

Her expression didn't become pained as she said these words, though I expected it would. I found myself watching her upper lip, the darker hints of hair growing in there, the way the hairs moved like little antennae as she spoke. She was the woman who raised Abby, her legal guardian. Within minutes, I could already tell she wasn't the kind of grandmother who'd open her arms to you, who'd remove the cigarette from her mouth to say sweet things and offer you a cookie. She'd let me inside the house, though. At least she'd let me in.

"And you went to that camp together?" her grandmother asked for the third time.

"Yes," I said. "I was there. She never said a thing about running away. I know she had her wallet with her, and her purse I think, too, but she left all the rest of her stuff there, you know."

"We know," she said. "They shipped it back to us. Of course we know."

Her grandmother's lips drew in on the butt of her cigarette, ballooning up her old lungs with the last of the smoke. She was smoking indoors, windows closed, slowly killing anyone who came near her, and as she tapped the ash I could see the similarity between this plastic-entombed room and the rooms in the house where my dream kept taking me. It was the air. The haze of it. A feathery, caustic mist of lavender-blue.

"This is a girl who ran away before," her grandmother said. "This is a girl who stole money from her own poppop's wallet when he was taking his afternoon nap in that very chair." She was pointing at the sunken armchair I was sitting in. I imagined it would be soft to the touch, but I couldn't tell, because it was encased in a skintight layer of clear plastic.

"No," I said. That didn't sound like the Abby I knew.

"Dear," she said, "the girl you met at that summer camp wasn't the same girl she was at home, with us, you can be sure."

I was sensing there were things Abby hadn't told me. A grave, troublesome part of her story she'd completely left out. When had she run away before? Why hadn't she mentioned this? What more didn't I know?

Abby's grandmother's eyes flicked to the side table beside the couch, and mine followed. There was a frame standing upright, a two-in-one. The frame met in the center, drawing the two sides together and connecting them symbolically.

Almost as if her gaze had given me permission, I found my hands reaching for the picture frame. I picked it up.

On the left side of the frame was Abby; I recognized her immediately. It was the school portrait, the same one used for her Missing flyer, but this was the first time I was seeing it in color. Her skin had a pink glow she didn't have anymore, and her teeth were extraordinarily white. Someone must have said, "Cheese!" to her before snapping that photo, someone must have forced her to have a smile that showed teeth, because as I held the picture close I could see how wide her lips were opened, how prominent her teeth were made to be, like an unseen hand was holding a hard, cold object to the back of her neck and telling her to grin or that would be the end of her.

On the right side of the frame was a woman with a pigtailed little girl in her arms. Abby's mother and young Abby.

Abby hadn't told me what happened to her mother, and now I wondered. Because she wasn't in this house, was she? She wasn't in Abby's life. She wasn't here.

Her grandmother sensed the question. "I'm sure Abigail told you about Colleen."

"A little," I said.

"Abigail is exactly like her, I should have guessed. Colleen ran off and Abigail gets it in her head to do the same."

"How old was she, Colleen, her mom, when she . . . ran off?"

"Old enough to know better. Twenty-three."

So she wasn't one of them, then. "That's awful. I mean it must have been, for Abby."

"Drugs," she said, and snipped it closed. "Miss Woodman. Lauren, may I call you Lauren? Do you have a mother?"

It took me a moment to nod. Of course I had a mother.

"And your mother, she's still with you?"

I nodded again.

I expected her to say, *Good for you.* So I could then say, if I dared, how it didn't matter: Having a mother couldn't stop it, and not having a mother wouldn't make a girl go. Having brown hair wouldn't make it happen; having black hair or yellow hair or green-dyed hair or a shaved head wouldn't keep a girl here, in this world, if she was destined to go. Staying home every day or going out every night. Taking drugs or not taking them. Wearing that or wearing this. Talking to strangers or talking to nobody. Hooking up with boys or hooking up with other girls or saving herself for "the one." There was no way to know. If a girl was meant to go, she just did. I believed that.

Abby's grandmother stubbed out her cigarette. "Abby always did want to be like Colleen. Let's hope she has fun." She breathed out, and the last of her smoke made its way toward my face. I coughed. I could see she'd decided what had happened to Abby a long time ago, and that was why she wasn't even reported missing for more than a month.

But I was there. I was there for a reason, and maybe it was only to say this:

"Mrs. Sinclair," I said, "I have to tell you. She didn't run away. Abby. I know her mother did, but she didn't. Something happened to her. She went missing. You have to keep looking. Please believe me. Please."

My face was on fire from letting those words out, my breath gone heavy and hard to catch, but all she did was shake her head. Then she had her hands out for something, and it took me some moments to realize she wanted the picture frame I was holding.

"Give it here," she said.

Before I did, I looked one last time, not at young Abby and her lost mother but at recent Abby. Abby at sixteen, maybe, in this photo, maybe even just turned 17. Abby forcing a smile that showed all her teeth. She was wearing something around her neck in the photo, but I got only a glimpse of it showing through the open collar of her shirt, before her grandmother was on her feet and rescuing it from my grasp, then snapping it closed.

I wasn't sure, because I had only a moment to see it, but I thought the pendant she had on was a swirl of smoke inside a stone. Round and gray.

"If she sent you here to get any of her things, let's stop this right now," her grandmother said. "I'm not letting you up there, in her room."

"She . . ." I started, beginning to deny it. But I did want to go up there; I did want to see her room.

"No," her grandmother said. "Absolutely not. I knew you were after those earrings. She thinks she can send you here to get them and sell them? No. Lauren, it's time for you to go."

Abby's grandmother led me to the door, and only after I stepped through it did she say to me, "When you see her, tell her we assume she's not coming back. Tell her we won't wait all those years like we did for her mother."

"How long did you wait for her mother? Did she ever come back?"

"Oh, she came back. She came back in a box."

– 38 –

OUT in the driveway, Abby's grandfather was shoveling snow. He had his back to me, his shoulders hunched into the work, so I wasn't sure if he saw me coming, if he'd overheard our conversation and the decisive click of the door closed in my face.

Even so, I was aware of him plunging his shovel closer and closer to where I was walking. He was moving down the imaginary line he'd drawn in the white powder, straight for me. If he kept it up, we would soon cross paths.

When we did, the shovel paused in the ground at my feet and I heard him speak. "How's she doing?" he asked, just loud enough for me to make out, and just quiet enough so his wife wouldn't hear.

He kept his back to the house and his head down, but though he leaned toward the snow at his feet, his eyes weren't on the ground. They were lifted up, to my face.

"You've seen her," he said—not a question. "She all right? Doing okay?"

There was no true way to answer this. She was intact, with both her arms and legs, and with hair on her head and no wounds gaping open, none I could see.

But *how* was she doing beyond that?

Whenever I saw her, the expression on her face was a different one altogether from the school photo in her grandmother's frame, the face photocopied on the flyer. Not smiling. Not even pretending to. No hint of teeth. Instead she wore a faint question mark of an expression, one waiting to be filled in by the numbers with paint.

I could sense only echoes from her. The echo of sadness. The echo of longing to go home. The echo of craving a peanut butter sandwich.

Sometimes she showed herself to me, so why wouldn't she do the same now, here, for her grandfather who surely loved her, and had certainly known her longer? She could set a whisper sailing on the wind. She could simply wave from the window of the van if she were in there again. Yet she did neither of those things. She wouldn't set foot near this house at all.

Her grandfather had asked how she was doing, if she was okay. I didn't want to say something cruel, but a big and blazing part of me did want to alarm him. Her grandmother hadn't listened; maybe he would. I locked my eyes on his, and I put as much weight into the words as I had in me, and I said, "No. I don't think she is."

I expected him to ask more of me, but he didn't. The shovel went down and he moved along the line with it, putting distance between us. I had the sudden vision of jumping into a snowbank like this one as a little kid. How it felt to throw armfuls of bright white powder up into the air and let it sprinkle down all over, to lie flat as it buried me, and then to stand up and shake it off and set myself free. Whose memory was that, mine or Abby's? It could have belonged to either of us.

I sensed his wife at the window, watching, but still I called to him, "Are you the one who put the flyers up on the telephone poles?"

"Up north," he said. "A whole lot of 'em."

"I saw one," I said. "Up in Pinecliff."

He nodded. "Nobody was doing a thing. I talked my wife into putting in the report, but the police say they don't have time to chase after every runaway, so . . ."

I had to do it again, even though I failed the first time. Now I was the one who stepped closer to him, walking into the pathway he was making in the snow. "She didn't run away like you think she did."

He eyed me, his pupils held low under a surface of shining water. "She tell you that?" he said.

"Not exactly," I admitted. "But you should call the police. Please. Call the police. Ask them to keep looking. Find out what happened to her."

He stopped for a moment and then said one last thing. I wasn't sure if it meant he heard me or he hadn't. He said, "You have to let them know you miss them. That's why I did the flyers. Even if they don't ever think about coming back. You gotta make sure they know they can."

–39–

MY mom was waiting in the garage when I came home from New Jersey that night. I hit the garage-door opener to see that she'd found what I'd hidden behind the lawn mower. I'd gotten the tire patched at the bike shop in town and she'd wheeled it out and was playing with the bell on the handlebars. When I pulled in and cut the engine, the first thing I heard was its tinny little *ding*.

"There you are," my mom said lightly, though behind those three light words were more words, heavier words. She was going to confront me about not telling her where I was all evening, and I was going to have to come up with an excuse that didn't involve a drive out of state to ask after a so-called runaway I'd never met, not in real life.

But all my mom said was, "I feel like I never see you anymore."

Get used to it.

I heard that. That was my head thinking it, or it was a familiar voice warring to be the loudest thing in my head. Fiona Burke had also heard my van pull up, so she'd come out to talk to me. She wanted my mom to leave the garage, but she wouldn't.

Maybe we should give my mom a warning on what to expect, now that I was 17 like the others. A little head start to begin planning out the design of my Missing posters. Hopefully she'd do something eye-catching, a Missing poster to frame and be proud of, to admire long after I was gone.

That was what Fiona Burke wanted me to say to my own mother.

"Where'd you get this old thing?" my mom said, nudging Abby's borrowed bicycle. "So retro. It's darling." She was straddling the Schwinn now and testing out its wheels.

"You shouldn't touch it. I'm holding on to it, for a friend."

She let go and climbed off, and I caught hold of it before it propelled itself into the wall.

"What friend? Deena?"

I shook my head.

"What's going on, Lauren? What was so much more important than being in school?" Seeing the surprise on my face, she raised an eyebrow. "Your school called. I told them you had a dentist appointment."

"Thanks for covering for me."

"Sure thing. Now you tell me where you were."

"New Jersey," I said, before I, or anyone else, could stop me.

"Excuse me?"

"I drove down to New Jersey, and then I drove back up."

"*New Jersey?*" she said, more to herself than to me. "Who do we know in New Jersey?"

I could have said no one, or I could have said someone, but my mouth didn't want to keep opening, and my body wanted to move instead. Before I knew it, I was grasping the bike's handlebars and wheeling it out to the center of the garage.

"You just got home, where're you going?"

She didn't say I couldn't go. She's never told me I couldn't do something. She didn't ground me or give me curfews. She covered for me when the school called and said I'd cut class. She trusted me—or she wanted me to think she did.

If there was any mother in existence who I should be able to let in and know all, it would be this woman. This woman, here.

"I want to try the bike," I said. "I'll just ride it along the train tracks to the bridge, then I'll turn back."

"It's too cold."

I shrugged and pulled down on my wool hat so my ears were covered.

"Besides, when's the last time you rode a bike? You were maybe ten and you skidded off the embankment outside and skinned both knees."

"I guess you never forget how to ride. That's what I heard."

"They say that." She was floundering here. She didn't know how to discipline me because she never had to before.

I straddled the bike and tried out the brakes, testing the bounce of the tire. It seemed as good as new. The snow had been cleared off the road and I could coast down it without sliding on ice. Not two miles away, down the hill, the train tracks ran north and south, following the river. I could follow those tracks for days. The line headed straight up to Montreal.

What could my mom do if I told her the truth? Tie me by the wrists to my bedposts each night, lock me in our basement and lower food through the vents so I didn't starve? Could she save me and could she save Abby? Could she save Fiona Burke years after the fact?

Once you were tagged to disappear and join the others, I don't think you could be saved at all.

My mom said my name, softly. She reached out, as if to touch my hair, and when I flinched, she lowered her arm.

"We're going to talk when you get back," she said, as if prophesizing our future. "You're going to tell me what's been going on and why you went down to New Jersey."

Very quietly, maybe to keep Fiona Burke from hearing, I said, *"Okay."*

"I just want you to know you can talk to me if you want to talk to me," she said, keeping it going and coming close to ruining it. "I'm always here, if you want to talk. I can see there's something, Lauren. I just don't know what it is yet."

For a moment I wondered if mothers *can* see. Maybe once you've made a person, you can see through the skin you shaped to what's in there hurting without anyone having to tell you, *Look here.*

I stood up straight with the bike in my hands. I stood in my mom's direct line of sight. There I was: Girl, 17. Girl, hair not so long anymore, but long legs, my mom's same long nose. Girl wearing black boots and black jeans. Wearing the pendant I found on the side of the road, a pendant like the one I thought I saw on Abby in that photograph, like the one Fiona Burke had on the night she ran away. I actually never took it off.

Wearing also a flashing sign that said I was in trouble. Wearing it on high for heavy traffic so it could be seen far out in the lanes in the distance. Letting it blink and beep. Letting it shout out what I wanted it to say because maybe someone would know how to make it stop.

Girl, not yet missing.

Easy target of a girl, standing out in the open right here.

But all my mom said was, "When you get back? We'll talk." All those psych classes weren't teaching her when to keep pushing and when to let go. She'd come so close, and too fast she'd let go.

"Don't you have homework?" I said. "We can talk tomorrow—it's not urgent."

Liar, said Fiona Burke.

My mom looked relieved. "I do have a paper to write, but Lauren? We'll talk tomorrow about all of this."

I got the bicycle gliding and hopped on. It balanced perfectly and didn't topple over. I hadn't forgotten anything I'd seen so far. Not even how to ride a bike.

I pumped the pedals until I was out of sight of my house and the Burkes' house and could let go and have the spinning tires do it all without me having a say. I thought of Abby on this bicycle, on the way to meet Luke. Then there was Abby leaving Luke's house on foot in the warm summer's night, there was the road, there were the pine trees, and beyond that I guess there was something I wouldn't get to know. There was a dark night sky starred with questions, and she was one of them. I kept thinking if I looked hard enough maybe I'd be able to pick out her point in the constellation.

Or more likely I'd keep getting it all mixed up, like how I could never seem to find the Big Dipper, even when it was right there, screaming out its existence in the sky right over my head.

Then I changed the story. I imagined Abby on the way to meet Luke, but never stopping, never bothering going to his house and instead riding a wide circle and making it back safe to the grounds of the summer camp that night.

I imagined her still alive.

I kept pedaling and soared around each coming turn. I sped past mailboxes. I flew over humps in the road. I somehow managed to avoid slicks of ice. I pedaled so fast, I didn't know how I'd ever get the bike to stop.

When I reached the railroad tracks, I saw the light in the distance and heard the rumble: a train was coming. It sped closer, rattling the air, a freight train that didn't look to be stopping at the commuter Amtrak stop at Pinecliff. I pumped the pedals and steered the bike down the narrow road that ran alongside the tracks. I was ahead of the train, but I felt it gaining on me, a hulking monster I was too small and insignificant to think of ever beating.

The train was just behind me and then it was beside me, and for a single, perfect moment the freight train and I were matched, its nose even with the bike's front tire.

Then, fast, it overtook me and thundered past me and I was left behind.

– 40 –

SHE was waiting for me in my bedroom, watching in silence as I shook out my legs, my muscles burning after riding her bike so hard and for so long.

Her eyes held on me, and the weight of that gaze felt like she was pressing her entire body down on top of me, caked in mud and littered with burrs and twigs, scraped raw in places, as heavy as a sack of bricks.

"I tried," I said.

She kept staring.

I sat on the end of my bed and watched her in the vanity mirror. It was easier than looking directly at her. Talking to her reflection came easier, too.

"I told them," I said. "I told them you didn't run away. That's what you wanted me to say, right? But, Abby, I don't know if they believed me. And that Cassidy girl from the summer? Don't even ask me what she said. I went down there and

I told them . . . I don't know what else to do."

I tried to keep my voice down, so my mom wouldn't hear, but why wouldn't Abby say something? Anything? Why wouldn't she blink or nod or give me a sign?

If she told me what to do next—where to go, what to look for—all of this could be over by morning. Any one of the girls could give me a little push like that if she wanted. I mean, if that's why they contacted me, why wouldn't they do the simplest, quickest thing? It made me question them, and myself, and all of this. It made me wonder about the dreams and the house that contained them. Either I was meant to stay outside and help, or I was meant to join them inside and never get out. This dark thread of tightrope between the two options couldn't keep me upright for long.

Abby, though. Abby was different. She would be the one to give me her secret and let me unravel the answers. Why else stare at me like that?

I took in all her details in the mirror: the mud spatter and the pieces of road and nature melded to her skin. The center hole in her throat had a faint glow, like she'd taken my pendant and swallowed it. Her lips were a thin, grim line, closed to air and words.

"It would help if you told me," I said. "What happened when you were walking back from Luke's house?"

I watched as she turned slowly, in small, jerky increments, until the back of her body was what faced the mirror and the front of her faced away from me.

I hadn't done what she wanted. I'd visited her grandparents—I'd done that—but maybe I should have said more. Maybe I'd been a coward. Maybe I knew how her grandmother would have responded if I'd told her the disconnected spirit of her lost granddaughter was communicating through me, a complete stranger, from some open gateway between this world and the next. And that I didn't know what this meant about where she was now, and I didn't know what that meant for where she could be found in the future. I barely knew how to explain it myself.

Really, that would have gone over well.

I was going to say this when Abby suggested writing the letter. She'd turned her body deliberately, and I saw what she was facing now: the open notebook on my desk, the pen pointed to the page. When I sat down at the desk, she came closer, and when I picked up the pen she was at my elbow, smoke-gray breath singeing my skin.

I couldn't mimic her handwriting, and this wasn't a session of automatic writing in which I sealed my eyes, cleared my mind, and let the barest touch of her ghostly hand guide my own. I simply wrote down what she wanted to say for her, because she couldn't hold the pen and write it herself.

For the return address, I used the one on Dorsett Road. I borrowed an envelope and a stamp from my mom's desk in the kitchen downstairs, and then I carried the letter up to my room to mail from a public post office box in the morning.

But as I was pulling the covers to my chin and curling up to go to sleep, I felt her still there in the room, as if I could do more even than that, as if I should be trolling the back roads in my van, calling out her name, pasting her poster on every telephone pole, visiting the police station every day until they reclassified her case as possible foul play. I thought of Fiona Burke, who I felt sure was observing from a perch somewhere in the shadows, and I thought of how I'd never wondered what happened to her, before this winter, and how I should have. How heartless it was for a girl to be forgotten and buried before there was even anything of her to put in the ground.

I wouldn't let that happen now, again. Not to Abby Sinclair.

– 41 –

FRIDAY was Deena's eighteenth birthday party at her boyfriend's house. It was also the night I lost any control I had over this. If I'd ever been in control.

First the noise. Not all in my head this time—also in the room around me. It was a raucous party as Deena had been hoping. All the activity didn't drown out the insistent whispering in my head but drew it out, made it frantic. So much seemed to be happening, and there I was in the midst of it, sitting on a sagging plaid couch with a spiked jug of cranberry juice. I was a part of things in the way any piece of furniture would be.

I'd forgotten anyone could see me and flinched when two girls from school came up asking if I was still into Jamie.

"Wait, is Jamie here?" I said. "Have you seen him?"

They said he was around somewhere, or I thought that's what they said, but before I could ask why, they'd moved away and somehow taken my jug, the one between my knees that I'd been lifting up, again and again, to my mouth.

It was here that the party turned from me. I became completely detached from it as if a scissor had poked through the page and removed me from the scene.

I realized two things: One, that cranberry juice Deena left me with sure had a lot of vodka mixed up in it. And two, none of these people would notice if I went missing.

Flash, I'm gone, and they'd keep partying.

It could happen to me here, at this party, at right that very moment: There'd be a girl in my spot on the couch and then no girl taking up space on the plaid cushion. The seat would stay open for a minute or two before someone snagged it. And that would be the last of me.

I checked to see what clothes would be listed on my Missing poster: black boots; black cargo pants; ugly flannel shirt I forgot I even had on; under that, a V-neck gray shirt with a rip in the shoulder; black tank top underneath it all. Would anyone remember any of those details when asked?

That was when I noticed it, the pendant, how it wasn't tucked under all the layers of my clothes the way I liked it to be. It had been pulled out, and I hadn't noticed. It was hanging down over my chest. Glowing a milky, fizzy white.

I stood up. I grabbed my coat. Of course no one stopped me. I took a step toward the door, and everything went on just as it was.

It was when I was pushing through the crowd to get to that door and to the front porch and then past the porch to where

I parked my van outside. It was right then. The shadows. I noticed them at the edges of the room, down by the floor, near the heating vents, and up by the ceiling, where the stucco met the plain white walls. These shadows formed themselves into thin tendrils, like fingers. And the fingers grew, coiling into long, snakelike arms. Reaching. I knew if I got close, they could grab me.

Maybe this was what each of the girls saw before her time came. One of the shadows was directly over my head now. It could let go at any moment. It could drop and take me down with it.

No one else could see them. Everyone from the party was oblivious: Chugging cups from the keg. Smoking up in the corner. Dancing to bad music on the worn rug. Making out against the wall. Picking a fight near the windows. Ordinary things on an ordinary night—and Happy Birthday, Deena, you made it—all while something terrible was coming for me, about to swallow me and make me gone.

It couldn't be my time yet. Could it? I had people to help, girls to unearth and keep track of, girls who needed me out here, alive. Didn't I? I had to leave this house. I knew how hot the shadowy hands would be, from the fire, how their grip would singe through my flannel shirt and my cotton shirt beneath it and even the shirt beneath that, to what's left, which was my skin.

Once they touch your skin, you're theirs.

– 42 –

I was facedown in the snow, and there was a boot planted before my eyes. Something damp was in my mouth, but it wasn't a tongue. It was the sopping-wet finger of my own glove. I think I might've been sucking on it.

I pulled out the finger, spit out some lint, and looked up. The sole of the boot had a red stripe, and ice and snow were crusted into the laces. There was another boot exactly like it beside the first, and far up above both the boots was a set of shoulders and, above that, a head. The head was shaking with laughter.

Then he reached out a hand, stretching out his arm so it was close enough to be grabbed by mine. "C'mon, let me help you up."

This wasn't Jamie, but it was a guy I knew. Really, it was a guy I'd talked to only recently, a guy I wouldn't have known if not for knowing the girls.

"You're plastered," Luke Castro said—Abby Sinclair's Luke. He grinned when he said it, and I couldn't see his face to tell if this was all a joke to him or if he really cared.

"No," I mumbled, "it's not that." Because it wasn't. It wasn't the spiked cranberry juice that made me run out of Karl's house—or if it was that, it was only partly that. I remembered the shadows, targeting me and descending fast.

"Sure," he said sarcastically. "You're perfectly sober. Sure."

"I'm fine," I said, and I shook off his hand and stood up on my own. I wobbled and tried to hide it. "Are you a friend of Karl's or something?"

"You asked me that already," he said.

Wait. I did?

"Tell me again," I said. "Tell me again you didn't do anything to her." I was back in our first conversation, asking after Abby Sinclair, and it took him a few moments to get there himself, even though I was the one who'd so obviously been drinking.

"I didn't. *Do* anything. To her," he said.

We were off to the side of the house, away from the windows, like we meant to sneak over here for a reason. Did I? Did I find Luke at some point and lead him out here? Did I do anything embarrassing? Did I say something stupid? Did he hurt Abby and all along I didn't know it? Did anyone see us go out here? How many of those things did I say out loud?

There was a motion sensor and not a regular light, which I didn't realize until it flicked off and dropped us into darkness. I couldn't see the puff of breath trailing from his mouth, though I could feel it, since his face was so close to mine. He smelled the way I remember Abby remembering he smelled—or else it was the way he'd smelled when I made that visit to his house weeks before. Her memories were cutting into mine, lifting up out of nowhere and confusing me.

She thought I'd been ignoring her. And maybe I was. It was just that there were so many, and my head had been crowded up with them, like a smoky, dim room at this party, except my head was filled with girls. And also with myself—because I was a girl, too. I was 17 and maybe in danger, just like they were.

A flicker of shadowy movement caused me to look toward the woods. And there she was, the dark shape of her at least, shaking her head no.

"No?" I said aloud.

Luke said something I didn't catch, and a voice in my head said, *It wasn't him.*

"Are you sure?" I asked to the trees.

Yes, she answered sadly. *Not him. Not him.*

She meant he hadn't hurt her, not that I ever really thought he did—besides how she'd gotten her heart broken. Hearing her made me know they were outside with me now. All of them.

I could see a girl. Then two more girls. Then another. Another. Girls I recognized, and some girls I didn't. There were so many girls I had yet to meet.

The lost girls' eyes glowed, fire-lit, from the sweep of pine trees nearby. How far were we from where Abby went missing? It was close, I realized. So close.

If Luke could see them there, he'd be scared the way I should have been scared. I squinted and tried to picture the girls as he would: the one girl with the glittering shards of broken windshield encrusted into her cheeks; the girl with the frost-blue lips; the girl soaked through her clothes, dripping from an absent rain. Then the two girls melded together as if their bodies met in the most intimate tissue- and sinew-filled spaces that Siamese twins share, shoulder muscle growing into lungs and liver, their sides fused hip to hip.

These two girls were motioning to get my attention, waving at me to stop, waving at me to get away from him, to get in my van and get away. I should have listened, but what struck me was how it looked like they had three hands. Two individual hands of their own, and the third hand, the one they shared, far larger than the other two.

"What are you looking at? What's over there?" Luke asked.

"Nobody," I said.

"Aren't you happy to see me? You sure seemed to be two minutes ago."

"Yeah, right." But I didn't bother arguing. I heard what the girls were trying to tell me, and I was feeling around in my pockets. The pockets of my cargo pants—there were many—and my coat pockets, too, inside and outside, every last one. Then I was down on my knees, there at Luke's feet, searching the snow to see if I'd dropped them when I passed out. I was drunk, probably, and I was seeing ghosts, definitely, and now to top it all off I'd lost my van keys.

With my movement, the motion sensor made the back

porch light flick on. It spotlit us, beaming down on the crown of my head.

Luke laughed again, and I realized how this looked to him, where I had myself positioned on the ground, with such easy access to his zipper. "You're something else, aren't you?" he said. I had absolutely no idea what Abby saw—sees, even still—in the guy, why she got so intoxicated by him and took off in the middle of the night on her bike to see him and let him stomp on her heart.

But then I wasn't looking up at him anymore. The side door of the house had come open, and the person standing there let go of the door and let it swing closed.

When it slammed, Luke turned toward it, too.

"Hey, man," Luke said, all nonchalant, when he saw it was Jamie. "What's up?"

This was what the two girls had been trying to warn me about. Now I knew. Nobody wanted Jamie to get the wrong idea.

"I was looking for you," Jamie said—to me, not to Luke. His voice was flat; I couldn't decipher any emotion from it. His hair had fallen over his eyes like it always did.

"Oh, I've got her," Luke said, a game in his voice and a hard hand on my arm, pulling me up to my feet so he could jerk me closer.

I pushed him away and disentangled myself, fumbling on clumsy legs but at least standing on my own without his help. "He doesn't," I told Jamie. "This wasn't . . . It's not, it's not anything. What?" I turned fast, in the other direction. One of the girls was talking to me, trying to tell me what to say to fix this, but I couldn't make out the words because there was this panic in my chest and it was cold and there was all the wind.

"That's not what she said before," Luke said.

I turned around to see Jamie backing up, away from us. That was it. He was going to believe that liar over me, thinking I'd gotten together with this sleaze so soon after our breakup. He was watching me with a strained, strange look on his face. But he didn't leave.

Luke cracked up laughing. "I'm kidding, man. Dude, just kidding. She's all yours. I'm going inside for a beer."

Jamie stepped away from the door and let him through. But he didn't join me in the pool of light, where I was still standing.

"I . . . that wasn't what it looked like," I told him.

He didn't say anything.

"I'm only talking to him because she wants me to."

"She, who?"

"She . . . oh." I stopped. I had to quit saying things out loud. I couldn't talk anymore about her or about the others. Not then, not to him. "Never mind. I'm not supposed to say."

He shifted a little, a flinch almost. Like I'd said something that scared him.

I found myself longing for it. I longed for the motion sensor to come on in another part of the yard and show him. There'd be Abby, moving fast across the snow with one flip-flop and one bare foot, but not fast enough. Natalie's long hair would hide her face, but a shimmer of glass would shine through. Shyann would be concealing herself in the branches, well-practiced from her days of living off nature in the vacant lots of her city. Madison would speak first before anyone, saying could we hurry it up already since she had somewhere to be, and Isabeth would have the most concern in her eyes, thinking of how it feels to lose the people you love, so she'd tell Madison to be quiet. Eden wouldn't care about any of this. She'd just want me to find my keys so we could go home. Kendra would want to leap out and go, *Boo!* And Yoon-mi and Maura would be shaking their heads because they tried to warn me; they tried to wave me away.

And the others? It was unbearable to think of how many girls the dark expanse of woods could contain.

Then there'd be Fiona Burke herself. She wasn't really one of them, but she was more like them than she was like me. She was missing, and I was still here. She was a ghost, and I was alive for however much longer I was allowed to be. She'd try to talk me out of him. *We don't need him,* she might say. *Walk away, Lauren. Walk away.*

But none of the girls came out, and no one spoke up from the vacant darkness. And so Jamie kept on disbelieving me.

So I tried to correct it. "I lost my keys. It's just that I lost my keys." I started looking again but came up with nothing.

"Fuck it," Jamie said—to the sky, or to someone, something I couldn't see. He said it while looking upward, as far away from me as he could. His body went rigid and I thought he was going to kick something. Then he let out a long breath and said, "It's too cold out for this shit. C'mon, I'll take you home. You're too drunk to drive yourself anyway."

He took my arm. It was the first time he'd touched me in days and days.

– 43 –

WE were silent on the drive home. I was cursing myself for losing my keys, and Jamie was next to me probably cursing himself for caving and being nice to me.

When we got to my place, Jamie turned to me in my driveway and said, "You're freaking me out a little, Lauren. It's like you're this whole other person all of a sudden. Or else you're just trashed. Is that it? Is it that you're just really drunk?"

If only that's all it was. If only I could sober up and take an aspirin to erase this tomorrow.

I leaned forward, and this wasn't Abby's memory or any of the other girls' memories cascading over me—it wasn't their wants but mine. I wanted to feel my lips against his neck, or his neck against my lips. I wanted to remember for one small second what there was before the shadows blotted it all out. I wanted to know if his mouth still tasted like cinnamon.

But he pushed me away. "We broke up," he said. "Remember?"

For an increment of time in the darkness of his car, I didn't. But it passed and then I did.

"I have to ask you something," he said. "It's about this."

From his pocket the folded Missing flyer emerged, and he didn't have to open it all the way for me to know Abby's face would be on it.

"You left it," he said. "In my hoodie."

I nodded. It was still in his hand, and I absolutely needed to take it back.

"What's up with this girl Abigail? For real. Is that why you were with Luke Castro?"

"Abby," I corrected him. "But I wasn't *with* him. I told you, I dropped my keys."

"You don't really know that girl . . . Do you?"

I took the folded flyer from his hands and protected it in mine. "Jamie . . . what if I told you something and I couldn't explain it and you couldn't ask me why or how I know or anything? What if I told you that Abby is here in the car with us, right now? What if I could see her sitting in the seat behind you and she's waving at me to stop talking now, but I'm not going to, I'm going to tell you. What if, Jamie? What if I told you all that?"

He shut his eyes and held them closed. At his back, in the seat directly behind his, Abby Sinclair glared at me. I could see the dirty reflection of her face in the rearview mirror even if I didn't turn around to be sure.

Finally Jamie spoke. "I'd say you were really trashed and you should go in and have a glass of water and go to bed."

"Okay," I said. "I'm glad I didn't tell you then."

There was a stunned look on his face when I slammed the car door and headed up the walk to go inside.

– 44 –

MY mom knew I'd been drinking before I'd even taken off my coat. She wasn't going to punish me over it, but she did remark on it, and she did ask how I got home and how I was going to get a spare key for my van if I couldn't find the one I lost, and she did comment that I deserved a hangover if I got one. She said that last thing with a vindictive little sparkle in her eye.

It was when she was asking me about the party, when she was saying something that required an answer from my mouth, that the room cracked open and the voices came out. They weren't slivers of whispers like usual. They didn't take turns, and they didn't play nice. I couldn't see them, but I could hear them, closing in on all sides, voices gone raspy and hoarse from breathing fire and hoarser still from all the screaming.

Aren't you going to go look for her?

Your mother. She knows.

You haven't said hello to me yet. Can't you see me?

You're a nasty ho. And you're not that cute, either.

You lie. You lie. You lie.

HOW LONG DO I HAVE TO STAY HERE!

You don't have much longer.

You said you were going to look for her. You're not looking for her.

Hi. I'm saying hi. Hi. Do you see me? Hi.

You don't have much longer.

Hi.

My head hammered with the girls' voices, more than I could have counted, more than I even recognized, proving there were lost girls I hadn't gotten to meet yet and that I hadn't been imagining them in the woods. I screwed my eyes shut as if that could stop them and it did, for a moment. Then it made it worse. One story drowned out the next story and capsized the story that followed and took over where the last story left off.

New voices. A new girl named Jannah wanted to tell me about a boy named Carlos—how she was supposed to meet him, and she never made it before she got taken, and how he had the most intense brown eyes. And another new girl named Hailey did some things she wasn't proud of, and who am I to judge? And a girl named Trina hated every single person who laid eyes on her—she hated every girl here; she especially loathed me.

Hailey had run away before. She had a chipped tooth from the first time, a pierced belly button from the second time, a prostitution record for the third time, but this time, the fourth time she went missing, she hadn't run away at all. Jannah loved Carlos and she ran away to have a life with him—or she meant to, before her family caught her and punished her for what she did. Trina ran off because no one was even looking. She ran simply because she could. And good fucking riddance.

Do you think he waited for me?

They think they know. They don't know. No one knows.

Going, going, gone. How you like me now, huh? How you like me now?

Are you listening? Why aren't you listening?

Do you think he waited?

Can't you hear me? Hi, hi.

She's out, idiot.

Wake her up, wake her up. Someone wake her up.

Then—in a gap between the noise—she spoke. Louder than the others, closer somehow, more urgent.

Help.

I knew that voice. That was Abby Sinclair.

– 45 –

WHEN I opened my eyes, I was across the room, on the couch, with our cat, Billie, before me on the coffee table. The cat stared intently at a spot just behind my head, and my mom hovered over me, in crisis mode. She had my two hands by the wrists and there was a sore spot on the side of my skull from where I'd been pounding it, I guess with a fist. She was making a soothing sound in her throat, and hearing it calmed something in me. Calmed the noise and lessened the panic. The girls responded, too, and soon we were all still, listening to my mom's tuneless humming.

When she saw this, she let go of my arms and took a seat beside me. "Tell me," she said simply. She said it with the look she used to give me when I was little, when I was the only person in her world and she in mine. I focused on one of her tattoos, the flock of soaring birds on her neck. I counted them for comfort, the way I used to when I was younger: nine. Nine birds. Or was it ten? Ten. I'd forgotten the tenth bird on the back of her neck, hidden now behind her ear.

Ten birds, like always. Ten birds, as I'd remembered.

This was all it took for me to begin telling her.

"There's this girl," I started. "I found her Missing poster and then I read more about her online. She's not from here, but she went missing from somewhere close by. They say she ran away, but she didn't. Something's happened, she needs help, I know she does. But no one's looking for her. No one cares."

My mom kept all expression from her face, but, twitching beneath her skin, there was something. The birds fluttered as the tendons in her neck tightened, and I kept my eyes on them and kept talking.

I spilled everything about Abby, except how I'd talked to her myself; I'd seen her and I'd heard her and I'd been close enough to her I could've reached out and touched her, but I didn't say that. I didn't say how I hadn't touched her because I'd assumed she was a ghost. But I started to wonder if maybe there was a way—when you're in trouble, when you're caught somewhere and you can't get out—that you can reach out to someone. Maybe it happens when you're sleeping, that you project a vision of yourself to anyone who can see, and I can see. I didn't have the rational, scientific explanation for seeing the apparition of a lost but maybe-still-alive girl in my van and in my bedroom, and without it I didn't know how to explain that piece to my mom. So I skipped that part.

But I gave her other pieces:

I admitted that I'd talked to the boy Abby had been hanging out with. That I went in to talk to the Pinecliff police, not that they helped. And that I'd even been to talk to a counselor from the camp and to Abby's grandparents, and that was the real reason I drove down to New Jersey. I had Abby's bicycle, the one she left behind, the one I was storing in the garage. (I had her pendant, too, but this I couldn't say.)

When I stopped talking at last, my mom had her eyes down, considering all of what I'd told her. Billie didn't blink. Her bright gaze bored into me, as if she'd been trying to decide how to respond, too. She sat poised on the coffee table, a slight tremor in her fuzzy tail.

My mom chose her words carefully. "You say you know? *How* do you know?"

"I just . . . know."

"How, Lauren? Explain."

"I have a feeling." The expression on her face didn't change, though the birds on her neck jittered. "I had a dream."

"You had a dream or you had a feeling? Do you know something you're not telling me?"

"No." Yes. "Both. I had a dream *and* a feeling. She's not okay. Something happened. I know."

"Do you want to call the police again? Do you want me to call for you?" She believed me. My mom believed I was telling the truth.

Relief washed over me, and I wanted to lie back and let that be enough for tonight, and I also wanted to keep talking, now that I'd started, to tell her more about the dreams. About the other girls. About everything I knew that I shouldn't know, every memory that had been shared with me.

Then I remembered something. She made me think of it when she'd suggested calling the police. "Maybe we could ask for Officer Heaney this time. That's who I met when Jamie and I were looking around that camp place. He was there—he found us. He made us leave, you know, for trespassing. But he remembered Abby. He knew she'd gone missing. He knew about the bike. We should call him. I didn't get to talk to him at the station."

"All right," she said. She grabbed a notebook and wrote it down: *Heaney. Heeney? Heeny?* We weren't sure how to spell it.

I still couldn't read her expression. "First show me this girl," she said. "This Abby Sinclair."

I found the folded flyer in my coat pocket and smoothed it out to show her. Abby's face had faded away to a white space as if she could be anyone, a fill-in-the-blank face surrounded by a block of dark hair. Showing her flyer felt like exposing a page from my middle-school diary; it was that gooey and personal and important and tinged with shame.

"It's hard to read," my mom said. "Is this online?"

Now she was acting like she might not believe me, and a little trickle of doubt hooked itself to the lobe of my ear, hovering there, breathing, waiting to hear what she'd say next. Did she think I made this flyer on my computer for fun, invented a missing girl's name and hometown and decided what clothes she'd be last seen wearing?

"It's just hard to read," my mom said, seeming to sense what I was thinking.

"It's online," I said. "I'll show you."

As we went into the kitchen, the girls' voices in my ears stayed ominously silent. No shadows skirted the walls. They must have been angry with me. I might be barred from the house if my dream took me there again in the night—but would they forgive me if I found Abby? Would that be enough? Or was it that I needed to save all of them, retroactively, every last one?

On my mom's laptop I brought up the missing-persons page: proof Abby was an actual girl and I didn't make her up. This was not imaginary; this girl really was missing.

She read it carefully and clicked on the photo to enlarge it and see her face more clearly. Abigail Sinclair, 17, of Orange Terrace, New Jersey. The pendant was a gray shadow in the hollow of her neck, and her eyes were black pools full of secrets, not all of which I knew yet.

I found my voice. "That's her."

"You dreamed about this girl," my mom said, as if she wanted to get the facts straight.

Can a dream be happening when you're fully conscious of it? I wanted to ask her. Because, if so, then I did dream about this girl. All the time. And I dreamed about the other girls; I dreamed about them all the time, too. And these were dreams when I was sleeping, and these were dreams when I was awake. *This* could have been a dream, I realized, sitting there at the kitchen table before my mom's laptop, the cat having followed us in and still watching me intently, pointing her fuzzed tail. The dream could have been this night, this room, this conversation, and the reality could have been the broken house on the cracked street under the dark smog, with those girls. The reality could have been that I was trapped inside that limbo with the rest of them, and there was no true sky above us, and there were no roads leading to us, and the side-walk ended, and the house was about to burn down with us in it. I could have already been taken.

"What else?" she said. "Does this girl . . . talk to you? In your . . . dreams?"

The way she said it—condescending, like she'd added invisible quotation marks around choice words—I could see her reciting it as instructed from one of her textbooks. This was what a doctor might ask a psychotic person. *"Let the patient think you believe her. Don't affirm the delusions, but don't let her feel attacked."* She was treating me like I'd gone mental.

I met her eyes. "Yes," I said.

At this, my gaze was pulled away from her to the window over the kitchen sink, the small one that looked in the direction of the grand old Burke house next door. The view was of the side of the house near the laundry room, where the fire had burned all those years ago. I knew there was snow outside, and the temperature hovered near freezing, but the window didn't have a pattern of frost on it like the others in the kitchen.

The window was fogged in the center into a round, warm shape, almost like a pair of lips. Like someone had pressed her glossed mouth to the window glass. And breathed.

My mom was taking out her cell phone and dialing the

number for the Pinecliff Police Department, the one that was listed on Abby's Missing notice. She was making the call for me, like she said she would. She believed me enough to make this call.

When someone answered, she said she wanted to find out more about a missing-persons case in the area. It involved an underage girl named Abigail Sinclair. She wanted to know if there was an active investigation, because she had information that led her to believe the girl didn't run away, as suspected. After a few questions, and discovering she should call back in the morning when the day shift was on, she asked if she could leave a message for a specific officer, one who had more knowledge of the case. Officer Heaney, she said.

A pause.

"Yes," she said. "Heaney. H-E-A-N-E-Y, I think, or maybe H-E-E-N-Y? You don't have a large department; surely you know who I mean."

Then she got quiet. She was completely silent as someone on the other end of the line spoke, and I wasn't close enough to make out what they were saying.

"What's going on?" I said. She waved at me to give her a second. "Did he come to the phone? Is he there?"

"No," she said into the phone. "No, I'm afraid not, no."

"Can't you leave him a message?" I asked. She didn't respond.

"I understand," she said at last. "All right. Okay. Yes, thank you." She left her name and her number. She was in this now, too.

When she ended the call, she took a long moment before meeting my eyes.

She'd spoken to the police on the phone as if she absolutely believed me, had not a single doubt, and would go to bat for me if she had to. But now she was full of doubts. They flew and flapped all over her, making grim shadows darker than the tattooed birds that lined her neck.

"How tipsy are you right now?" she asked.

"Only a little," I said. "I know where I am. I know what's happening. I know who I'm talking to. What'd they say? Tell me."

"Besides tonight," she said. "Besides whatever you had to drink tonight. How have you been feeling lately, Lauren?"

"Fine," I said, in growing confusion.

"Are you sure?"

"Why wouldn't I be?"

The question hung in the air, unanswered.

"All right," my mom said. "Just making sure. I'll tell you what they said. They're opening an investigation."

I breathed a sigh of relief.

"Not because I called," she was quick to add. "Not because of us. Turns out the case was just reopened, actually. Just this morning. Because her legal guardian called. Her grandfather, they said. From what I understand, he called out of the blue and said the family had reason to believe she didn't run away and they wanted her case recategorized."

There was a warmth inside me, and it wasn't the pendant heating up; it was knowing Abby's grandfather had heard me.

He did what I'd asked him to do. And, because of that, someone would be searching for her now. They hadn't given up.

"But," my mom said, and lingered there like she didn't know how to finish.

"But?"

"But there's no Officer Heaney at the Pinecliff Police Department, Lauren. I don't know who you met that night, but no one by that name or any name like it works at the station. Are you sure he was from the Pinecliff station?"

"Yes," I said.

"And you're sure you got his name right?"

I nodded. "He said. Heaney, he said. Pinecliff police, he said. I think. I'm pretty sure. He was going to arrest us for trespassing on private property. He said."

She shrugged. Then said what she really meant. "Are you sure you talked to someone that night? Are you sure you're not . . . confused?" There they were again. The shadows on her face that showed she doubted me. Now she thought I was having imaginary conversations with authority figures and lying to make my story more convincing.

"Jamie was there with me. He met the guy. He talked to him. Officer Heaney. He had on a uniform. He . . . I think he had on a uniform; it was dark."

"It's okay," she said. "It doesn't matter. They've opened an investigation, so if she's out there and needs help, they'll find her, okay?"

I didn't feel okay.

Not anything close to okay.

Yes, I wanted them to be looking for Abby, but there was more to this. There was the fact that I didn't know if I could trust my own mother.

That was when I saw it on her chest. The hint of red. Bright and searing red. Like a patch of flames.

My mom had new ink. Did she get another tattoo while I was out at the party? Because a blazing crimson thing was newly visible beneath her collarbone on her chest. Her shirt was open beyond the third button, and somehow I'd missed what looked to be an unfamiliar picture there, until now, because now I couldn't seem to see anything else. The tattoo was a fiery heart above her real heart.

"Mom," I said carefully, "you didn't tell me you were getting a new tattoo."

"What?" she said. "But I'm not."

"You already did. Can I see?"

"What, when? I didn't. What do you mean?" And right then, so I could see her do it, and so the shadows watching us could see, my mom took her hand and held it over her chest. Covering the new tattoo.

It was here, while studying her, while paying attention, that I noticed the difference in her face. It was very slight, and there was a good chance I wouldn't have noticed if I hadn't been concentrating. But I was. And my mother—the one I've had all my life—has a beauty mark on her left cheek, just beside her lips. So black it's almost blue. I always wanted one of my own, and when I was little she'd pencil one on me with her eyeliner and say I was just like her, except mine washed off in the bath at night.

This mother, this one sitting at the kitchen table with me in the early, early hours of a dark morning—she had a beauty mark on her *right* cheek.

Same spot and same color and same shape. Wrong side.

She saw me staring and rubbed her cheek. "Have I got some food on my face or something?"

"No," I said, "it's nothing. I'm tired. I should sleep."

But, oh, it wasn't nothing.

The secret tattoo was one thing, but now this? This made me question everything about her. It made me wonder if telling her about Abby had really been the right thing.

I shouldn't have asked for help, should I? I shouldn't have trusted her. I should have done this on my own. With only myself. And the girls.

MISSING

JANNAH AFSANA DIN

CASE TYPE: Endangered Missing

DOB: April 4, 1995

MISSING: January 2, 2013

AGE NOW: 17

SEX: Female

RACE: Middle Eastern

HAIR: Brown

EYES: Brown

HEIGHT: 5'3" (163 cm)

WEIGHT: 135 lbs. (62 kg)

MISSING FROM: Clarkestone, MA, United States

CIRCUMSTANCES: Footage of Jannah was caught on surveillance video at a gas station in Clarkestone, Massachusetts, in the early-morning hours of January 2. She may have been meeting someone but appears to have left before that person arrived. She was wearing a white coat, blue jeans, and a Red Sox baseball cap. Jannah also wears contact lenses.

ANYONE HAVING INFORMATION SHOULD CONTACT

Clarkestone Police Department (Massachusetts) 1-617-555-4592

HAVE YOU SEEN THIS GIRL?

Please help find my sister Hailey Pippering.

She comes here or she used to all the time.

If you see this flyer and you know anything, e-mail me PLEASE!!!!! You don't have to use your real name! I won't call the police. I just want to know where she is!!!!

helpmefindhailey@fastmail.com

(Trina Glatt: disappearance unreported)

–46–

THE house was waiting for me. Always there, when nothing else was. The girls were gathered—the newest of the girls, Trina, at their center. She was flashing something that caught the firelight. A blade of some kind . . . sharp, silver. A knife.

No one knew how she smuggled it in, and everyone wanted to hold it, but when she said maybe it'd be for the best if they avoided getting their prints on it, they stopped reaching for the contraband and they stopped asking.

Trina told us that it all began when she got that knife. Before it came into her life, she felt helpless. She felt like a *girl.* She spat out that word like it was the worst insult in the world, to be what we all were, and so she offended every one of us.

The knife itself was titanium, the blade and handle coated in a silvery finish. It was a butterfly knife that folded in on itself so it could fit in the crevice of a clasped hand.

Trina had stolen the knife from a boyfriend who'd himself shoplifted it from an army-navy surplus store. She couldn't explain why she'd swiped it from his pocket while he was sleeping—better would have been to rifle through his wallet—but she wanted to take something from him that would really bother him. Something he'd notice, something he couldn't replace. She'd planned to return it, maybe a week later, but once she had it she found she couldn't part with it. The knife was so compact, it could be tucked into her front jeans pocket, and the secure sense of it under her pillow helped her sleep at night.

After she dumped him—all right, she admitted, *he* dumped *her*—she realized the knife was hers forever. She'd find herself playing with it, like in school or at home in full view of her mom's boyfriend on the couch. What was to keep her from plunging it into someone who tried to mess with her? Nothing. Not saying she did or would. Just having the weapon and knowing she could use it was enough.

The thing is, she never once made use of that knife. Not technically, because slicing incisions into the arms of her mother's couch didn't count. And making snowflakes out of loose-leaf paper for her little half sister didn't count, either.

She never made use of the knife on a person.

That was her biggest regret. She could have done so much with it! When she leaped up while telling this part of her story, the other girls backed away. Not like they could get hurt in the smoky house, which was more charred and patterned by fire each time I visited—because this house held them close, kept them safe—but they remembered being hurt and reacted like they still could be.

Maybe it was talk of the knife that brought her out after all this time. She shifted from the curtains, and before anyone knew what was happening, Fiona Burke's arm reached out and smacked the silvery butterfly knife from the new girl's hand. It went sailing and landed with a *thunk*, spinning on the blackened wooden floor far across the room where no one could grab for it.

It doesn't matter, Fiona Burke said to Trina Glatt, as if they were the only two lost girls in the room. *You know it doesn't matter, don't you?*

It matters, Trina growled. *Give it back.*

You can't have that here, Fiona Burke said. *None of us can have any of the things we had.*

It happened as we heard her say those words.

One of the girls, Eden, crept over with curiosity to retrieve the butterfly knife—though it wasn't clear who she planned to give it to, between Fiona and Trina, or if she meant to keep it for herself—but before her fingers got close enough, Fiona Burke had her foot in the fray, stomping down on the knife to keep it from being rescued. Trina got in the mix, lunging forward to kick away Fiona Burke's spindly leg. But when she did so, there was no knife beneath Fiona's foot. There was the blackened floor, and the dusted ash from the fire in relief against the shape of Fiona's foot. But no knife.

Fiona Burke wanted to teach the girls a lesson.

You couldn't hold on to what you loved—unless you were

Yoon-mi or Maura, who loved who they brought here.

You couldn't have a keepsake in this burning house. All you could have were the clothes on your back, and even those were illusion because they were the last things you remembered wearing. (When she said this, I caught a flash of them, of all of us, ghostly gray and naked in the smoky night. Then it passed. It passed, and I looked down and my dream-self was still wearing pajamas.)

Fiona Burke continued with her lesson. All the girls couldn't help but listen. She knew more than anyone, and this was the first time she'd shared this information.

It didn't matter what you had before, or who you were before, or what you did in the moments leading up to being here. If you fought or if you let go and watched it happen. If you were the one who turned down the dark road on your own, or if someone led you there.

Because you could be pissed off, you could stab everyone in sight with your boyfriend's stolen butterfly knife, and yet you could still end up here.

You could come here quiet, and you could come swinging punches. You could come and sleep for a week. You could come here and try to leave, but you couldn't make it back down the stairs and out that door. You could come here and wonder what happened. You could come with questions. Or with that night's homework half done. You could come here the day you turn 17, and you could come here on any day before you're 17 no longer. You could come here any one of those 365 days.

You just couldn't come here after your eighteenth birthday. Not one girl ever has.

That's what Fiona Burke told us.

Then she said one last thing. Being here meant you couldn't be out there anymore. She counted us all on her fingers and then settled her eyes on me. Strangely. Being here meant you were dead—or soon would be. Didn't we—you, *me*—get that yet?

– 47 –

TRINA'S knife. I had it. Outside. Here, now, in my hand.

Or a knife almost identical to it, one with the silvery coating and the blade that tucked to hide inside itself but that could snap out quick when needed. Because you never know when you might need it.

The butterfly knife was there in the bathroom medicine chest when I'd opened it in the night. It was late, closing in on morning, and the dream had woken me up. I couldn't get back to sleep and was looking for nail clippers, which was random enough, but in their place on the bottom shelf was this knife. I'd patted it at first, to be sure. Removed it from the medicine chest and studied it in my palm. Closed the cabinet and looked into the mirror at myself and what I had in my hand:

Yes, a knife. So much heavier than the nail clippers. Larger. And with so much more possibility.

I couldn't deny that a pair of ordinary nail clippers had somehow transformed themselves into Trina Glatt's most treasured possession, the one she was banned from keeping inside the house. The one I'd last seen under Fiona Burke's foot.

The blade slid out and begged me to extend a fingertip to touch it. Just to feel. Only to see how sharp it really was.

And it *was* sharp.

But then the knife slipped and time slowed and I could see what was about to happen.

How my fingers would lose their grasp on it. How the knife would flip in the air, blade side aimed down. How my arm would be in the way. How the impossibly sharp blade of the knife would land, perpendicular to my arm, slicing my wrist, and how it wouldn't hurt at first, not until I saw the blood.

Then I was feeling so much. This rush of pain, all at once, radiating out from that one line below my wrist and coursing through me, pulsing in places the blade of the knife hadn't even touched.

It shouldn't have been bleeding so much—it was one little slice. I rinsed it in cold water until it numbed some. I lifted my arm over my head because I heard somewhere that if you get a cut that won't stop bleeding you should hold it high over your head. Gravity will pull the blood down to your feet and if you hold it up there long enough, it'll slow the bleeding.

But, this time, gravity didn't make it stop.

Blood came pooling down my arm, dripping all over the white sink.

The mirror showed me a gruesome image of myself, the way the girls might have seen it, if they were there watching.

I must have been making noise, or else my mom must have woken from her own sleep and needed to visit our shared bathroom at just the exact moment I needed her. Which at first felt like some far-off answer to some unspoken plea buried inside me. And then it flipped and felt like the exact opposite.

Because next thing, my mom was bursting in and there I was, dropping my arm and hiding it behind my back, forgetting there was a pool of blood in the sink.

Don't let her think— Fiona Burke's commanding, distinctive voice started to say inside my left ear, but that was drowned out by my mom's shrieking.

Before she wrestled the arm out from behind my back, and before the blood started coursing out quicker than before and running in thick rivulets to the tiled bathroom floor, before her eyes alighted on the knife and the mess of the sink and then shifted fast to me, growing wide, and wider still, I think I knew what she was thinking. And so I knew just what she'd say:

"Lauren! Honey, what— Oh my God, baby. What did you do to yourself?"

It wasn't possible to be a girl with a bloody arm and a dirty knife in my mom's world without having done a sick and twisted thing to myself. To her, this scene she stumbled on starring me and the butterfly knife in the upstairs bathroom could mean only one thing.

She'd read all about this. She'd gone over the case studies in her textbooks and written papers about adolescent depression and done all that research to get an A on the last one, and she was hunting for signs she must have missed.

I would have argued it. I would have explained, even if I couldn't tell her about the missing girl this knife belonged to.

But when I looked down into the sink, I saw the blood-smeared nail clippers. That's the thing: They really were only nail clippers. And then I saw the shards all over the bathroom, on the sink and the floor and the shelf and even the top of the toilet and the bathtub. The sharp, bloody pieces of glass that reminded me of Natalie Montesano, who still wore bits of broken windshield in her face.

Oh.

Oh no. The mirror. It had been shattered. It was beginning to look like I'd broken the mirror and sliced myself up with it. *Did I?*

One glance at my arm told me I did.

Realizing this, there was a growing sense of heat building up the length of my body from the floor. My skin went feverish with it; my gaze went red. I was all red, inside and outside and everywhere.

My mom was in shock, and so she didn't stop me when I reached out and did what I needed to do next. I pulled open her nightshirt, bursting the buttons, to expose her chest. I had to see the secret tattoo, the new art she'd had permanently etched onto her body without telling me first. And I didn't know for sure what I expected to find there: my own Missing poster, done up in crimson Gothic lettering with my measurements and my eye color for the world to see? Or instead, a My Little Pony, a shriek of hot pink like a stove burn? A cartoon heart, the exact size and shape of the true heart my mom carried inside?

It wasn't any of those things, my mom's new tattoo. That was what startled me. It wasn't a tattoo at all.

It was skin. Her bare skin. Blank as a porcelain sink before all my blood messed it up.

She pulled herself away from me, closed her ripped shirt, and then came for me again, arms out, wanting to hug me, I think, or wanting to stop me from doing much worse than I'd already done.

The heat in my head.

How it buzzed, centering in on my brain like I was about to lose my own signal. An infestation of wasps expanding up the walls of my mind and burrowing into all my corners where I hadn't lived enough years to keep any thoughts yet. They dislodged pieces of me. Like how one time I was stung by a wasp in the backyard and my mom cradled me in her arms like she was doing now and pressed a package of frozen peas to the sting, and the peas really did make the pain ease away and now whenever I eat frozen vegetables I feel a sense of deep comfort, of love, because it reminds me of her. But why was I thinking of the frozen peas at that moment? And how come there was so much blood? And why couldn't I feel my—

So dizzy.

Needed to sit down.

When my mom started shaking me, saying, “Stay awake, baby, stay awake,” the lost girls chose to remain silent and refused to come out.

They kept silent as the room went black.

And I guess they keep silent now, too, because of what came after. Because they’re afraid. Because we all are.

– 48 –

WHAT do you do with a girl who's slit her own wrist with the shards of a mirror? Who's done it vertical, like she knew what she was doing, and had every intention to die? What do you do with a girl who hears voices whispering secrets in her ears? Who believes she's chased by shadows? Who has an unnatural, unexplainable connection to a host of missing girls?

Ask my mother. I know what she'll say because I woke up with the blue lights of the ambulance dancing over me, easing out all the bad red, and I heard her talking to the EMTs. She'd say you send that girl away.

You send her away.

AND THEN

– 49 –

IT takes some time before I realize the words they're saying aloud are meant for me.

"We're going to take care of you here, Laura, hon. Just rest."

"I think her name is Lauren."

"Sorry. *Lauren.* Your mom brought you in to us. Do you remember? Do you remember what happened? What you did?"

"Have you ever tried to hurt yourself before, Lauren? Lauren?"

"All right then, I see you want to sleep. Just sit up and swallow this."

"She won't sit up."

"Just help her. There. Let her lean on your arm. There, Lauren. Here you go. This will make you comfortable. Good. Swallow."

"Who was that you were talking to just now, Lauren?"

"Did she say something? I didn't hear."

"She's talking to those girls again . . . What girls, Lauren? I don't see any girls."

"Let's leave her be. Don't encourage her. Let's just let her sleep."

The two nurses shuffle out the door. They leave it open—it's a door that doesn't seem to ever be able to close—and they wander back, every so often, checking on me as I pretend to sleep. Soon the pill they had me swallow makes it impossible to keep pretending. The pill makes the sleeping turn real.

My head thickens with the quiet. The lost girls who've come out to visit with me slip under the bed to hide. Or they've gone somewhere else, behind the curtains maybe, where the shadows gather—all I know is I can't see or hear them anymore.

The next time my eyes close, I can't get the lids to lift open.

This is the psych ward of the hospital and I don't know how many days I've been inside.

–50–

I don't dream. I don't wake up coughing, and I can't smell smoke.

I've been across the river, in the hospital's adolescent psychiatric ward, for what feels like a week's worth of nights, though it could be fewer and it could be more, I'm not sure. The sun streaming through the window feels like afternoon sun long left over from morning, or the dreary start to a new day. I'm in a long, narrow room, in a long, narrow bed against a wall. The bed on the opposite wall is empty. So is my head.

There isn't a voice rattling around in my mind that doesn't belong to me—which, after all that's happened, is a foreign and noticeable thing. Whatever they give me here at night knocks me out and steals the dreams away, also the voices. I'm wiped clean and returned to who I was before I ever spied Abby Sinclair on the side of the road.

Except for the bandage wrapped around my left arm.

I don't want to unpeel the bandage to see what I did. I lie still on the bed and wait. My limbs are heavy, and I can't seem to do much else. Surely, if I wait long enough, one of the girls will visit me.

Someone has to.

But no lost girl enters the room, and no lost girl finds her way through the quiet caverns of my head to lift her lips to my ear.

I need to get out of bed and go out there, see if someone can get my mom on the phone. She'll believe me if I could only get a chance to talk to her. She'll come right away and she'll take me home.

On the ride back, we'll laugh over this. We'll be sure I'm far more careful in the future with mirrors and fingernail clippers. If I missed too much school, she'll cover for me as she has before. Maybe we'll say I came down with the flu.

No one will ever have to know this even happened.

– 51 –

MY mom seems afraid to look at me and yet all she can do is look at me, so there's the constant swish-swishing of her head as it turns toward me, then away, toward me, away. Not to mention her hands, which keep smoothing the hair from my face, or grabbing my fingers and squeezing, or rubbing circles upon circles on my back between my shoulder blades even though I'd rather she didn't keep touching me right now.

She clears her throat. "They're going to keep you here through the weekend, Lauren," she says. "Then we'll . . . we'll decide more on Monday."

When I speak it's my voice that comes out, but it's slower than normal, which makes me think my ears have gone bad. The meds they keep giving me whisper through my system the way the voices used to, but in dumb, dull sounds I can't translate. "Monday?" I say. "I think I have a big exam on Monday. I can't stay through Monday."

"I'll bring your schoolbooks and whatever you need from home, if that's really what you want. But are you sure? I don't want you worrying about school after, after . . ."

She can't say it.

"I didn't try to kill myself, Mom. It was an accident. I told you."

"Do you remember what you said?" she asks tentatively. "About Fiona Burke?"

I sharpen. "No. What did I say about Fiona?"

"You were . . . It sounded to me like you thought you were talking to Fiona."

I shake my head. "I don't remember that at all."

She changes the subject. "How do you feel?"

"Fuzzy."

"Does it . . ." She points at the arm.

"Hurt?" I finish for her.

She nods.

"Not really. It's barely even a scratch. Can't I go home with you? I have shifts at work all this week."

"No, you don't. I called in for you already. And it wasn't a scratch, Lauren."

Now she's not meeting my eyes at all. She looks like she's about to burst into tears. She turns from me in the chair to survey the common room we're sitting in, this sad space meant for sad people. Blinds block out as much sunlight as possible, and puke-and-blood-proof couches and chairs covered in scratches aim away from one another, making it possible for a dozen people to sit in this room at once and not have to talk to one other person, which is a miracle in furniture arrangement. A large woman guards the common area from inside an adjoining office. The window between her desk and the rest of the room has a shutter over it that can be closed, so if the place falls to chaos, she can abandon ship and blockade herself in.

A boy shuffles past the common room just in time for my mom to see him—how both of his arms are covered in the kind of bandages that cover just my left forearm—and how slowly his legs move, barely lifting off the floor as he inches down the tiled corridor. He walks like he's been filled with cement. Maybe that's what's in the pills they make us swallow here. Carefully I lift my arm to see how heavy it is, and then with a *thunk* I watch it drop back down onto my lap, the way a sack of cement might drop.

When my mom turns back in my direction, a perfectly positioned beam of sunlight from between the blinds catches her in the face. It lights her up as if someone in the clouds has aimed a spotlight down to reveal something of significance to me.

Pay attention, it says.

My mom's beauty mark again. Just like the other night, it's on the wrong side of her face and I'm left wondering. Am I looking at her in a mirror? Has my memory gotten dislodged and confused? Or is this woman—this beautiful woman with the mark on the wrong cheek, the one who keeps nervously touching me, the one who locked me away supposedly for my own good—is this woman even my mother?

I want her to speak. I need to hear her voice. Then I'll know.

She sighs. She says, "I'm so sorry I made you feel like you couldn't come to me, Lauren."

For a second I think she called me Laura, like I swore I heard the nurse call me the other night. But no. No, she knows my name, and she'd never make such a simple mistake as that. It won't be so easy.

I'm second-guessing myself again. I'm not sure who she is now: the one I know and have always known, or someone pretending to be that person, trying to trick me. I decide to take careful stock of her tattoos, but she's wearing a sweater, and the sweater strategically covers them up with overlong sleeves and a bulky turtleneck that doesn't allow even a peek of vine to be seen. Of the birds on her neck, only two can be made out, the last two closest to her ear.

Should I ask her to take off her sweater? To undress and prove herself to me?

Then I remember how I tore off her shirt in the bathroom the other night and how frightened she seemed of me after, like I'd attacked her with claws out and teeth bared, ready to rip into her skin. I remember the sight of her chest. Her breasts. Her ribs. Her stomach. And I hang my head, ashamed.

"What?" she says. "Tell me what you're thinking, honey."

"You should probably go," I say. "I'm having weird thoughts right now."

"Like what weird thoughts?"

"I shouldn't tell you."

"Are they telling you what to think?" She's leaned forward

and whispered this, like someone might overhear. "Did they tell you not to tell me?"

I think at first by "they" she means the doctors, but then I get it. She's regurgitating rote from those case studies in her books again. She used to make me read them aloud to her so she could guess the right answer and prep for her exams. Because that's the kind of question you'd ask a patient you're trying to categorize, ticking off all her symptoms until the winning diagnosis dings and lights up the game board. If I tell her that the alien-vampires who've come down from the galactic heavens are telling me what to think and what to do and what to say, she'll win the prize refrigerator.

I give a tiny shake of my head. That's the only answer I can offer right now.

"Oh, Lauren," she says, a hint of pity in her voice. Her mouth crumples, showing me how defeated this makes her feel. She asks if I need anything from home and I describe what she can bring me: my textbook, for the test Monday; some books to read, anything really; my gray notebook with the doodles on the front and I think I left it on my desk; my eyeliner and the rest of my makeup; more socks.

Then I make myself ask, "Did they call you yet? The police? About Abby?"

What I know from my last night at home—and my last visit to the house before Trina left me her knife—is that Abby might still be out there somewhere. It's possible. I can't give up hope on that.

She's hesitating, so I really do begin to think it's about to happen, the truth, the end of the story, the end. And will I be allowed to be sad about my friend while in here, will they let me have that emotion? Will they even let me call her my friend?

But my mom shakes her head. "No news," is all she says.

"Do you want to call them and ask, maybe? For me?"

I think she might agree to it. Then she veers around and completely changes the subject. "So I called Jamie. I thought he should know."

"About Abby?" I ask, confused.

"About you," she says. "I called and told him you were here."

My real mom would have called Jamie. That's something she actually *would* do. This is her, isn't it? This *is* my mother, and this crazy girl is me.

"He picked up your van from that party for you. He said he found your keys."

"Please tell him thanks for me," I say.

"He might visit. I hope that's okay."

I don't want Jamie to see me like this; it's bad enough he knows, and I don't know how much my mom told him, so I can't be sure how much he knows. It could be all; it could be every awful thing. He's probably so relieved right now that we broke up; he's probably eternally grateful to be able to stay out of this. Away from me.

— — —

Soon it's time for good-byes. There's the hug, never-ending so I feel like I can't breathe, and there's the remembered scent of my mother's hair, which brings me back to childhood, and I'm thinking randomly about the wasp sting and the frozen peas, and I feel worse again for doubting her. I don't know what's happened to me. To my head.

I let her go without standing up, as my legs weigh twice as much as they did just minutes before and my left arm feels too weak to lift. Only my right arm can be made to move, and I wave that at her until she disappears down the hall.

It isn't until she's gone that I think to raise my right hand to my throat. I feel the exposed skin at my collarbone, tracing my fingers around the base of my neck like I'm aiming a guillotine. I let my hand go lower, feeling for it. The pendant isn't there.

I don't remember seeing it here, in the hospital. I don't remember feeling it, against my skin, all those days I spent in bed. Was it on me when they brought me in? It should have been around my neck, but what if something happened when they carried me out on the stretcher? What if it fell off? What if it got caught on something and it broke? I have to go after my mom and get her to look for it at home.

I stand up.

I try to remember which direction my mom went down the hall.

It takes me a moment and then I see the exit—of course, that's the only direction she could have gone; that's the one exit. There isn't another one on this whole ward.

I walk toward it, but the walking is a difficult thing to manage. I feel sure I'm being faster than I am, except the tiles under my feet are changing too slowly and the window in the wall is the same window that was there before.

It takes me a long time to make it even a quarter of the way down, and it's here that I come upon the sounds of them talking. There's an open, unguarded door and two voices thrown out into the hallway. The first voice, the one I recognize, belongs to my mom, and the other voice, the voice that sounds only barely familiar, must be one of the doctors. They're talking about something that confounds me at first: They're talking about my dad. The last time I saw the guy, I was three years old, which for all intents and purposes means I have no memory of ever seeing him at all. And yet here's my mom telling some random doctor all about him.

"And he wouldn't come to the phone," she says. "And I've called around, but I haven't been able to find where he's staying since. I mean, I have no idea. He could be out on the streets again. He could be sleeping under a bridge. He probably is. I don't know. It's not like anyone would tell me."

"So was there ever any diagnosis? Did he tell you?"

"He didn't." She sighs and stays silent for a long while.

I'm hovering just outside the door and I wonder if she can sense I'm here. Then she starts talking again, starts saying these things she never bothered to tell me. Her own daughter. About my own dad.

"He never said anything to me about it. But there was the medication he was taking when I knew him. He left an old prescription bottle in the house when he took off, and I found it after. I remember seeing the label. Thinking, *What are these for?* So I looked them up. Antipsychotics. I mean, schizophrenia, could that have been it? How could he not tell me? I know it can be hereditary. Doctor, with Lauren, I mean she's too young yet, but do you think—"

I lose track of the rest of it when an orderly takes my elbow and says, "Are you confused? Do you need to go sit down?"

The orderly spoke loudly enough to bring my mom to the door, and the doctor, and there's a nurse, and there's a shuffling patient coming this way, and some other hospital person in hospital clothes, and they all see me and they all know I heard.

My mom looks stricken.

"Lauren, do you need something?" the doctor says. I don't know her name, but she knows mine.

"Mom, I was going to ask . . ." I settle my eyes on my mom. Apparently she thinks my absent, supposedly homeless dad is a certified lunatic and she's been keeping this little detail from me for my whole life. "My necklace. My gray one. Could you bring that for me from home, too?"

She glances at the doctor. The doctor nods. So she turns back to me and she says sure, she'll look for it at home and bring it with everything else tomorrow.

"Lauren, did you—" my mom starts to say, but the doctor there beside her is shaking her head. "I'll see you tomorrow, Lauren, honey," my mom says instead.

I nod and make my way slowly back down the hallway to stare at the wall while sitting in an uncomfortable, antisocial vinyl chair.

– 52 –

A new day, but I haven't been staring at the wall. I've been staring at the girl. She hasn't noticed because she notices nothing. She hasn't moved since the nurse led her in and sat her down, not just not moving from this chair to another chair, but at all. Not even to fidget or scratch an itch. Not to blink her eyes or adjust the piece of fire-red hair that's fallen in front of her nose.

Maybe she is sitting very, very still in the hopes that I notice her. There are other patients who are louder, and flail more, and in the midst of all that she stands out. Or there could be another reason. She must think we're being watched here—she must know for sure if she's keeping herself that still.

Her voice won't reach me through the drugged confines of my head, so she's come here in the flesh. It's the only way.

"Fiona?" I prompt her.

She doesn't stir.

I try her name again, louder. "Fiona. I *see* you, okay? I see you there."

Her body betrays no movement. She's catatonic, if you can be in that state with your eyes still open. There she sits, as if formed into the vinyl chair by a mold of wax.

I move chairs so I'm right beside her. Then I reach out and shake her knee, but it's like playing with the CPR dummy in health class. Deadweight.

"Can't you talk?" I whisper. *"It's me."*

Her eyes are still open, and I wedge my face in front of them, so she *has* to look at me. Even then, the brown irises seem to cast straight through me, as if my body has lost all its skin and bones and bloody, bubbling organs so the blank wall behind me holds more space in this world than I do.

"Blink if you can hear me," I say.

She blinks.

Then I get an idea.

"Write it down if you can't talk," I tell her. I pass her my gray notebook, which is the only thing besides the socks that made it through to me on the inside. The nurses' station acts like the TSA at an airport. Everything must be checked, and since they have no scanners, that means by hand. They've only given me two things from the bags my mom brought me for now, and say they have to go through checking the toiletries and all the rest.

I place the open notebook on her knees. She doesn't flinch. The lock of hair in front of her nose doesn't shift, so I'm not positive she's even breathing.

But she blinked. I did see that.

I take the pencil in my hand and place it into hers. The nurses wouldn't let me have a pen, but they let me use one of their own dull-sharpened pencils. It barely writes, but I tighten her fingers around it so it doesn't fall. I position the hand holding the pencil on the paper. Then I step away and wait to see what she'll do with it.

Which is nothing. The pencil drops and rolls across the floor.

The screams that come next aren't from her mouth, or mine. A wailing can be made out down the hall, and it's getting closer. When the new patient—some girl I don't recognize—is walked through, struggling with two male nurses as she's led past the common room, I cover my ears and watch her go. She flails and lets her hair fly. I uncover one ear for a second to see if she's stopped and quickly plug it closed again; it sounds like she's yodeling. *That's* someone with problems.

When I look back to Fiona, I see she's moved. She isn't catatonic, as she wants everyone to believe; she's lightning-quick and on alert. She's the girl I remember from the house next door, who pitched her bags down the stairs and locked me in the closet. She's the girl who always thought of running, one eye on the road. Even now, escape plans hatch in her mind, but I'm not sure they're for her to follow—I think this time they're meant for me.

Somehow she's gotten herself to the wall behind the nurses' station. She's pulled the fire alarm. And she's returned to her statue pose on the vinyl seat, her mouth slightly open now so a nice, telltale line of drool can emerge. Her eyes focus on nothing but the dust motes floating around her face in beautiful snowflake patterns, mimicking what's coming down outside. All within an instant, before the nurses react to the alarm and come to line us up and check with the fire marshal to see if we need to evacuate. That's how fast Fiona Burke moved.

– 53 –

I don't run.

I can picture what Fiona wants from me: a daring escape while the hospital staff is distracted. She longs for the sight of me leaping over the half door that divides the patients from the so-called healthy people on the other side, making it out to the elevator, and riding it down to freedom. But she's forgotten how slow I am.

There is the moment in which I could make my escape.

And then that moment passes.

I do make it downstairs, and outside, but only with the nurses and the orderlies and the other patients. A group of us takes the back stairs, the emergency exit I didn't even know was so close to the common room, and we are made to do so without getting our coats, though it's still only January.

It had been snowing before, I think, but now the bleached-out sky spits up only a few damp flurries. So we stand there shivering in our cotton shirts, with a lucky few in sweatshirts. We watch the parking lot in a daze.

Fiona is at the end of the row we've formed against the hospital's back brick wall, near the shadows and out of reach of the sun. No one's guarding her, and someone should be. Her spine is slumped and her red-dyed hair hangs in her eyes. She wears the clothes she always wears, the last outfit I remember seeing her in and the outfit she wore through the ashy rooms of the dream: the too-short shirt and the too-tight jeans. Her bare stomach is exposed to the biting cold. She makes no movement, doesn't even shiver.

They're saying it's only a fire drill, but I know better. We wait outside longer than any drill should last, wait until someone inside gives the all clear. Then we can go back in. We pile up, one behind the other, pushing into the oversize elevator, enough of us inside you'd think we'd make it sink instead of rise.

Fiona is between me and the paneled wall, and as the elevator doors fold closed I feel how hot her skin is up close, how it roasts against mine. I don't move away, because I want the mark on me after. I want the proof we've both been here.

The adult ward has also been evacuated—in a time of emergency, no one would be left behind—and some of their patients are on the elevator with ours. One of the women has suddenly taken a liking to me. She's sandwiched beside Fiona, but she ignores Fiona entirely and focuses her attention on me. Her blue hair is cotton-candy soft, and hollow punctures in her earlobes show where thick piercings used to be.

When she speaks, her voice is fainter than I expect. Gentle.

"They're wrong about us," she whispers, her heated words in my face. The elevator, so fully loaded, takes its time lifting us between floors.

"Who is?" I say back.

"In another place, in another time, we'd be shamans," the woman whispers with shining, truth-telling eyes as blue as her head. *"We'd be gods."*

I turn to Fiona to see what she thinks of this nonsense. There is a muscle in her cheek that jitters—if she lets it go, it would allow her mouth to smile.

A nurse takes the blue woman by the arm and says to me, "Don't you listen to Kathy. She knows that's all in her head. And she *knows* she's not to talk about such things with the other patients."

The blue woman knows no such thing—her blue eyes tell me so—and then when the elevator doors open and she leaves, she takes everything she knows with her.

I can tell Fiona thinks she's insane.

We've returned to our side of the floor, to our vinyl chairs and to the hour before it's time for dinner, which we look forward to and dread all the same. My gray notebook is where I left it, open to the page I'd given Fiona to write me a message, though the pencil has vanished from the room.

She's left me a drawing that's been scratched into the paper, like with a fingernail. I can see it if I turn the page this way and that, let it catch the light. It's a hard, jagged line that rises high to attack the edge of the paper, like a burst of flames.

This is when the understanding leaks into me, faster and so much more welcome than a sedative. Fiona is trying to communicate. She drew me this symbol, and she pulled that alarm. In doing so, she showed me the way out.

Because there it is in the paper carving she did for me:

Fire.

She wants one.

But she hasn't said why yet.

-54-

MY mom's wardrobe choices for me make me question *her* mental state. Once the nurses let me have everything she's brought for me, I discover that she's packed me more socks and also the ugliest sweaters and sweatshirts I own, ones she would have had to go digging through my drawers to find, and more than I'd need for staying only through the weekend. For my therapy appointment, I'm encased in a bright orange sweatshirt, the cautionary color of traffic cones, and if there's anything that says I'm not myself, it's this. Only a very sick person would wear this shirt.

The one thing my mom didn't send was the necklace. It wasn't anywhere in the bags she packed for me, not even in the pockets. It's all I can think about now, how I've lost it, how without it I've broken my connection to the other girls. Fiona is here with me, but the others—I can't hear them, and I haven't dreamed them, and it's Abby I keep wondering about, Abby I miss most of all.

"How are you feeling today, Lauren?" the doctor is asking me. Or she may have asked this minutes ago, and I still haven't formed my answer.

Some days I see one doctor in a group with the other patients, and other days this doctor, alone. The last time I was in here alone with this doctor I was asked all about wanting to harm myself, which I denied, and I'll say the same today.

This time, though, when I say I'm feeling better, the doctor asks about the voices. "The girls," she calls them, as if she was pleasantly introduced to each of them before I came in the room and they've stepped out for a moment, perhaps for tea.

How long have they been talking to me? she wants to know. Do they ever ask me to do things, things that scare me or upset me? Things I'd rather not do?

"Like what kinds of things?" I ask.

"Violent things," she says carefully. Her hair is layered and cropped short, and her pantsuit is wrinkled in only one spot as if she ironed everywhere else but the left knee. This mistake in her pants seems violent to me.

"No," I say.

"Such as trying to hurt your mother?" she says, and waits.

"That's not what happened," I start, getting upset. "I'd never hurt my mom. Who do you guys think I am?"

"Of course you wouldn't," she says, then switches gears. "Tell me about this party where you lost your keys. That was a bad night, wasn't it? What happened?"

"I lost my keys." She stays silent, so I keep talking. "I guess I dropped them. I don't remember. I kind of blacked out."

"Do you have blackouts like this often? When you wake up and don't remember what you've done? Or maybe when people tell you that you've done things and you have no memory of doing them?"

I'm not sure what someone told her I did beyond losing the keys; my mom wasn't even there that night. Has she been talking to Jamie? Did Jamie say something?

"That's like something I saw on TV once," I say. "Multiple personalities, I think. Is that what you mean? Like I black out and someone other than me takes over and makes people call me by a different name?"

"I'm not saying that at all. Is that what you're saying?"

She leans forward and the large button earrings she has fastened into her lobes droop low, skimming her shoulders. The earrings themselves are bigger than her ears and must weigh a ton. It's like she's decorated herself with two plates from her kitchen.

I think of the blue woman from the elevator, how the giant empty holes in her ears might have once held earrings as large as this.

"No," I say. "I'm not saying I have multiple personalities. Of course not."

If she knew more about the girls, she wouldn't have even asked that. The girls may tell me things, and let me walk through their memories, but I don't *become* them. They're them, and I'm always only me.

I fold my arms over my chest and play with the caution-orange cuffs on my floppy sleeves. The sweatshirt smells musty, like my mom wanted to dress me as a whole other person and had to search for the costume in the back of my closet. Or like she's some other woman, come to impersonate my mother, wanting to dress a girl who's impersonating me.

"Do you ever see things you think might not be real?" the doctor asks.

"What do you mean by 'not real'?"

"Hallucinations. Things or people no one else can see."

I'm silent for a long time.

She's not asking any more questions, so after a while I speak up. "Can you be a psychiatrist and believe in stuff?"

"How so?"

"If you had a patient," I start, "and if she said she saw a ghost, if she said she could talk to the ghost and the ghost talked back, would you automatically give her medication and call her crazy? Or would you consider that maybe some kind of supernatural explanation is possible? What I mean is, do you believe in things like that? Are you even allowed to?"

She skirts the question. "We never use the word *crazy* here."

"But would you? Would you say that seeing something like that is only a chemical imbalance in her brain?"

"Seeing hallucinations can be a symptom of mental illness, yes. Seeing a 'ghost.' Talking to the 'ghost.' Having the 'ghost' talk back . . . Yes."

"Like what?" I say. "Like which illness? Tell me one."

"We don't insert labels so soon in the process, we never—"

"Schizophrenia," I insert for her. "Like my dad."

She pauses and absently touches her wrinkled knee. "So you *did* hear what your mother and I were talking about. That was not about you. You understand that, right?"

I shrug.

"Schizophrenia isn't something that can be diagnosed after just one episode. A diagnosis can take years. And I want you to know that one person's experience isn't necessarily like another's. Experiences can vary, and nothing in psychology fits neatly into a box and gives us such easy answers."

She's being vague. I don't respond, so she keeps on.

"There are many things what you're going through could be. You say you're not depressed, but that's something we need to explore. There has to be time for therapy, time to adjust to different medications, to—"

More things, she says more things. She keeps talking. She could be talking about shamans and gods, for all I know—I suspect she talks simply to hear herself talk. What I'm waiting for is another voice, an answer in my head. A voice of a lost girl to tell me all of this is what's crazy. My being here. My having to listen to this. While outside they're being taken and I'm the only one who knows. The meds aren't making me as slow and sleepy as they were in the beginning, but they do something far worse than that. They make it so I haven't heard a voice in days.

At some point I realize the doctor has gone silent.

"Who are you listening to?" she asks.

I'm confused. "I'm listening to you. You were talking."

"You turned and looked over there"—she points at the

potted plant in the corner—"is someone there, talking to you? One of the 'girls'?"

The plant is a plant, a fern in a pot of dirt. If I insist that the plant is only a plant, will she wipe my slate clean and send me home? If I say the plant speaks in the voice of a girl, will I stay locked away here forever? Or maybe I have it in reverse. Will she think I'm lying if I deny the plant can talk? Will she think I can't ever be "cured"?

I turn back to her and there she is. Not the doctor—she hasn't moved from her plush chair, where she sits with her leg folded up, daring me to notice the wrinkled knee—but Fiona, no longer faking catatonic and instead faking a trigger with her finger and pointing her imaginary gun to the back of the doctor's actual head.

–55–

FIONA'S here with me now. She pretend-shoots the doctor dead and then she's motioning for the window, like I should make a leap for it, or push the doctor through the glass to see if her enormous earrings will break her fall. I'm not sure what Fiona's getting at, but I'm not about to do anything stupid, and I need to keep all reactions off my face so the doctor doesn't know.

With Fiona's arrival, the doctor's office has darkened at the edges, bleeding shadows in the corners and on the ceiling tiles. I see our time is running out. Not just on this session. On the girls.

Then I catch what Fiona wanted to show me: She's not motioning at the window; she's motioning at the desk beside the window. The pendant is on the doctor's desk. It's been here this whole time.

I point to it. "That's mine. Can I have that back?"

The doctor gazes over at her desktop, but she doesn't move closer.

"I'm glad you brought that up," she says. "What is this little collection?"

I don't understand what she means by "collection." There's one thing: the necklace. There's the necklace I wore around my neck, and that's all.

I can see it there, out of reach but in the same room with me now. Close enough that I could stand up, and take a few steps, and have it in my hands. I study it as if for the first time: The stone is gray but not completely gray; really, it doesn't look like a stone at all but a breath of smoke that's been caught inside a bubble of glass. I think of breaking it open, to see if that's what's in there. Because it can't be. Because it's heavy, heavier than something made of smoke should be, and when you hold it in your fist it grows hot, or your fist does, and if I had it now I'd practically be burning.

"It's just a necklace," I tell her.

"Is it?" she says oddly.

I watch as she raises herself from her plush chair and moves for the desk, gathering up some papers in her arms and my pendant on top. She walks it all over to me and places the pile neatly on the small table before the chair where she has me sitting. I'm about to grab for the necklace first, but she blocks my hand.

"Is that what you meant? This 'necklace'?" She points, and again I notice how she's careful not to touch it.

Her tone is confusing me. Also confusing is when she asks

me to describe it for her, as if she can't see it on the table before us, right here. I tell her about the smoky gray stone, which gleams in the light and swirls with movement, coming alive at the sound of my voice. It's like a mood ring, the kind they sell at gas-station registers for five bucks. But it never changes color, and you wear it around your neck instead of on your finger.

"Where did you get it?" she asks. "Did someone give it to you?"

I avoid her eyes. "Not exactly."

I'm worried she'll make me tell the whole story before I'm allowed to have it back. And if I told, I'm not sure I'd get to keep it.

"I . . . found it," I say weakly. What I *should* say is that it belongs to a missing girl. I should be confessing that it might be a clue, and should be turned over to police, if my wearing it against my skin all these weeks hasn't contaminated it. But if I could only get it back, I'd have my link to her again. To Abby. Because she hasn't finished telling me her story. None of the girls have.

"Lauren," the doctor says, waiting until I meet her eyes. "What I see there isn't a necklace like you're describing. What I see there is a rock."

A rock?

"A rock," she repeats. "A rock from the ground, which looks to be tied with a string."

I lower my eyes to the pendant, and there's the swirl and the gleam and the shimmer, and then a flatness and a stillness that wasn't there before, and a darkening that wasn't there before, and a rock. There's a rock. The pendant has turned into a rock.

I flash back to the side of Dorsett Road, the gully filled with snow where I found the pendant that night. I see my hand reaching out to pluck it from the ground and I see my fingers wrapping around a dirty rock from the side of the road and lifting this putrid thing into the palm of my hand like it's something beautiful. I see it clear, and my throat chokes up, and my eyes burn, and I'm not so sure anymore about anything.

"What did you do?" I shriek.

I have it now, in my hand, and it's still a rock. No matter how many times I turn it over, rubbing it in my fingers, it doesn't change back. It's as gone as the girls are, as gone as I should be soon, if the shadows gathering by my feet under the table are any indication. Gone, and this dirty, lumpy rock is all that's left.

"I didn't do anything to it," she says in a quiet voice. "You know that."

I put my head down, which is why I don't see the next thing she's trying to show me. There's the sound of shuffling papers and some movement on the table before me, and then she says, as if this is a portfolio showing at the end of art class and she wants to know my artistic influences regarding my still life of grapes: "Now tell me about these, Lauren."

I won't look.

"Your mother found them in your room, in your dresser,

she told me, and under your bed. Your mother said there were a lot more than what we have here, but she brought in a few to show me. Can you tell me about these posters, Lauren? These 'Missing' notices? It looks like you've printed yourself up quite a collection."

On the top is Shyann Johnston, gone missing from Newark, New Jersey, at age 17. Beside her is Yoon-mi Hyun, gone missing from Milford, Pennsylvania, at age 17, but I don't see Maura Morris's flyer, which bothers me, because I always like to keep them together. And then poking out from beneath Shyann is a girl I haven't found in the dream yet, and edging out from beneath Yoon-mi is a girl I looked for and didn't ever see and there are so many, all age 17, and these aren't even all of them.

I wonder what Fiona will have to say about this—or, more, what she'll tell me to say in my own defense. She stands far across the room, beside the potted plant the doctor accused her of being, and the look on her face is something terrible.

I've seen that look only once before, years ago, when she wanted to get me away from that little man and did the only thing she could think when his back was turned, which was hide me, fast. In the moment before she shoved me in the coat closet, I remember how she looked this sickened, this afraid.

I turn back to the doctor. Fiona has given me no words, so I have nothing to say.

It doesn't matter. The doctor has glanced at the clock. She gathers my girls off the table and holds them in her arms. This is enough, she says, for today. We'll talk some more next time.

We'll have time to go through all of this—we'll have lots and lots of time to talk in the coming weeks.

"*Weeks?*" I say. "I thought I was getting out on Monday."

She won't confirm if I am or not, only that we'll talk more soon. Then she tells me I can go now. I can go out with the others and line up now, because it's time for lunch.

– 56 –

THE girl who I witnessed yodeling when she first arrived has the other bed in my room now, but she sleeps with her face to the wall, so all I have is a view of the back of her head and the lump of her body. She sleeps day and night, night and day, and there's nothing that can wake her, not even when I bolt upright in the dark, shaken to consciousness by a bad feeling I can't name.

This isn't a dream—those have been taken from me. This is something else. I let my eyes adjust in the darkness and stare directly overhead, at the ceiling speckled with midnight static. It takes some moments before I start to be able to decipher them. The shadows.

The ceiling and walls are clean and unmarked where my roommate is sleeping—no shadows there. That's because they've all gathered on my side of the room, staining the wall beside my bed and clawing upward to bloom in the darkest spot directly over my pillow, where my head is now resting.

"You have to get out of here," a voice says.

It wasn't one of the girls' voices sidling through the slurred spaces of my mind. It wasn't Fiona's voice, her body appearing suddenly beside me in the bed, her mouth tilted to face my ear. It wasn't even my neighbor, spouting out a random lucid sentence in her sleep. It was my own voice. I'd spoken those words aloud. To myself.

– 57 –

JAMIE has come to visit, and he's driven my van. He tells me he'll go drop it off at my house after. A friend will come pick him up, and he'll leave the keys for me in my room.

I don't know why he's come all the way over here to tell me about his transportation arrangements, or why it's so important to him that I know he got my van off Karl's back lawn. He goes to the window of the common room to point out the van in the parking lot, and there it is, at the curb beside a low-hanging tree, black and menacing and mine, and if only I could be in it now, going anywhere, just driving.

Jamie's back is to me, and I can study the set of his shoulders under that old peacoat he's still got on. His thin legs in those big black boots. The curls of his hair sticking out under that knit cap. If this were the last time I ever got to see him, I'd be okay with it. This memory of him here at the window would be a decent one to hold on to.

Then he turns, and the memory I'm making of him shifts. The pain in his eyes is more emotion than I've felt myself in days. It's like they carved all feeling out of me and handed the gore over to him, as my guest, to carry through the halls on my behalf until his visiting time is up and the dinner hour begins and they make him leave empty-handed.

He takes a seat in a vinyl chair beside me and turns it so we face each other. "I've been thinking about what you said," he starts. "That night. When I drove you home."

It's kind of him, only I can't remember exactly what I said that night. Bits and pieces like that have been smudged away.

"So that really was what you were seeing?" he goes on. "That girl?" And that's how I remember I told him about Abby Sinclair.

I have the very strong feeling that he shouldn't say her name here, so I put my hand on his arm to stop him, the first touch we've had between us since he arrived. Unfortunately I've used my left arm, and some of the bandage peeks out from the edge of my sleeve. He sees it and freezes. I pull my arm away and put it back where it was.

Jamie and I aren't together anymore, and I'm not sure if we're friends, but we're something. He wouldn't be here if we were nothing. He starts talking about some random thing and while talking he fidgets—I think the other patients in the common room are making him uncomfortable—and it's while his mouth moves that time slows around him and he doesn't seem to notice. I'm slow enough to see through it, and what I can see is Fiona standing up from the chair she's been parked in all afternoon and walking with purpose over to us. She's behind Jamie's chair now. Now she's reaching out her arm and slugging a hand into Jamie's open coat pocket.

So slow, and also fast. Too fast. In no time, Fiona has picked Jamie's pocket and rescued my van keys.

I don't want her to bother me with this now. She's easier to deal with when she stays catatonic in the vinyl chair in the corner, barely blinking. Yet now she's dancing behind Jamie's back, making a game of it, and when he whips around to see what's got my attention she rises to her toes and throws them.

She doesn't know me so well. If she did, she'd know I can't catch any objects pitched straight at me, which is why I always do so dismally in the forced ball games during gym. But what she's done has surprised me, and in the shock of realizing she's tossed my keys over Jamie's head, I have this vision of my good arm shooting out on instinct and my good hand opening. I can see it like it's already been done and happened: the keys landing there, perfectly timed and well-aimed. It makes as much sense as if I'd simply reached out myself and plucked the keys from Jamie's gaping pocket when he wasn't looking.

I can't fault her. When Fiona sees an opportunity, she takes it. Maybe that's why she ran off with those two guys all those years ago. It wasn't either of them she wanted to be with—it was that they had a truck, they had the means to get her out of there, and so she gambled on it, in case she never had another chance again.

I don't mean to get Jamie in trouble, or leave him stranded, but if this is my only time to go free, shouldn't I take it? Shouldn't I catch the keys in my open hand and wait for a moment when no one's looking and find my way to the back stairs I remember taking in the fire drill? Shouldn't I follow her lead and go?

– 58 –

I'M 17 now, I have been since last month, and I think it must have changed me like it changed Fiona all those years ago. It's made me shrink away from the people in this world who care about me, and obsess over people I've never met in real life.

It's put me in danger, the way it did her. But it's also opened my mind, and my ears, and I don't think there's a way to close either now, after this. I've been changed down through to my bones.

Fiona likes me better this way, I can tell. We're the same age now, but, still, she wants to protect me. She won't say so aloud; she doesn't have to. It's clear from how she refuses to leave my side. I know she doesn't want the shadow-fingers in my hair, playing with the jagged wisps at the back of my neck, tugging a little, trying to get a good grip. She doesn't want the shadow-hands tightening in a stranglehold around my throat.

She's broken me out of the psych ward to *help* me, she says, to keep me from getting stuck in that house and ending up lost the way the rest of them did, the way *she* did, she reminds me.

And I did want out. It's the only way I can help the others. And Abby. Abby especially. Fiona keeps assuring me it's not too late.

The plan forms as we drive. Its pieces click together almost too easily, as if in her quiet stupor in the corner of the common room she was devising this outing all along. There's something we need to do; and tonight is the night we must do it.

There are certain things we agree on, philosophically: To save myself, we have to save the others. You can't have one and not both.

To save Abby, we must pinpoint her location first. Fiona assures me we're gaining on her; we're close.

We agree that the lost girls can't be left in that house. Whatever kind of limbo it may be—made of charred wood and tattered curtains, burned things and ash—it's still a place that's not here and not there. It's the in-between, and whoever's shown her face there is stuck in the smoke where no one can find her. Where no one can know her end.

Isn't it better for people to know? Fiona says. And I think of her, wrapped in mystery, how her parents still don't have a clue what became of her. And I think of Abby Sinclair, her fate unspoken, and I think of the others, their gaping stories without any definable finish. It's better to know, I decide, than to never.

Fiona and I agree that the hospital was not the place for

me. We agree I should be allowed to stop on the road for a burger and fries, because she might not be able to eat solid foods, but I still can, and we agree it was a good thing I only pretended to swallow my last round of pills. Fiona says her head feels clearer already.

We do agree on so much. But there are other things I sense Fiona wants to keep to herself until the time comes, possibly so she won't scare me off. Details, mostly. Like not mentioning exactly where we're headed. She directs me on a circular route through snowy back roads, avoiding fallen trees and numbered highways.

They'll be waiting for us, she says. All the girls will be; we just have to get ourselves to them. It's those pills. Whatever's in them kept me from visiting the dream. But it was also the hospital itself, the walls there that kept my dream-self from stepping in where it belonged. That, too, she says.

This has to be done, she says. This is the only way, she assures me when I ask if maybe I should look for a pay phone somewhere and call my mom. We can't call Mom yet. I won't be able to see the girls otherwise. But I have her, Fiona says, so it's okay. I have her, and she'll take me to them.

She stretches out in the front passenger seat of my van beside me, her legs up on the high dashboard and her feet pressed against the slope of the windshield like she might kick it out at any moment and cover us in glass, knowing it wouldn't hurt her, but it would hurt me. That's the old Fiona, I tell myself. She wouldn't do that to me now. She might tease, but she wouldn't actually kick.

She becomes more animated the farther we get from the hospital. Her voice is clear, her eyes bright. And there's a cunning curve to her lips sometimes as she points me down this road and that road, leading the way.

I keep an eye on her as I drive. It's late afternoon and already the light is falling fast, bringing with it a dark night. In that low light what I see is my former babysitter, the neighbor girl who ran off and left me suffocating in a coat closet for my own protection, a flash-point decision that proved to be the right one. Her flame-dyed hair reveals her natural dark roots as it did then. The *FU* scrawled on her thigh is now facing me, right side up.

Everything Fiona has said makes logical sense to me, until I see the road she has us driving. Dorsett Road is more narrow and twisting, coming from this end, which was closer to the side of the river where the hospital could be found, and the hills are all leading downward instead of up. The entrance to the Lady-of-the-Pines Summer Camp for Girls has been piled with snow, as if a snowplow gathered all the weather from every corner of Pinecliff and deposited it in this spot to keep me out.

I've slowed, but I haven't stopped. "Not here?" I ask.

Yes, here, she says. *Don't play dumb.*

There's nowhere to park near the gate, so I have to leave the van at the edge of the road, only half hidden in the trees, and I don't know how I'll get back out, with the way my tires are jammed in.

I shut off the engine. Still, I hesitate.

What? she says. *You were thinking we'd find that brick building with the gate? That we'd drive to some street and there it'd be? Popped up like a mushroom from your little dream?*

I don't nod. Then again I don't *not* nod.

She sighs, showing she's on her last nerve, then gazes out at the gate separating us from the campground.

It's where this all started, she says, waving her arm at it. *This sick, disgusting place where whatever happened to her happened. Do you want to help Abby or not?*

I nod. I do.

And the others?

I nod. All of them, I do.

Then we have to do it here. Where else?

– 59 –

SO much snow since I last visited. But not enough to keep us out.

We trudge through it to reach the gate. There, we discover that the broken chain on the fence has been replaced with a much thicker one, along with a more sturdy lock, a gold one, shiny new and too solid to get through without a big hammer. The top of the gate is still woven with coils of barbed wire, but Fiona is undeterred. I expect her to hoist herself up on the chain link and climb over—because how would the barbed wire cut through smoke, if that's what she's made of? How would it cut through a ghost, a memory, an idea? But she won't do it. She says we'll have to find another way in.

After maneuvering over a snowbank and circling widely past the first set of trees, we do find another entrance. Really, the whole pine forest is an entrance. We come in through the back way, past the offices and a maintenance shed made of gray concrete blocks. There are prints in the snow leading up to its door, there are prints to the compost pile, and there are prints heading into the darkened woods, but Fiona waves at me from far up the path. I'm slow.

Fiona isn't cold, but I am, and then, like it's been left out for me to find, I discover my own scarf lying in a knot in the snowy path—I must have dropped it weeks ago, though I don't remember walking this particular path at the edges of the campground. So how would I have dropped it here? It doesn't matter, because I pick it up and shake off the snow and wrap it twice around my neck. And it helps, a little.

It won't be so cold soon, Fiona tells me, making me shiver. I can't help but wonder if she means it won't be so cold after you die. If it's warm and snug when it's over, and the starshine glowing down over you warms your skin. If that's what she's telling me. If that's really what's about to happen tonight.

I follow her along a path and up a hill, made more difficult by the container of kerosene we discover and liberate from under a tarp near the firewood. She makes me carry the kerosene to the circle of stones, so we can build ourselves a fire. It's what will bring them out the quickest, she says. A fire, she says, to smoke out Abby and the rest of the girls.

A fire, like she was pointing to in the hospital. Fiona Burke has always wanted a fire.

I'm following her and doing what she tells me to do—just like that night when I was a kid. But also, I know she's right. I've seen the girls in reflective surfaces: mirrors and windows, and once in the exceptionally clean surface of a fork from the dishwasher. And I've seen the girls in small spaces, where they emerge only if no one's looking, and in the trees, where the shadows make good places to hide. But I don't know how being out in the open, with the pine forest all around and no roof above, will let them know it's safe to emerge. The only other way is the flicker of flame, the mask and smell of smoke. That's why we have to do it, Fiona says.

Once we do, they'll be lured out, and so will their stories. I think of them like apples bobbing to the surface of water, though these are real girls, and real girls' heads. Soon, families and friends will have closure. Mysteries will be untied and left out in the sun for the finding. I'll mourn every last one of them, hoping against hope I'm wrong.

And Abby Sinclair, the girl my thoughts keep returning to. The one girl whose end I can't see. Her story starts here, on this closed-off tract of land in the pines. She'll have to step out of the woods once the fire starts. How could she ignore us now?

When the fire catches the kindling and begins to burn, I warm my hands over the growing flames. I don't let myself think about Jamie, who I ditched at the hospital. Or my mom, who's surely gotten a phone call that I'm not there and is in a panic trying to figure out where I could be. I mean, I think about them, but only for a moment. Fiona stops me. She wants me to see . . .

At this high point, looking over the campground, all the dark, empty cabins can be viewed. The mess hall, the arts-and-crafts cabin, the chapel, the empty flagpole flapping its loose string in the billowing wind. Abby Sinclair spent her last days here, and now—side-eying Fiona, who drifts fire-bright at the edge of the stones—I wonder if this is where I'm about to spend mine.

The fresh night air clears my head. It's cold, but it's cleansing, and I can think again the way I used to.

I stand up. I pat my pockets, feeling for a cell phone, and remember I had no cell phone at the hospital, so I have no cell phone here. For a second, I'm on a frozen, windy hill in a vacant, forgotten place on a late January night and I don't know why.

Then I see what Fiona has been trying to show me.

The snow has disappeared to make way for the sidewalk. The cracks are the same, and I avoid stepping on them, and the black iron gate swings open with a shriek and a creak, the way it always does. The stairs don't crumble under my weight the way I sometimes suspect they might as I approach the door, and the door pushes open, because it's never kept locked, not for any of us, not for me.

Inside the house is a wall of heat, from the fire. It climbs high to eat a gaping hole out of the ceiling. I duck when the chandelier drops and falls. I'm so deep in it, the heat should blister my skin and catch and blaze up my clothes, but I can't feel a thing. It doesn't touch me.

That's when they start to come out, one girl from behind the banister, and one girl from another room. One from within the folded curtains, and one from the floor, since there's no furniture to sit on. They come from upstairs, where their rooms are, and they gather here with me.

There's a flicker, and I lose sight of the house and can see only the quiet campground again. The fire burns from a pit of ash and sticks and branches at my feet.

But then the night flickers back to what it was, to what Fiona knew would happen. They've been smoked out, as she said they would be. Smoke clears to show that the girls are here. The girls I haven't seen since getting sent away. Now they surround me.

Natalie Montesano, who thought for sure her friends would come back for her, who never thought they'd leave her behind in the crushed car on the sleek, steep road after the accident, but when they did, she took off and she didn't look back. Even when she wanted to.

Shyann Johnston, who sometimes fantasizes she could glide through the school hallways again, but this time with a sawed-off shotgun tucked under her arm, because they'd see it and they'd shut their mouths. And when the hallways emptied, she'd put the gun down on the floor because it's not like she'd ever use it and she'd get a drink from the water fountain, which she's never been able to do before without getting shoved in, and she'd smile.

Isabeth Valdes, who thinks she wouldn't have gotten in the strange car if she hadn't been carrying all those books in the rain, and she wouldn't have been carrying all those books if she didn't have three tests on Monday, so if she didn't have three tests on Monday she might still be here.

Madison Waller, who bought herself three fashion magazines for the bus ride into the city, who's practicing her face for the camera even now, even though nobody who's anybody can see her.

Eden DeMarco, who only wanted to see the Pacific Ocean, who only wanted to touch it with her toes, that's all.

Yoon-mi Hyun and Maura Morris, who both think love changes a person for the better, and both agree that it *is* possible to find your soul mate at age 17, no matter what your parents may say when you bring the girl home.

Kendra Howard, who expects she's the bravest, baddest, most kickass girl those guy friends of hers have ever known, and bets they still spend nights talking about her, still toast her memory over cold beers, saying how high she leaped, how far she fell, how she had balls, and she'll never be forgotten, RIP.

Jannah Afsana Din, who believes starting a new life with Carlos in Mexico wouldn't have been as impossible as people said—they could have lived on the beach together and raised chickens; they could have sold the little cakes she makes on the streets and survived, even flourished, even found happiness.

Hailey Pippering, who's done some things she can't say out loud because it'd make her sick; she only wants her parents to know that she didn't run away this time, even if they think she did. This time, she wanted to stay.

And Trina Glatt, who always meant to track down the father who abandoned her when she was a baby, so she could throttle him and blame him for every bad thing that ever happened to her, but also, secretly, so she could hug him, and admit she missed him, and if he invited her to a baseball game, or to the backyard, to throw a Frisbee around or something, she'd probably go. She'd tell him that, if she could.

There are a lot of things the girls would tell the people they left behind, if they could.

All those girls. So many to keep track of tonight, my head swirling. Only, something's missing. Something's not right here. The circle of girls comes close and then weaves tighter around me. I can't tell if I'm at the center or if the fire is.

The night flickers.

What I thought were the soot-streaked walls of the house are the tall stalks of the pine trees; the staircase to the upper floors is the side of the mountain leading up to the looming ridge; the ceiling doesn't end because it's the night sky. Pinpricks of flurries rain down, as soft as ash but cool on my cheeks. My surroundings keep shifting: I'm at Lady-of-the-Pines, in the ring of stones where the campers toast marshmallows in summer. Then I'm in the house in my dream. My dream is here, or this place has become a part of it; I don't know the difference.

The girls' hands are tightly clasped, though there's no singing. This isn't summer camp. This isn't the kind of night for belting out "Row, Row, Row Your Boat" and holding a flashlight to ghoul up your face and tell ghost stories. The ghosts tonight have already told their stories.

I cast my eyes around the fire. I still can't shake that something's not how it's supposed to be. Madison's bright-blond hair seems wild in the fire, and there's an uncountable number of stars in her eyes, but it's not her. Trina shoots me a threatening glare, but it's not her, either.

Then I know: Yes, the girls have come out. Some (Jannah, Hailey) have only recently become familiar and I barely know their full stories yet, and some (Natalie, Shyann) are girls I feel like I've known since first grade. But there's one whose face I can't find in the roaring glow, one I keep looking for in the hissing, dizzying circle of smoke, thinking I must have missed her. Thinking they're moving too fast, and if they'd only slow down or stop so I could see her.

Where's Abby?

She doesn't step out of the smoke. She still hasn't come. I haven't gotten her out. All this, and I haven't found her.

I turn to Fiona to ask what happened. I see Fiona now, at the edge of the ring, not holding a hand, not taking a step inside, only watching. Only waiting. An observer to a disaster about to occur, standing back so she can wipe her hands of it after.

She wants me to join the girls. It's not fair that I've been living my life out in the daylight, driving my van down any road I want, walking into any house I want, seeing the people who love me at any moment, on any day. She's forgotten I've been in the hospital, unable to have any of these things, either. Because surrounding us is an entire sky made of shadows, and there's no escaping your fate.

I'm 17. Like she was, like they all were.

Then Fiona meets my eyes, and I question my distrust of her. I question everything.

Because no, she didn't bring me here to get rid of me. She expected Abby to come out, just as I did. She's looking at the fire, waiting and wondering where she is, too.

Then she makes a decision.

She grabs my arm. I can't tell if I'm feeling her touch or if what's come back is a memory of her touch, from before. Her hand has a hard grasp of my arm, reminding me of that night when I was still eight and she was 17 as she is now, when she grabbed me and shoved me in the closet. But tonight it hurts so much more than it did then because she's grabbing my left arm, my bad arm.

We've got to burn the place down, she says.

No, no, wait, we can't yet, I try to tell Fiona. Abby's not here. Aren't we supposed to find Abby first, and only after can we—

But I'm not fast enough to catch her. Fiona's racing down the hill with the bottle of kerosene in her arms. It's too late. She will start the destruction without me.

– 60 –

SHE'S telling me to do it. She's telling all of us, pulling our strings and giving commands. Soon the girls have sticks gathered from the outskirts of the woods that they raise to light the way, and soon the kerosene can is in my good arm and the spout is open and the liquid is dribbling out on my toes.

I start to wonder: Is it too late for Abby? Fiona is acting like it might be. And if we destroy this place, this last place Abby stayed before she disappeared, will we set her free? Maybe we will. Maybe doing this will set us all free. Even me.

First go the cabins closest to the hill. We set fire to the empty beds. Next is the camp office, a small building with a wraparound porch, and we run a line of kerosene all around the porch, from end to end. The canteen is a tiny outhouse of a structure and we leave a fire at one corner, like a bird's nest. The canoes go up as if they were doused already and were just waiting to be set alight.

Smoke is in the air the way it always is in the dream; it smells just the same.

But then something's not the same. Something's off, and calling to me through the smoke. A voice. And not a voice in my head or a whisper at my ear or the girls with the torches at my back.

This is an actual voice shouting out into the actual night. Someone is on the campground with me.

I'm afraid it's a delusion, that my mind has shattered and scattered all over the snow. And when he reaches me and he's been running and the panic colors his face and he says, "Lauren! Are you okay? Lauren?" it takes me a long moment to realize he's not a ghost or an escaped piece of a dream. He's Jamie.

Jamie's been here with me once before, so I should have guessed he'd know where to find me.

He's shouting. At me. "Did you do this? What did you do?"

He means the fires. When I glance back behind him I expect to see a tidal wave of fire, the coiling, curling lip edged with girls holding torches as tall as their arms will lift, so if they reach high enough they could catch the night on fire. They could destroy the whole world they've been stolen from. They could end everything.

But there are only the fires in the places where I set them myself, and there is a trail of kerosene in the snow that no one's dropped a match to light. The fires are burning, and letting off black puffs of smoke, but they're not near as large as I thought they would be.

The girls are nowhere to be seen.

"Why'd you do this?" he says quietly, taking one wide step closer to me.

And I take the next step, to close the gap. "I had to," I say, the words thick in my throat, forcing me to choke them out. Also the smoke, coughing from it. Making it difficult to speak. "She . . . They . . ."

He holds me, and I have his arms around me again. I know what I should do is shove him into the pines and tell him to start running. *Get away from me, Jamie. I'm burning. Get away before I burn you, too.*

But there's the way his body feels pressed to mine. The way his fingers brush away my tears when I didn't even know I was making any tears and the way his mouth says the things that calm the blazing fury in my head and there's everything we used to have between us, not dead and trampled in the snow, but here, somehow still among the living.

I have his voice in my ear, and it's not a phantom, not a demon, not a hallucination. His voice that I lock on to so it's all I'm hearing.

"It's okay," is what he's saying. "Look at me. Lauren, look at me. They're not real. They're not real. *I'm* real. I'm right here."

– 61 –

WE break apart when we notice a flicker of movement down the hill. There's a figure in the distance who I think at first must be Fiona herself, come out to lure me away from Jamie and back together with her and only her, the way it was when this night started. But the figure is in dark colors and appears much larger than Fiona ever was, even in my memories.

It's a man. And I'm afraid I know who it is.

"You called the cops on me!" I hiss at Jamie, horrified, but he appears just as shocked as I am, pulling me off the pathway and into a thicket of trees.

"I didn't, I swear," he says, close up against my ear. "Quiet."

"But you called my mom." I whisper it as if I can worm my way into his head for the answer, the way I have with the girls. I watch his face as he stares down the hill.

"Yeah," he admits, "of course I called her."

"So she must have called *them*," I say, indicating the man at the bottom of the hill. "The cops."

The dark-clad figure's movements against the white snow are impossible to miss. The man looks up, toward the fires—he doesn't seem to see us hiding in the trees. Witnessing the fires blazing appears to make him move even faster. But not toward them. Toward something else.

He's headed for the maintenance shed, along the path where I found my fallen scarf. My stomach sinks when I realize: the footprints in the snow, not an animal's, a man's. The one who called himself Officer Heaney. Is that what he said, *Officer* Heaney, or did I mistake him for something he wasn't? Did I assume?

Jamie echoes what's coursing through my mind. "You think that's the same guy?"

I nod.

"I've been thinking. About him. That night. I'm not sure he was an officer . . . A security guard, maybe. But police?"

"My mom said he wasn't," I say.

Whatever his name is, whoever he is, we watch him struggling with the locks on the door of the maintenance shed. Pushing the door open, disappearing inside.

"You saw that, too?" I say quietly to Jamie, wanting to be absolutely sure. My eyes can't be trusted. I'm not positive if any part of me can be trusted from now on.

Jamie only nods, watching. He stays very, very silent. His body straightens and I swear he goes cold, colder than the snow we're knee-deep in right now.

Near us, the fires continue to burn. But if we walk the path down and out of the campground, we'd have to pass the maintenance shed. I know now that the man isn't a police officer, and I feel very sure that we don't want him to see us.

He comes out carrying some things in his arms—papers? A bag, or some kind of blanket? We're not close enough to see what—and then he turns fast, down a side path and into the trees, which I guess is another way to get on and off the campground that I didn't know about. He's gone, just like that. He came here only to take some things from that shed, and he left with the fires still burning.

Jamie's focus is all on me now, saying we have to go. We have to call 911 about the fires, and we have to get me out of here, and he's torn, I can tell, not sure what to do first. I'm reeking with kerosene, my face surely blackened by fire smoke and ash—I can tell when I cough and wipe my mouth and a streak of soot comes off on my sleeve. But when we reach the bottom of the hill, when we get to the turn that will take us to the camp exit, where my van and whatever car Jamie used to get himself here is parked, I stop and ground my feet in. The door to the maintenance shed is no longer locked. In fact, it hangs partly open, as if there's nothing in there to hide.

Of course I have to see.

Jamie doesn't understand; he's still pulling me away, saying we need to get out of there, I'll be caught, they'll know I did this, I'll be arrested for arson, and more things I can't hear. The fires are burning. And yet I won't budge.

I feel sure I'm going to find someone inside that shed.

I imagine her: Abby Sinclair, in the flesh. I imagine with so much of me that I even begin to think I can hear her voice. That she's in there. That I've brought her to life. That now she's calling out—for help, from me.

Fiona Burke was right: Setting the fires has led me to her, the real girl she is apart from her Missing poster. It's happened as Fiona told me it would. Even Jamie should be able to see.

But now the image before me flickers, and it's not the dreamscape that comes back to me this time. It's the questions.

In a rush I think about what the doctor said. Those nurses at the hospital, the ones who couldn't remember my name, who gave me the pills in the little paper cup. Does this mean they're right about me?

This girl shouting for my help, she's a voice in my head—that's what they'd tell me. They'd tell me Fiona Burke is a figment of my imagination, one grown from a traumatic night in my past and turned real. They'd tell me all the girls are visions I've brought to life from the Missing notices I found online and on bulletin boards and in the post office. Those girls may indeed be real, but my dreams that star them, my conversations among them, the memories of theirs I've walked through, all of that, every detail and flash of color and cough of smoke, every ounce, is a delusion I've concocted. Isn't that what the doctor would tell me? These girls don't know I exist. They don't know I've claimed them and made them a part of my life, sleeping with their photocopied faces under my mattress every night. That this is my psychosis.

That I was—and continue to be—making this all up.

But then I have to answer the questions with more questions: What if that voice calling for help *is* real?

What if I've found Abby Sinclair, who went missing from this place months ago and who's been kept here, a prisoner, all this time? What if I made everything up except for this?

All I have to do is push open that door to find out.

And if there's no one inside, if there's no body attached to the voice that's screaming and I turn around and I feel my throat and I discover it's my own voice, my delusion, my dream come to violent life, I'll admit I'm wrong.

I'll be what they say I am, and I'll disown all I've seen. I'll swallow the pills for the rest of my natural-born life.

-62-

WHEN the door opens to silence—and darkness; and no girl, alive or not alive; no girl at all—I think I've lost everything. Most of all, my mind.

Because I was wrong. Everything about me is wrong.

Maybe that's why I'm not able to see the shine of it for some time. But when I do—when it catches the light somehow, when it flashes, brighter than the fire outside and brighter than all the snow—my breath goes with it.

It fell, I guess, on the ground, when he was carrying out whatever he had in his arms. It fell facedown, splayed open on the concrete.

I am holding it in my hands when I hear the sirens. When the fire truck comes and the police after that. I am holding it in my hands.

It's made of plastic; it's purple, gaudy, and shiny, with glitter sandwiched between the translucent decorative sleeves. Its pockets are stuffed full, so the single snap doesn't work to keep it closed. And inside there are pictures of her and her friends, and a mass of loose change that spills out all over my boots, nickels mostly, and there's an ID card from a Catholic school in New Jersey, and ticket stubs and clothing tags and little scrawled notes for things she may have wanted to remember and a dollop of chewed gum making some of the contents stick together forever.

It's Abby Sinclair's wallet, and I know this before it comes open because of what her former camp counselor told me about the things she took with her the night she went to meet Luke. And I know simply because I *know*, in my gut. As if she reached out from the ether and told me so herself. I knew it as soon as I had the thing in my hands.

It's over soon after I find it.

The fires lured them all here, and with them comes all the noise.

The shouting. A dog barking. Sirens. The door being kicked all the way open. The men bursting in. Hands up. Knees in snow. The fire truck, the firemen. Lights. Confusion. The wallet being taken from me. A girl's name on my lips. Police on the way, and then here. My mom. The feel of my mom's intact and pounding heart through her coat. Lights. A blanket wrapped around me. The tight ties around my wrists. Questions. Losing sight of Jamie. The backseat of a police car. Lights. The sound of fires being put out. The darkness as the lights go down. The remembered feel of that wallet, that old chewed piece of gum. The smell of kerosene on my clothes, in my hair. The taste of it on my tongue.

Out the window: the calm, blue sign that says LADY-OF-THE-PINES SUMMER CAMP FOR GIRLS fading away and the quiet oasis of my mind that shrinks off with it.

Then pine trees. The pine trees of Dorsett Road as I'm carried away. The same stretch of pine trees Abby must have seen the last night she was here.

– 63 –

THERE are things I don't understand, things I was a part of without even knowing I was taking part. I guess I was one girl trying to make sense of them. And trying to fight them, in a way that made sense only to me.

"How did you know to go looking in that shed?"

I'm asked this again and again, the night of the fires and in the days after. By firemen. By police. By my doctor, once I was returned to the hospital. By my own mom. Never by Jamie, though. He doesn't ask me how I knew to stay and search in there—I guess because he saw the force that propelled me that night, couldn't help but see the living fire of it in my eyes.

Because that's the thing: I thought it was over. I thought finding something that belonged to her (and the glittery purple plastic wallet with her school ID inside did belong to her; police verified that) meant the worst I could imagine, and I did imagine. I thought it was too late. I thought she was dead. I held something of hers in my hands and then I held only my hands in my hands, when they took the wallet for evidence, my arms wound around my back and zip-tied there as I waited inside the squad car to be taken to the station and charged with arson. I told myself awful things. Convinced myself she was gone. My voices told me, or some voiceless part of me told me, or the synapses in my head broke open and trotted out a song-and-dance made up of kicking legs and flapping lies to tell me. It doesn't matter how I thought I knew.

I was wrong.

Turns out Abby Sinclair was still alive.

Officer Heaney was no police officer—he's a man who worked maintaining the campgrounds, who visited often during the off-season, who lived nearby. He's a man who was working at Lady-of-the-Pines the summer Abby Sinclair disappeared. What was found in that maintenance shed, what I handed over to police, with my descriptions and Jamie's of the man we saw, led to uncover who he was, and where he lived, and what—*who*—he'd stolen.

I was told she knew him. All the Lady-of-the-Pines girls did. So when she was walking back on foot after overhearing Luke on the phone with another girl, after stumbling off her bike and leaving it behind at Luke's and rushing off into the dark to get away from him, she ran into this man on the road. I don't know where on the road; no one told me so specifically. But I can imagine it.

Like Isabeth, she got in the car. Even though, like Shyann, she wanted to run off and hide forever in the trees, because her heart was broken. Like Jannah, she went off with someone she thought she could trust. And like Hailey, she was assumed to have run away . . . even though all this time she was really missing.

The car pulled over, and the man leaned out an arm. "Hey, hey, Abby— Your name's Abby, right? What are you doing out there? You okay?"

And she was nervous at first—anyone hearing a car stop short on a lone road at night would be—and, besides, she didn't want him to turn her in to the counselors. She'd get kicked out. But his face was friendly enough, and she'd talked to him before, that one time the sink got clogged full of hair and he came to Cabin 3 to fix it. Not to mention, she'd skinned her knee when she fell off the bicycle in Luke's driveway, before she left the bike there and took off on foot, and she still had another mile to walk back to camp with her knee bleeding.

He said he wouldn't tell on her. He said he'd help her sneak back in.

I wish Abby didn't believe him and accept the ride that night, but she did. She did.

Parts of this I tell myself, and parts of this are unalterably true—news articles and police officers have told me.

I don't know what happened to her all the months she was kept by him, and I can't make myself ask. The horror of it gouges me open.

How easy it was for the man to get away with taking her and keeping her—because everyone so quickly believed she ran away. It was never questioned, not by anyone who knew her, not by friends or family, not by the girls she spent her summer with, not by the boy she kissed under the stars.

It was questioned by no one—until me.

At some point, and I don't know if it's the night of, or a different day, someone approaches to tell me something important. One police officer remembers me from when I visited the station asking about Abby Sinclair and her bike. He comes over when they're processing me for setting the fires, and he takes one of my hands, even though it's got ink from the fingerprinting on it, and he tells me some things.

Thanks to me convincing her grandparents, Abby's file was reopened. He says that my visit to New Jersey, not to mention the letter I sent Abby's grandparents—creepy as it was, upsetting them as much as it did—did have them looking into it, but it was my finding the wallet that broke open the case. My poking around, my insisting no one give up looking, that's what did this, he says. He was telling me I helped save a missing girl.

I don't see her myself, but I think of her. I am always thinking of her.

She's Abby Sinclair, 17, of Orange Terrace, New Jersey. Abby with the cubic zirconia in her nose. Abby who's afraid of clowns. Abby who can't whistle. Abby who chews her nails, just the ones on her thumbs. Abby who can tap-dance. Abby who doesn't mind when it rains. Or maybe she does mind. Maybe she isn't like any of those things, since I made that all up.

But she is Abby Sinclair, for sure. She was reported missing September 2 and her case was officially closed on January 29.

She's 17 still, and she's alive.

So how did I know? The truth is that I only hoped. That's what I did. There was no disembodied voice whispering the truth of what happened to Abby Sinclair into my waiting and willing ear. And if there had been, if ghosts walked and communicated with me, if lost girls really did reach out to me across the smoky abyss—I wonder, wouldn't I have known the truth so much faster? I could have saved her two months ago.

I could have helped end this before the fires even got set.

Which is what I keep going back to: the fires. It's all I dream of now, since the house is gone. This time it's not wishful and imaginary, it's a memory of something I did with my own two hands.

Besides, I know it now for what it was: a girl's attempt to call for help. A need to be listened to. To be *heard*.

I know what she was saying—what I was saying, even if I had trouble articulating it in words then:

Don't give up.

Don't give up on her, or any of them. Keep looking. Always *keep looking.*

No girl—no missing girl, no runaway—deserves to be given up on, just like I wouldn't want anyone to give up on me.

The blaze was red and ferocious in the snowed-out night. Before the fire truck came to douse it and darken it, it was brilliant, it was blinding. It was unforgettable. No one could ignore it. I bet it woke people in their beds at night, so they stood at their windows wondering. I bet people could see that fire from miles and miles away.

THREE MONTHS LATER

IT'S my first week back home. The insurance company decided my stay at the hospital was over, even if the doctors hadn't, and I was signed out and left in my mom's care as of Monday. There are things outside our small house that look different now, and I'm spending my time noticing. There are colors that are brighter, and patches of sky that seem lower, and there's a tree on the lawn that I don't remember seeing here before.

Since I've been gone, spring has come to Pinecliff, and our cat, Billie, has lost some weight and is shedding tufts that drift through the rooms. In the quiet, it seems as if the house has been capsized and I've woken underwater, seaweed and minnows slowly circling me. I know it's only Billie shedding, but I let my imagination idle as I watch a bit of hair float by. There are other things I notice: how my bedroom looks smaller than I remembered, the bed taller. Things like that. But I'll get used to them.

Another one of my letters got turned in to police, the postmark tracked down and pointed to me, which is how my mom discovered I'd written to more than Abby's grandparents. I'd been writing other girls' families, too, when I could find them, telling them what their missing daughters and sisters and nieces would have wanted them to know. The things the girls told me in my dreams, when they let me coast through their memories, a visiting observer who never tampered with their lives but who paid attention, who remembered. I'd write to a girl's mom, saying she meant to visit her in prison, even one time. I'd write to a girl's boyfriend, saying she still loved him and she didn't ditch him at the gas station and she did want to go to Mexico with him, if only she could. My mom wanted to know how many of these letters I'd sent, whose mailing addresses I'd found and what stories I told them, even if I had the addresses and the names wrong, even if my letters never reached who I intended.

When I confessed, I could see from her face how serious she thought this was.

"These are real girls," she told me carefully. "Those girls you found online, they *are* real. With real lives. And real people at home wondering what happened to them. But the part about you knowing the girls, talking to them . . . Lauren, sweetie, you know that's not . . ."

"Real," I said for her, so she wouldn't have to use such a dangerous word. "Mom, I'm sorry. I know that now."

It hurts to know. It mortifies me. But all of what my mom says is true; the doctors have made me face it and say it out loud and admit to everything.

Since that night, I have a court date coming up because of the fires, and Jamie does, too, which isn't fair, but my lawyer says I can explain everything when I plead guilty. He expects community service, since he'll be arguing that I was mentally impaired.

And Abby has gone back home to New Jersey. I've watched what I could about her on the news, as much as they'd let me, and I recall being hung up on the fact that she didn't look the way she did in my mind. Her face was mostly the same as the one on the Missing poster, but her body was different. She was shorter than I thought, from those visions of her gliding away on the Schwinn, and her hands didn't look the way I remember her hands looking, and her hair was curlier and, from the side, there was an unrecognizable slope to her nose. Also, when she spoke for the cameras in an interview my mom saved for me to watch, I was struck by how her voice wasn't the voice I heard in my head. It was the voice of a stranger.

But she was found, and she was alive. And the man—whose name wasn't even Heaney—was arrested, charged with a list of crimes my mom wouldn't read aloud to me from the newspaper. His trial is coming up soon.

This is not a part of the story I invented. Not pieces of my mind come loose. Not flashes from dreams. People keep assuring me that Abby was found, and they have the same response every time I ask, so I'm choosing to believe them. It's not like the rock that still hasn't turned back into the pendant, even when I look at it from all angles, upside down, sideways, with lights on and lights off. It's still a rock I found on the side of the road.

Also, I have the letter now. It was waiting for me when I was released. I think my mom held on to it for a long time, not sure if she should show me. I'm glad she did, even though it shoves me right back into everything whenever I read it.

Her handwriting slants forward, and her round letters bubble, making me think she was a cheerful person, or is trying to be. She used green pen and a piece of ruled paper from a notebook instead of stationery. I've let my fingers run over the ridges on the back of the paper, feeling where her pen pressed down, feeling for the words that were heaviest to write, the worst ones. I like that she wrote it all down. She could have e-mailed, and this is so much better.

Dear Lauren, she starts. *I keep trying to write you this, but it's hard because I don't know what to say. The police told me what you did. My grandma told me you visited. I know we never met or anything and this feels really weird, but I need to say thank you.*

She goes on, telling me how hard life has been since she's come home, fitting back in with friends who don't understand, who look at her differently now, and how she tries to forget things, but she can't and wonders if she ever can. I'm not sure how much she knows about me—she doesn't say explicitly—but she seems to be aware that I've been sick and that I was sent away. There's a line in her letter about hoping I get to come home soon and that I feel better.

She signs the letter Abby, not Abigail, like we're friends.

I'm not sure if I'll ever be able to write her back.

I fold up the letter again and slip it into the drawer of my nightstand. I'm looking out the window and I'm thinking how happy I am she's alive and then I'm thinking how I'm still alive myself. Still intact and in this body and breathing through these lungs. Still here. Two twists I wasn't expecting.

It's a Thursday now maybe, or it could be a Friday. I don't have to go back to school until next week. My mom has taken a semester leave, saying she can't juggle classes on top of her job and wanting to be home to take care of me right now. I joke with her about how she could have asked for extra credit, since she can do a home-study of a mental disorder under her own roof and hopefully I'm enough to fill a thesis paper, but she barely cracks a smile.

I shouldn't be joking about it. She doesn't even want me to say the word in front of her (schizophrenia), though doesn't she know how an unsaid word (schizophrenia) holds more power the longer it's kept from touching your tongue? The fact that it's unsaid, and that it could be years before I get an official diagnosis, makes me wonder about it all the more. In the night, I tiptoed downstairs to pore through her college psychology textbooks, seeing what the "positive" and "negative" symptoms are and ticking off how many I've had. I also read about how it doesn't go away, how there's no cure. People who have this spend their whole lives on antipsychotic medications to keep the delusions and the voices away. And even then, the meds don't always work. The cocktail can change often—it's never the same mix for everyone. There's no way to know.

It's realizing all this that scares me more than anything supernatural ever could. The concept of a ghost, I can understand; the misfiring synapses of my brain, I can't. One is outside and apart from me and something I could run from, but the other *is* me. The other is what I am. So I've been thinking on it for all these months, and I've decided.

I just have to play along whenever my mom's around.

Now she's fluffing my pillows. She's asking me what I think of couscous for dinner tonight. I'm not sure if that's what we want to eat, but I say it's fine.

After my mom watches me swallow today's dose of meds, she says she'll go make dinner in the kitchen now. But she lingers, at the doorway, blinking her eyes so they don't water. She does this more and more, this staring, like she can't believe I exist. It's how I used to look at the girls, before I got used to them.

"You can go," I tell her. "I'll just be in here, reading." I hold up a novel I've barely started because I can't pay attention to books right now beyond page one. I use my bad arm to lift it, and she flinches, even though it's just a few Band-Aids now, only to keep the scars covered.

I've been wanting to tell her so many things about how lucky I am to have her, but I can't seem to get out the words, so I haven't said any of that yet. I only hope she already knows.

She's gotten a new tattoo, to commemorate this, which is a strange thing to do, but she says it's a healthy way to handle trauma. It's not on her chest. That's still clean—I keep checking. It's on her arm. So when I see her walk out of the room, I also catch my own face staring back at me, like a stunted anthropomorphic owl perched on her shoulder. I also always check to make sure the beauty mark is on the correct side of her face, so I'm sure the person wearing my image is really her. It says something to me, that she's done this, tattooed me on her body. It says she'll be here for me no matter what, and I know for a fact that some of the girls can't say that about their mothers. Not all girls can.

If I'd been one of the missing, my mom would have never given up on me. Never.

Once she's gone, I don't touch the book. I watch the window for some time. She's closed the window again, when she came up here, but I go over and push it open once more. I have to leave it open. The tree I don't remember, the one right outside my window, rustles with the lightest touch of wind. It's an oak, I think. It's older than I am and will still be here long after me.

There's a knock on my bedroom door, even though the door is open. I startle, thinking thoughts I shouldn't. When I look, I see it's a girl, just a different kind altogether from what I expected.

She steps in the room, the freshman, Rain Patel, who lives nearby and has somehow finagled herself into bringing me packets of homework for next week, even though we barely spoke in school. "Your mom sent me up," she says.

She gives me a stack of papers and a new book for AP English, though I'm so far behind I'm probably not in advanced placement anymore, and then she bursts out with some random updates, like how Deena Douglas got mono and the wrestling team won some trophy at state.

Then she weaves awkwardly around my room, not wanting to leave yet, lifting things off my dresser and setting them back down. I don't stop her. But I do flinch when she finds it and holds it in her hand, playing with its smooth, round surface. "What's this?" she asks.

"Oh, just something. Something I found."

"Like on the beach? When my mom and my dad and my brother and I went to the shore, I swear I collected, like, *hundreds* of stones like this. Okay, maybe not hundreds, but you know. I liked ones in prettier colors, though . . . white, blue with speckles, pinkish pink. This one's just gray."

In the mirror, for an instant, what she's holding in the palm of her hand goes bright, like it's no rock. It dances with a smoky, sultry light. Then it's dark again.

"Put that down," I say.

"It's special," Rain says, setting it back on the dresser. "I can tell. Where'd you get it?"

It's so special, I can't seem to get rid of it. Maybe I'm supposed to keep it, give it a permanent place in my life to commemorate my trauma, like my mom has hers. Or maybe I'm meant to wear it until I know for sure it's over. Then I can bury it in the yard. Or throw it on the tracks when a freight train goes past, though even the wheels of a train couldn't crush it. Maybe sometime this weekend I should drive over to the bridge and throw it in the Hudson. No one could get to it then.

"It's from here," I say. "From right here in Pinecliff."

"Oh," she says, seeming disappointed. She glances in the

mirror because that's where I've been staring, and then she comes closer, sitting on the edge of the bed.

She whispers it: "Are you seeing them *right now*? Your mom told my mom, so I know about the, *you know*." Her dark eyes are very wide, the long lashes creating a dusting of spiderwebs on her cheeks. I can tell by the way she's edged forward, inching along the end of my bed, that she wants me to say I'm seeing them. The lost girls.

I shake my head.

"Oh," Rain says. "Okay."

Her face falls. I think she's the only person who believes that I've seen ghosts. She must think I'm psychic, a medium for the undead or something, like the blue woman on the elevator all those months ago might say we are. For this, I like Rain a tiny bit more. I look at her carefully. She's so young, so open. All I can see on her face is that any possible thing in the world could happen to her—her fate is completely unwritten. That's not me being psychic; that's me being kind and not corrupting her with what I know.

There's another knock on the door, and then he's here. He seems surprised to find Rain in my room with me, also disappointed he hasn't found me alone. But he still comes in; he still leans up against the wall beside the bed.

There's a difference in what Rain believes about me, and what Jamie believes. Rain *wants* to believe any wild thing to the point that I could tell her there is, right this very moment, a shrunken shadow crawling on the ceiling directly over her head, about to bound down to her shoulders, about to come and curse her future, and she'd believe it because she wants to believe. But she only wants the horror-movie shiver, so delicious because it can be turned off when the lights go up and the movie's over.

Jamie believes that *I* believe, and that's all that matters to him. He knows what the doctors have said; my mom told him. Besides, I can tell by the way he looks at me sometimes, the unsaid diagnosis scuttling beneath his lips. How terrifying that must be for him, to not know for sure what's happening to me yet.

"Oh hi, Jamie," Rain says, blushing. "I should go."

She slips out and pulls the door closed with her, so now it's just Jamie and me.

He edges closer until he's beside the bed. I move my book so he can climb up, and he does, leaning against the pillows propped up behind me so our shoulders touch. "So glad you're home," he says. He takes my bad arm and holds my hand.

"Me too," is all I say. I don't apologize again about the arson charges; he's told me to stop bringing it up. I don't say how even though I'm home from the hospital, that doesn't mean I'm cured. Because I'll never be the way I was before, and there's a reason I know this, there's a reason I hold it like a whisper in my ear, hearing it again and again, even when I tell myself not to listen. There's a reason.

"How're you feeling?" he asks, his fingers laced in my fingers, his wrist against my bad wrist.

"Tired," I say. "It's the meds. I don't know if they're helping, except that they make me tired. So tired I can't even read this book."

He sits up straighter. "They're helping," he says. "They're not helping?"

"Sure. They've helped a lot." I turn to the window.

"What's out there?" he asks. "What are you looking at?" Whenever I look at anything, anything at all, he's going to ask me what I'm seeing. I need to get used to it.

"Just that tree," I say. And I *am* gazing at the tree I have no memory of standing so close to my house in the backyard, the tree brushing its branches against my window. How is it I never realized a tree was right beside my bedroom before? A whole tree?

I don't want to say what else I'm seeing.

"Did you find out about any others?" I ask, changing the subject.

He hesitates. "You sure you want to know?"

"Always."

Jamie's been helping me. My mom keeps track of what sites I visit on the computer, but he understands my need to know what happened to them.

"Shyann Johnston," he says, pulling a printout from his backpack to show me. "She made it home. See?"

I take in a breath, holding my mind very still in fear of its reaction, as I read the story he's printed out about her. Apparently she won a prize at the senior-class science fair, and this is dated just last month, which means she couldn't have frozen to death in a vacant lot in Newark, she couldn't have died. It's always a beautiful thing when a girl I thought had found a tragic end turns out to still be alive. I feel choked up about it, in my throat, and I hold my hands there, hovering, letting the relief sink in.

I felt the same when I learned about Yoon-mi Hyun and Maura Morris, who ran away to Canada and did make it up there together before they got sent home.

Some girls don't have such good ends. Hailey Pippering's remains were found in a landfill during the time I was in the hospital. And Kendra Howard was pronounced deceased even though she hasn't washed ashore yet. The lake is deep, and town officials say they may never find her body.

Whenever I learn a bad thing about one of the girls, it breaks me up some more. Which might be why Jamie usually only brings me the good stories, the happy ends.

Besides, I won't need his help soon. I'll have private access to a computer again, and I'll be able to take up the searching. I'll keep checking, with or without him.

Silently, to myself, I've vowed to check up on all the girls. Whether we had a true connection or not doesn't much matter to me. These are real girls. They're important. The runaways, too, even if the police don't act like it. Even if the girls' families don't care and don't go looking, I vow to. These girls matter. I need to know what happened to every last one of them.

"Thank you," I tell Jamie. Knowing about Shyann has lifted my spirits a little, and I find myself turning to the window again, almost smiling.

Jamie's eyes follow mine, but he says nothing. It's best if he doesn't ask what I'm seeing out that window or what I'm thinking.

Because I'm thinking how I know what's going to happen. I couldn't see Shyann's true fate, not in the real world, but mine is another story.

The therapist will stop asking me questions about the lost girls, and I'll stop bringing them up. It's safer that way. Because even though the pills I swallow have taken the girls from me, it's not like I'm alone. Not entirely.

There's one girl who's always here and always will be. Even through the Brillo Pad walls the meds create in my mind—through which I can sometimes only see her in the space of the tiniest, fuzziest pinhole—she's here. She stays with me because she never felt at home in that house next door.

We'll grow up together, though Fiona Burke will stay perpetually 17, with the red dye never inching out of her dark roots, the *FU* never fading from her frayed jeans. She'll wear the scowl she always has; her mouth has grown into the shape of it, even though she's softened on me and I can make her smile sometimes.

That's something I can be sure of. I can see my life with Fiona cascading on into the distance, and I'm not so sure about my life with Jamie. We're back together, but I don't know how long he'll end up staying.

Fiona will stay. She'll be with me on my first day back to school next week, and she'll keep me company during summer school so I don't have to repeat the eleventh grade. Sometimes she'll whisper the wrong answers to me during trig tests, but mostly she'll sleep through class, as she did when she was a student.

If there were a way to sever the invisible ball-and-chain that connects her to me, and me to her, she'd be the first one there with the chain saw.

Fiona Burke will continue to be with me next year. Hers will be the first face I'll see on the morning of my eighteenth birthday, before I even look in the mirror to confirm I can still see my own. She won't make a big deal of it, even though my mom will bake up my favorite box-mix cake and bring out the balloons. But Fiona will be happy for me, to know I survived. I'll catch her staring at me, not only with jealousy, because she knows she'll always have a place at the table with me, even if my mom doesn't see her in the third chair and doesn't set out an extra piece of cake.

Fiona will join me at prom, meeting me in the bathroom when I go in to touch up my eyeliner, and she'll try and fail to keep quiet when Jamie tries to slow dance with me after spilling the spiked punch all over his rented tux.

She'll be in the back row during my graduation ceremony; when I cross the stage she'll be one among many who will cheer my name.

We'll spend years together, Fiona and I, like childhood friends who grow old side by side. Some might say that means I'll spend my life being haunted. Or that I won't ever be better because of her. Either way, whatever the explanation, I know I'll forever hear her voice thrumming through my head.

Still, I can't blame her for staying with me. She doesn't have a life of her own anymore; the only way she can live is to walk alongside mine.

There will come a day, decades from now, when I'm again in a bed much like this one. I might have cancer, I might be lucky and simply be dying of old age, I can't know that part of my fate yet. What I do know is that I won't be alone for it.

I'll look across the room and there will be the 17-year-old girl I've known all my life. Not a wrinkle or a mark of age on her. She'll want to jump on the bed. She'll want to poke the home-care aide with her needle and eat all my Jell-O before I can get to it. She'll simply be trying to lift my mood before I go. Because Fiona Burke will never grow up and she won't want me to, either.

This is what I don't tell Jamie. He's looking out the window right now, and he doesn't even see her.

She heaves a sigh, stretches out her arms, and cracks her knuckles, then balances on the branch of the oak tree to climb inside the room. She eyes the two of us sitting on the bed together and stays perched on the windowsill, not willing to get any closer.

You're not going to do it while I'm here watching, are you? Fiona says.

I feel my cheeks go hot and shake my head.

Can't we go out somewhere and have some fun or something? God! I'm so bored. You were in that hospital so long, I thought I'd go INSANE, she says. She giggles a bit at the last word. She enjoys using it around me.

"You sure you're all right?" Jamie says. "Do you want to get out of here, go for a walk or something? Get a coffee? Take a drive?"

"Maybe later," I answer them both.

Fiona sighs again, loudly, letting me know her deep discontent, but Jamie leans forward and brushes my hair from my face, and by the way he's sitting, his shoulders are blocking the view of Fiona at the windowsill. "Hey," he says, "we don't have to go anywhere. We can stay right here."

"Yeah," I say. "Okay. Let's do that."

The vanity mirror over my dresser reflects this scene back to me:

Jamie with his arm over my shoulders and his other hand keeping ahold of my hand. A lock of curly hair drops forward into his face like he can't ever stop it from doing. Beside him is a girl with choppy, dark hair with lighter roots growing in, and her eyes are wide open, and her cheeks are a little hollow, though there'll be couscous for dinner later and she'll eat two plates. She's wearing black and gray, like she does most days, and the room she's in is brightly lit by the sun streaming through the window. There are no shadows. There are no voices. There is no flame-haired visitor on the windowsill waving an arm and giving the finger. There's just a perfectly normal girl with a boy in her bed and a book on her lap and no hint of what's kept hidden away in her mind where no one can see it. There's a girl.

She's 17, and she's still here.

AUTHOR'S NOTE

This novel evolved as I was writing, leading me to discover what I was meant to be telling just as Lauren discovers the truth of what she's seeing amid the scattered stories of the missing girls. So much of the ultimate story for *17 & Gone* stemmed from my own research into experiences of teens living with mental illness and the visions Lauren could be seeing and the voices she could be hearing.

There is no single way to portray the symptoms or experiences of a teenager facing early-onset schizophrenia or any mental illness—and I can only hope that my portrayal of Lauren's story will come across as distinct to her, and most of all respectful and true.

If you are worried that you may have warning signs or symptoms that might prove to be a mental health problem, please consider reaching out and talking to someone and getting help.

If you are thinking of running away or if you have left home and don't know how to go back, there are resources that can help you and even assist in finding a safe place for you to go.

Here are some resources in the United States that could be a lifeline when you need one:

- *National Alliance on Mental Illness (NAMI)*: A national grassroots organization providing resources for teenagers and adults affected by mental illness. www.nami.org • Information Helpline: 1-800-950-NAMI.
- *National Runaway Switchboard:* A toll-free number to call if you're thinking of running away from home, have run away and want to go back home, or have a friend you want to help. www.1800runaway.org • 24-hour Crisis Line: 1-800-RUNAWAY.
- *National Suicide Prevention Lifeline:* Free and confidential support for anyone facing a suicidal or emotional crisis. www.suicidepreventionlifeline.org • 24-hour Hotline: 1-800-273-TALK (8255).
- *Safe Place:* A national youth outreach program for teenagers and runaways who need a safe place to go. nationalsafeplace.org • If you are in trouble or need help, text SAFE and the location where you are (street address/city/state) to 69866.
- *The Trevor Project:* A national crisis-intervention and suicide-prevention organization for LGBTQ youth. www.thetrevorproject.org • Trevor Lifeline: 1-866-488-7386.

ACKNOWLEDGMENTS

I am in awe of my editor, Julie Strauss-Gabel. I truly can't fathom how she is able to see the story I am trying to tell and know exactly how to coax it out of me before I'm even able to articulate it myself. With every round of revision, Julie puts me through the paces and inspires me to dig deeper and fine-tune and be clearer—and through all this hard work she helps me transform my ideas into something to be proud of. My writing is far better thanks to her extraordinary talent, and I know for a fact that this book was able to emerge into what it was meant to be thanks to her passion, attention, and skill. I wouldn't be the writer I am today without her.

Throughout the doubts and struggles and ensuing madness that was the writing of this book, I have been grateful to have my fantastic, dedicated literary agent, Michael Bourret, at my side. He is the calming magic to my anxious frenzy, and has talked me through so many dramatic moments that I'm pretty sure I've lost count. I am so lucky to have him in my corner and grateful for his energy, honesty, and wisdom. This is only our second book together, and I hope it's just the beginning.

From what I said above, you may have guessed that this book was not easy for me to write. I look back and it seems like I was working on it—or trying to—constantly, in multiple locations, throughout the past two years. This book was written and revised in numerous significant places that all seem connected to the story in personal ways maybe only I can see: The very first words of the very first draft were written at Yaddo (thank you, Yaddo staff and my fellow Yaddo-mates, especially in West House, where we sometimes shared a muse). A significant part of the first draft was written at the MacDowell Colony, in Omicron (thank you, MacDowell staff and my fellow colonists). This book was continued in secret writing bunkers at undisclosed locations and revised and revised and revised back in New York City, and could not have been finished without the space I found at the Writers Room, Think Coffee, the Housing Works Used Bookstore and Café, and other writing cafés scattered throughout the Village. Thank you to each of these places for putting up with me and letting me sit for hours upon hours at your tables.

I am so grateful to Libba Bray for her belief in me, her inspiration, and her guidance, and I am beyond honored to have the words of an author I admire so much on my book cover. I am still pinching myself that she liked this book.

I am floored by the generosity of Courtney Summers, who was there for me at so many moments during the writing of these drafts, and whose advice and support helped me make it to this point. I only hope I can do the same for her.

Thank you, Penguin and Dystel & Goderich Literary Management, for all you've done for my books. I've been honored to be able to work with such dedicated, passionate people, including Liza Kaplan, Lauren Abramo, Steve Meltzer, Rosanne Lauer, Elizabeth Zajac, Anna Jarzab, Emilie Bandy, Marie Kent, Danielle Delaney, and each and every person who touched my books in one way or another. As someone who used to work in publishing, I know how easy it is to feel unappreciated and crushed under the deadlines, and I hope they know that this author is astoundingly grateful.

I am also ever thankful for the support from the fellow writers in my life, and especially want to mention those who made an impact while I was writing this particular book: David Adjmi, Tara Altebrando, Joëlle Anthony, Bryan Bliss, Rachel Cantor, Cat Clarke, Camille DeAngelis, Gordon Dahlquist, Gayle Forman, Adele Griffin, Michelle Hodkin, Stephanie Kuehnert, Nina LaCour, Molly O'Neill, Sigrid Nunez, Laurel Snyder, Cheryl Lu-Lien Tan, McCormick Templeman, Lorin Wertheimer, and Christine Lee Zilka. And last but absolutely not least, Micol Ostow, who has been such a huge support to me, since before I even found YA fiction, that I will endlessly thank her in every set of book acknowledgments I write. Thank you also to my extended family and other mothers, especially Ethel Wesdorp, for her enthusiasm and willingness to go to so many of my book events.

And to my blog readers at distraction99.com: Your support over the years as I went from a struggling writer of literary fiction for adults to finding my place here as a YA author has meant the world to me. Thank you for reading and cheering me on along the way.

My family is small, but so very supportive. My brother, Joshua Suma, never wavers in his belief in me. And my sister, Laurel Rose Purdy, has been there for me through every low point, and to celebrate every high point, and I can't imagine my life without her.

My mom, Arlene Seymour, went above and beyond when it came to this manuscript. Due to her own work with MICA (mentally ill and chemically dependent) clients at her clinic, as well as with schizophrenics using art therapy, she became an essential resource during the writing and research of this novel. She was beyond generous with her time and attention in reading this book, and helped steer me in the right direction when it came to writing from Lauren's perspective. My mom is a true inspiration to me, a phenomenal woman who I know has changed the lives of many, not to mention her own, when she went back to school when I myself was in college. She was always there for me, while I was a teenager, and through to today. It's not an exaggeration to say I would be nowhere without her.

My other half, Erik Ryerson, who I've been with since I was eighteen, can surely see parts of himself in Jamie. I don't want to embarrass him by singing his praises (too much), but he really gave his all for this novel: He is the first reader for every single draft I write, even if that means staying up until five in the morning before one of my deadlines to do so, and it is thanks to his inspiration, his imagination, his sacrifice, and his belief in my writing that this book even exists at all.